DREAMS OF SHREDS & TATTERS

AMANDA DOWNUM

SOLARIS

First published 2015 by Solaris
an imprint of Rebellion Publishing Ltd,
Riverside House, Osney Mead,
Oxford, OX2 0ES, UK

www.solarisbooks.com

UK ISBN: 978 1 78108 326 0
US ISBN: 978 1 78108 327 7

A CIP catalogue record for this book is available from the
British Library.

Designed & typeset by Rebellion Publishing

Printed in the US

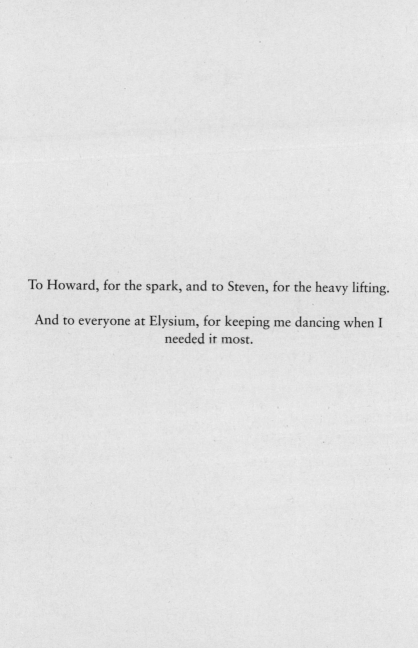

To Howard, for the spark, and to Steven, for the heavy lifting.

And to everyone at Elysium, for keeping me dancing when I needed it most.

Every angel is terrible.
Rainer Maria Rilke, *The Duino Elegies*

If every angel's terrible then why do you welcome them?
CocoRosie, "Terrible Angels"

In a perfect world, there are no bad dreams
We fall asleep believing in the same things
For it's not perfect where we are
No wishes come true from falling stars
God Module, "Image"

0

PROLOGOS

HALLOWEEN NIGHT, AND shrieks and howls drifted off Granville Street. Parties staggered in and out of clubs and down the sidewalks, a dizzying confusion of music and laughter and shouting, sequins and feathers, masks and paint. People dressed in shiny new skins, searching for opportunities to shed them. Groping hands and sticky candy kisses, tricks and treats in darkened corners.

Farther south, across the bridge, the chaos thinned and the night stilled. In the dark loft above the Morgenstern Gallery, Blake Enderly leaned against the window, staring through the ghost of his reflection to the street below. Black and orange flyers scattered like fallen leaves across the damp sidewalk, trampled into soggy pulp as a gaggle of late arrivals hurried north to join the press. A pair of pixies in glittering wings and too-short skirts huddled together beneath one umbrella, shouting at their companions to hurry. Their friends—a trio of pirates and a blood-splattered bride—only laughed. A figure in a black cloak and mask trailed behind.

Blake laughed too, a soft chuckle that fogged the rain-streaked glass. A sigh spread the mist further; he envied them the dark and cold and excitement. There were no costumes here tonight, no sweat-fog or throbbing speakers. Only soft music and conversation spilling through the connecting door from the next studio, muted laughter and the unsteady glow of candlelight.

Below, the pixies cursed and left the others behind, the clatter of their heels fading into the night. Their friends followed, until only the man in the mask remained, caught in the glow of a street lamp. He lingered there, looking up.

The tipsy warmth in Blake's stomach faded, replaced by a prickling chill. He raised a hand to wipe the glass and froze half way, unwilling to move, to draw attention to himself.

Just a man in a mask. But he wasn't sure it was a man. The mask was a featureless black oval that swallowed light. Everything about the figure was the same matte black, liquid and unbroken. The face had no eyes, but Blake couldn't shake the certainty that it watched him all the same.

Shuddering, he stepped back. His heel caught an easel frame, and the sudden clatter sent a queasy thrill of adrenaline through him. He grabbed the frame to steady it, saving a canvas from toppling over. When he glanced back at the window, the street was empty.

"Hey." A shadow filled the doorway, accompanied by a purposeful boot-scuff and the rap of knuckles on the frame.

"Hey," Blake said. He nearly laughed at himself as his panic faded, but the electric tingle in his fingers lingered. He took a deep breath, letting the layered scents of paint and chalk and chemicals calm him.

"Are you hiding in here?" Alain asked, stepping out of the fall of light into the cool shadows of the studio. His voice was dry and raspy, too deep for his narrow chest. A whiskey-and-cigarettes voice from a dentist's son who'd never smoked. He did a good Tom Waits karaoke. "You're not brooding, are you?" A joke, but his eyebrows quirked in a more serious question. *Are you all right?*

"I'm fine. I just needed a minute."

Alain moved closer, brushing his shoulder against Blake's. He held a glass in one hand, and the sharp, bitter fumes cut through the dusty air. "Disappointed?"

About the party, he meant, about the quiet night. Blake had told him stories about Halloweens in Connecticut, the old white house strung with purple and orange lights, bats and ghosts and guardian jack-o-lanterns. The costumes and parties and graveyard excursions. He missed it, missed Liz and all their friends. He caught himself twisting the silver ring on his right hand absently.

Blake leaned his head against Alain's, grounding himself in the familiar texture of his boyfriend's hair. Thick and soft, brittle at the ends from the bleach and dyes that stripped away his natural black. This month's brilliant peacock green had faded to a yellower absinthe shade. His own hair, plain brown and unbound, fell over both their shoulders. The window showed their reflection, faded as an overexposed photograph.

It felt unreal, like a snapshot of someone else's life. Eight months together, and they made it work. Blake had even stopped waking up next to Alain with the terrible certainty that *this* would be the day it fell apart. Most days, at least.

"No. I'm not disappointed." He was happy here. That thought scared him more than any ghosts or goblins or faceless monsters. Alain turned his face for a kiss, and Blake's nose wrinkled at the bitterness of alcohol and citrus. "What are you drinking?"

Alain raised his glass; dark liquor glowed sienna in the light. "Black rum, coffee liqueur, Campari, and bitters. I think I'll call it a bête noire."

"The bane of your existence?"

Alain winked, a sweep of black lashes and silver flash of brow ring. "If I have any more it might be." He threaded his arm through Blake's. "Come on. Rainer wants to talk to everyone."

"About what?"

"Dunno." His eyes narrowed. "The exhibit, I hope."

That tiny frown made Blake pause, ignoring Alain's attempt to steer him toward the other room. "What's wrong?"

"Nothing." A second later his cheeks darkened. "That's never sounded convincing from anyone, has it? Sorry." He scowled at his glass and tossed back the last swallow. "It's just... Rainer. And the way he looks at you sometimes."

Blake's cheeks stung as if he'd been slapped. He stiffened and jerked his arm free. "That's—" A denial died unspoken. It wouldn't have sounded convincing either. "Are you jealous?" he asked instead, and cursed his defensive tone as soon as he heard it.

"Oh, please!" Alain drew the word out in two drawling syllables. "He may have money and a sexy accent, but throwing me over for your patron—who I introduced you to—would be so tacky you'd choke on it." He grew serious again. "It's not that I mind him making eyes at you. I just wish he wouldn't do it in front of Antja. Even if she doesn't say anything—" He shook his head. "Damn it. I'm tipsy and stupid. Don't pay any attention to me."

He held out a hand like a peace offering. After a heartbeat, Blake took it. Together, they stepped into the light and warmth of the other loft, into the smell of wine and candle wax and soft perfume. The party was quiet, intimate, not one of the events that sometimes crowded the gallery beneath them. Everyone here was familiar—still more Alain's friends than his, but Blake liked most of them well enough.

Tonight, though, tension ran in crackling lines through the room. Robert and Gemma—the gallery's premier artists, and normally inseparable—sat together, but Robert looked everywhere but her. Everywhere but her and Stephen York. Stephen circled the edges of the room, sleek and amused. He raised Blake's hackles, but was also one of gallery's backers. Jason and quiet little Rae sat apart, baby-bat goths and the youngest ones here. Antja stood by a window, watching the night as Blake had moments ago. Streetlight kissed her cheeks and hair. Studying her profile, he felt a familiar spark of recognition—the weight of unhappy secrets. Alain's words echoed in his head, and he looked aside.

And in the center of them all sat Rainer.

The gallery owner glanced up as though the thought had summoned him. His eyes were vivid even across the room, a pale shade that wasn't sky or periwinkle or even non-repro blue. A blue like shadows on snow. Compelling and disconcerting, especially when they lingered too long. After a few seconds he smiled apologetically and looked away.

The song on the stereo ended and the last haunting electronic notes fell into silence as conversations paused. Rainer shifted in his chair, ice clinking as he tilted his glass absently in one hand. Heads turned in the lengthening hush, watching, waiting. Blake didn't know how he did it—the charisma that drew attention with the slightest gesture, the energy that pulled people close.

Rainer sipped the last of his drink and set the glass aside. The guests turned to face him as the silence deepened, and the lights dimmed as if they too were quieting to listen. Antja resumed her usual place beside him, one smooth hip propped against his chair. Stephen flanked the other side, his posture cool and removed, his dark eyes derisive as ever. The others moved closer. Robert and Gemma reached across the space between their chairs to hold hands, their tension forgotten. Rae curled into Jason's lap, black hair hiding her face. Alain settled in a corner of the sofa and tugged Blake down next to him. Like children for story time.

Rainer glanced around the room, his eyes catching everyone in turn. That was part of the magnetism—the sincerity, the way he made everyone feel included. It had been a long time since Blake trusted easy charm and kindness, but even after Alain's misgivings he felt Rainer's smile like sunlight on his face.

It was what connected them, all these disparate people, besides art. They were all waiting for something, searching for something. And they all thought Rainer might give it to them. Blake knew better—knew too well how badly that could go. But here he was.

"I'm glad all of you could come," Rainer said. "I know some of you want to talk about the next exhibit, and we will, but there's something else I want to show you tonight." Cloth rustled; a boot scuffed against the rug; breath caught and held. "Some of you have already seen it. The rest are here because I think you should. Because I trust you."

Again that rush of pride. Ridiculous, dangerous, but Blake couldn't stop it. He wasn't the only one—even Alain leaned forward, color rising in his cheeks.

"The gallery is only half of what I'm doing here. Art pays the bills—" Someone snorted, and Rainer tilted his head in a wry nod. "Sometimes, anyway. But I'm looking for another sort of talent, too."

Blake flinched, unpleasant possibilities strobing through his head. He knew Rainer provided the drugs that floated like party favors through the private events, but that didn't make him a pusher, didn't make him a—

Alain's hand clamped on his, interrupting his increasingly hectic thoughts. "What do you mean?" he asked, voice rasping deeper than ever.

Whatever Blake expected, whatever he feared, it was nothing like what followed.

"Watch," Rainer said with a smile. He reached out and traced a shape in the air.

No, more than that. He opened the air, opened the world along an invisible seam, and filled it with golden fire.

1

KATABASIS

THE PAIN BROUGHT him back.

Blake blinked, pulling himself free of the haze of shadows and slanting lamplight. Slow and dream-sticky like the edge of waking, but his eyes ached as though he hadn't slept in days. His hand cramped, the dull ache of old fractures pulsing in his wrist and collarbone. A brush he'd forgotten he held trembled in his grip, the sable tip clotted with yellowish-grey paint, a shade somewhere between ecru and old bones. Numb fingers twitched and the brush fell to the floor, leaving a comma-shaped smear as it bounced against the boards. He let it lie, lifting his gaze to the painting in front of him.

It was finished. The rush of completion drove away the aches and cramps and pins-and-needles fire between his shoulder blades. For an instant the canvas eclipsed everything. A door. A door on the verge of opening. He reached for it, imagining its texture, the loops and whorls of silky stone, the weight of it against his hand. It would open for him, if he could only reach through—

But he couldn't, not that way; his fingers hit paint and canvas, left tacky smudges in the thick layers of oils. He scrubbed his hand on his jeans. The fingerprints could stay, a subtle sort of signature.

Not just finished—it was perfect. As close as he'd ever come, at least, just for this moment. The flaws would surface later as they always did, the imperfections and imbalances he could never shake. But that was why he'd come here tonight, wasn't it? To finally escape them.

He dragged a hand through his hair, snagging sticky fingers in the tangles. He usually pulled his hair back to paint, but it was too short for that now, falling in waves around his ears and across his eyes. Seven years of growth gone—seven years of defiance, of spite against his father. A sacrifice or a severed fetter: he wasn't sure which.

His stool scraped the floorboards as he stood, and a hum of conversation he'd barely noticed faltered and died. Silence pounded in his ears. He stepped back from the easel, caught himself on the stool as his knees buckled. Lamp- and candlelight spun in lazy kaleidoscope swirls through the shadowed room. Terrible light for painting—no wonder his eyes burned so badly. He'd pushed himself too hard and the pharmaceutical daze was wearing off.

Thunder shook the house and he nearly fell again. The echo in his ears wasn't his own pulse but rain, drumming fierce against the roof and windows. Waves lashed the deck, and the sky was a swirl of darkness veined with lightning. The night had been clear when they'd arrived at the cabin, December-sharp and sweet, the stars a spray of diamonds without the city's glare to dull them, the light of the waxing moon a pewter glaze across the cove.

"What time is it?" That was what he meant to ask, anyway. His tongue was swollen, mouth parched, and all that came out was a sticky croak. No one answered.

The others watched him, silent as mannequins. Almost like a party, like the night five weeks ago that started this, but stripped of warmth and comfort. Robert and Gemma sat with hands clasped, while Stephen lounged, bored and indolent as a cat. Antja stood apart. Her face was smooth as a mask, but he read the tension in her shoulders, in the tightness of her folded arms. Only Jason and Rae hadn't been invited, and Blake was just as glad—they were kids. Whatever happened here, he wasn't sure they needed to see it yet.

Rainer's cabal. Everyone here tonight had somehow touched the secret things Rainer had shown them. The world that existed below the world Blake knew. But none of them—except Rainer himself— had ever attempted what he meant to do tonight.

None of them had needed to.

Another thunderclap and the lights flickered and dimmed. Blake startled, knocking over the stool. It toppled with a machine gun clatter, and a sliver of pain wedged itself behind his right eye. He'd seen more rain than he could have imagined since coming to Vancouver, but he couldn't remember the last time he'd heard thunder.

A footstep fell behind him, too close. He spun, fists clenching, but it was only Rainer leaning over his shoulder to stare at the painting. The fascination on his face nearly made up for the intrusion. It was certainly better than the pity and frustration Blake had seen so often in the last few weeks.

"Is it finished?" Rainer asked.

Blake nodded. The admiration warmed him; so did the mania lingering in his bloodstream. His senses reeled with the drug. Beneath the stink of linseed and turpentine, the smell of Rainer's aftershave made his head spin: pine and citrus and mint, and under that the warmer soap and musk of his skin. Blake wanted to lean into that warmth, to rub against him like a cat. He clenched his aching right hand and let the pain ground him.

"Well?" His voice cracked with thirst and fatigue and the insidious doubt he could never be rid of. "Will it work?"

Is it good enough? But he couldn't ask that, not for all the magic in the world.

Magic. The idea gnawed like nothing had since he first realized he could capture and change the world on paper, could capture and exorcise himself. But no matter how many times Rainer had tried to teach him even the simplest of tricks, Blake could never reproduce them. Weeks of failure had left him seething with all the bitterness and self-loathing he thought he'd put behind him.

I can't teach you, Rainer had finally said. *But there is another way.*

"It will work." Rainer lifted his hand just as Blake had, but let it fall again.

Blake turned away, searching for Alain. He found him standing alone by the windows. Stormlight gleamed in his blue-streaked hair, rinsing the warm tones from his skin until it was cold as silverpoint.

He turned, light sliding across his face, and reached for Blake's outstretched hand.

"Are you all right?" Alain asked as Blake leaned into him. Blake nodded against his neck, scraping his cheekbone against stubble, breathing in the unnatural sweetness of drugstore shampoo. Beneath layers of shirts and sweaters, Alain's shoulders were knotted tight. The tension had been building for days. Neither of them had slept well all week, tossing with dreams they didn't share, burying themselves in work. They hadn't argued, precisely, but Alain wasn't so eager for all the wonders Rainer offered.

But he was still here.

"What's wrong?" Blake asked. "You're the one brooding now." He hoped for a smile, a joke, something sarcastic to ease his nerves, but Alain only shrugged.

"I don't like the storm."

Rainer cleared his throat. "Do you still want this?"

This: mysteries, marvels, numina. A way to transcend his clumsy aching flesh, the scars and fractures and constant fear. The doubts and demons he could never shake. It had taken him years to learn to live with himself, with the scars carved in flesh and bone and brain. To accept that he would carry them always. He couldn't go back to that acceptance now, not if there was another way. Alain's long dark eyes narrowed, but he only squeezed Blake's hand in silent sympathy.

Blake swallowed and wished for water. He'd come this far. His free hand rose to tug at the ring hanging from a chain around his neck—a nervous habit, and he forced himself to let go again. "Yes."

"Then it's yours," Rainer whispered, moving closer. "You just have to take it."

"What—" Blake licked his lips and tried again, hating how small his voice sounded. "What do I say?"

"It doesn't matter. You don't have to say anything. He'll know."

With that, Rainer split the shadows open and filled them with fire, spoke a word that rang in the air like the toll of a cathedral bell.

The world unfolded, dissolved and ran like watered ink, and Blake saw the door. Just as he'd imagined it, slick as soapstone, warm as flesh. Just as he'd painted it. It swung inward and he felt it in his chest, something wrenching inside him. Disintegration: the falling away of drugs or sex or pain.

The door opened and he stood before an angel, beautiful and terrible, scalding his eyes. An arch of wing, pinions dripping flame; robes of smoke and light; a halo like the darkness between stars. He could only stand to see the edges, where its outline burned the world. Any deeper and his blood would boil.

The angel extended its cupped hands, filled with the fire of heaven. Filled with everything Rainer had promised and more. All Blake had to do was accept it, even if it charred him to cinders. The angel spoke inside his head, echoing through every bone.

Before he could answer, the vision fractured.

Thunder crashed and the shriek of splintering glass filled the air. The angel vanished as the windows shattered, taking his fire with him. The electricity, jealous or shamed, vanished too. The storm whipped cold and wet through the room, full of stinging shards. Someone screamed.

Monsters rode the wind. Inky bodies writhed through broken windows, darkness given shape—darkness with wings and claws. Rainer shoved Blake back, away from reaching talons. Everyone was shouting. Candles guttered and died and everything was shadows and lightning and screams. The smell of blood blossomed raw and metal-sweet, mingling with ozone and turpentine. Blake lunged for the painting, desperate to save it from the drenching storm.

Alain grabbed him first, pulling him away from the canvas, away from the monsters, into the teeth of the wind. Glass crunched and slipped under their boots and freezing rain slapped them, soaking to the skin. Lightning split the sky—split a tree in a shower of sparks. Wood groaned, flaming as it fell, and the deck buckled and shrugged them off.

Water hit him like a wall. Blake flailed, breathless and one-armed. Alain's hand clenched his, a lifeline—the current tossed them, but couldn't pry them apart. Instead it sucked them both down.

Brine seared his eyes and mouth, stole the heat from his bones. All that was left in the dark and cold was Alain's hand, and the picture still burning in Blake's mind. The door. A way out.

The door opened and the current pulled him through. Darkness filled his mouth, pushed down his throat. Coiling, solidifying, dragging him under. Swallowing him.

The last thing he felt was Alain's hand slipping from his.

THREE THOUSAND MILES away, Liz Drake woke gasping, still aching for breath. Adrenaline left her cold and shaking and she clutched the twisted sheets until the world stopped its seasick tilt and sway. The taste of salt filled her mouth.

Not again.

A week of drowning dreams, of watching Blake vanish into the darkness, unable to reach him. A week of waking breathless in the dead hours before dawn. Finals week, no less.

She sat up, breathing slowly until her heart slowed. The old white house sighed around her, the secret language of wood and plaster spoken only in the dark. December pressed cold and black against the window, stealing through chinks and cracks; the heater rumbled like a sleeping dragon. Alex's side of the bed was cold.

She wrapped her arms around her chest, goosebumps prickling through the worn-thin cloth of her T-shirt. Twenty-five was too old to be afraid of the dark, afraid of bad dreams, but she felt a fraction of that age, tiny and helpless and alone. It had been a long time since her dreams were so bad.

Fresh panic rose sharp as fishhooks behind her sternum, squeezing her heart and tightening her throat. Sweat slicked her palms and she wiped them on the sheets. It had been a long time since the anxiety was so bad, either. It made her want to call Dr. Matson, though she hadn't been to therapy in years. Any familiar voice to cling to, to reassure her that she wasn't alone in the night. That her nightmares were only that, only anxiety and bad brain chemicals and all the normal things that crowded her head.

Your dreams are just dreams, Elizabeth. The human mind excels at finding patterns and correlations, at giving weight to coincidence and hindsight. Magical thinking. You've studied that, haven't you?

But another voice, a wet, rasping voice, whispered back. *You know better than that, Lizzie.*

She did know. Something was wrong, and no reassurances would change that. She was too old for handholding, anyway. But Dr. Matson would also remind her that she wasn't alone, and that much at least was true.

She swung her legs off the bed, toes curling against the cold floorboards. Light from the hall spilled over stacks of books and papers, cast shadows like toppled pillars across the floor, ruined menhirs of ethnographies and grammars and dictionaries. The corner of a book bit into her instep and she winced—*The Consolation of Philosphy*, one of Alex's. She nudged it toward the foot of the bed.

The floor creaked as she crossed the room. Light welled up the stairs and the heater's dry breath gusted over her, but she couldn't stop shivering. She stared down the hall toward Blake's old room, still full of the things he hadn't taken with him, that she never got around to packing. She stopped herself before she opened his door.

He was nine months gone, thousands of miles. Her nightmares couldn't conjure him home.

The kettle began to whistle as she reached the bottom of the stairwell and the tightness in her chest eased. Sometimes she forgot how echoing and empty the house was without Blake. She should find another roommate, or another house, one that didn't swallow her up with its shadows and silences. She might ask Alex, but that hatched a whole different unsettled feeling in the pit of her stomach.

She found him puttering in the kitchen, still in boxers and a T-shirt, his dark blond hair tousled from bed. Steam coiled around one bony wrist as he poured water into two mugs. All elbows and knees and Adam's apple, but he moved with a lanky, water-bird grace. She paused in the doorway, letting the familiar sight of him take the edge off her nerves.

This is real, she told herself. Alex, school, friends. A life. This was real—not the dreams.

Laughter answered inside her head, soft and wet and mocking.

"Couldn't sleep?" she asked when Alex set the kettle down. The clock over the stove said it was just after two in the morning. Neither of them had been asleep for long.

Round glasses flashed white as he looked up. "After repeated application of your knee to my spleen, no."

Her cheeks warmed. "I'm sorry."

He bent to kiss her forehead. "It's not a mortal wound. I thought you might like some tea, if you woke up." Years in the States had worn the crisp edges off his Queen's English, but his accent was always stronger when he first woke up; he must dream in Received Pronunciation.

Liz leaned into his warmth, breathing in the smell of his skin—must and grassy sweetness, like tea leaves and used bookstores. The silver saint's medallion he always wore shone in the hollow of his throat. "Thank you."

Blue eyes narrowed as he traced a thumb over her cheekbone, below the bruised circles that branded her eyes. "It's getting worse, isn't it? The same dream?"

"Yes." She sank into a kitchen chair, pinching her nose against the ache building between her eyes. "But not exactly worse. Just the same." Every night the same—darkness and cold, water bitter as blood. Blake's pale face sinking into the depths, always out of reach.

Outside, branches creaked in the wind, rattling their fingerbones against the walls. Much too quiet for a Saturday night, but with finals over the neighborhood around campus was a ghost town. Even her neighbors had vanished—she hadn't heard the thump of their bass through the walls in days.

"Have you called him?" Alex sat beside her and slid a steaming mug across the table. Books and notes and graduate catalogues buried the nicked Ikea veneer, the carnage of another semester past. Only one more until her Master's and still no plans after that. Maybe that was a good enough reason for falling out of touch with Blake, but it certainly didn't feel that way now.

"And emailed. No one answers." She stared at the cup, at the leaves drifting dark as silt in amber fluid. No symbols to read in their eddy and swirl, no visions in the chamomile fumes.

"You think something's happened," Alex said, not a question. He never dismissed her dreams or hunches or magical thinking outright, but his eyes tightened whenever she mentioned them.

Liz lifted her cup, but her hands shook and hot tea slopped over her fingers. As she blew on her scalded knuckles, the unhappy chill in her stomach crystallized into something sharp and certain.

"I do. Something's wrong. I haven't heard from him since October."

She turned toward the wall beside the table, where framed photographs lined the worn white plaster. Her gaze settled on one of the newest, the three of them on Halloween two years ago—Liz as Alice in a starched apron and witch boots, Blake the Mad Hatter in a red leather straitjacket. Alex had dyed his hair orange and black but resisted all her pleas to be the White Rabbit.

"Something's wrong," she said again. "I need to find out what happened. I have to go."

"To Vancouver?" Alex's eyebrows shot toward his hairline. "In December?"

The skepticism in his voice woke all her own doubts. The money, the time—where would she go when she got there? What if Blake didn't want to see her?

"What if it's a false alarm?" Alex said, taking up where her second-guessing left off. "A new phone number and he forgot to tell you?"

"I need to know," she whispered, to Alex and herself. "Whatever it is, I need to know."

She didn't look at another photograph. Another Halloween, years before. Three Alices in that one, blonde and brunette and raven-dark, all their cheeks soft with adolescence. Liz on one end, Alis Park on the other, and Alice Ransom between them. Alice, whom Liz hadn't been able to help. Alice, whose drowned voice still whispered to her in the dark.

Her neck ached with the effort of not looking at the dead girl's shy smiling face. Instead she lifted her mug and took a determined swallow, exhaling steam from burning lips. "I have to go."

Alex stared at her for a long moment, thin mouth turned down at the corners, eyes blind and unreadable behind a glaze of light. Finally he sighed and lifted one long hand in a shrug. "It's been a while since I had a vacation."

She swallowed. Her throat had gone dry despite the tea. "You mean—"

"That I won't let you fly across the continent chasing another man by yourself?" He smiled wryly. "Yes. If you want me to come, that is."

"Of course I do." She reached out to catch his hand, a quick pressure of fingers. "Let's start packing."

2

TERMINAL CITY

Rae flew.

Thermals swelled, ruffling black wings. The city sprawled below, a web of glass and steel and concrete, softened along the edges with green, bounded by black water, and all of that enfolded soft and safe by layered clouds. Between those clouds the sun sank toward the sea, trailing veils of color—violet-grey and salmon and sticky marmalade orange. The cracks in the world that let the light in.

Above the clouds the stars burned. The stars called her and she flew higher, shredding vapor with every wing-stroke. East, where Taurus snorted and heaved himself over the horizon. Her blood itched, driving her farther, faster, closer to the blazing stars, where the Hyades sang wild cradle songs to their wild god. The god who waited for her in the heart of the Bull's eye.

Faster, farther, higher than she'd ever flown before, but her wings weren't meant for the icy void between the stars, for the solar winds that gusted around her. Pinions cracked, wax melted, and she fell screaming, a flurry of black feathers blinding her as she tumbled down.

Back into the prison of her flesh.

Rae moaned, her face buried in a mattress that stank of old sex and sweat, the cloying honey-sweetness of mania filtering through her skin. Human skin, wrapped around clumsy flesh and heavy bone, limbs so much dead weight. Wings clipped again.

She rolled over and wiped her nose with the back of her hand; three fingers tingled pins-and-needles as feeling returned. The room was black except for a glowing stripe under the door. She blinked watering eyes and turned away until her vision adjusted.

Shadows wept down the walls, puddled and bubbled on the floor. They whispered. Rae bit her lip to keep from whimpering, to keep from calling out. Only shadows and synesthesia. She pulled a pillow over her face and counted from zero to ten and back again. Only shadows. They couldn't hurt her.

Voices from the other room filtered through her frantic thoughts, drowning the whispers. These voices were worse and she hugged the pillow tighter against her ears, but they snaked inside anyway. Jason and Stephen, the conversation a blur of profits and costs that made her head hurt, that dragged her back into the cold, ugly world where one friend was dead and another in the hospital and her boyfriend was selling drugs to pay the rent. As often as she'd wished for Jason to find a decent job, she'd rather go back to busking and waiting tables to support them than have him working for Stephen York.

Very bad karma, her mother would have said.

She sat up, wrapping a sweaty sheet around her and waiting for the shadows to stop seething. If she stepped on the floor now they might stick to her feet, or crawl up her legs like spiders, and then she'd definitely freak out.

A little longer was all she needed. If the mania only lasted another hour, maybe she could reach the singing stars, understand their voices. The drug lingered warm and liquid in her veins, but she wouldn't fly again tonight. The curtains were pulled tight against the hiss of rain, no clock in the room to tell her how long she'd been out. Her bladder ached and her mouth tasted like old socks.

When the shadows finally stilled Rae stood by the door, almost-clean clothes bundled in her arms, waiting for the voices to stop. The cold floor sent goosebumps crawling over her skin, tightening her nipples around silver hoops. Her desire not to see Stephen overshadowed her need for the bathroom, especially when she was grimy and strung out and mostly naked. She'd nearly started to potty-dance when the front door opened and closed again.

Hinges creaked as she peeked out of the bedroom and Jason turned, matte-black hair falling over his eyes. "Hey, babe. Finally awake?"

"Maybe." She glanced past him, making sure the living room was empty. The curtains gapped here, showing black beyond the rain-fogged glass. Her broken-tailed Kit-Cat clock told her it was a quarter to eleven, which meant she'd been out nearly eight hours.

Longer and longer every time. But never long enough.

Jason crossed the room and bent his head to kiss her. She was still manic enough to see his aura without trying, a faint nimbus of color circling his head and hands. Murkier than usual, dull brown wicking through the blues and greens, but maybe that was just her imagination.

"You want to go out tonight?" He trailed a thumb over her collarbone and she shuddered as sensation rippled across her skin.

She shook her head, which made the colors swirl. "I'd rather take it easy. Maybe I'll busk a little if I'm feeling up to it. We can go out tomorrow."

His hands settled on her shoulders, pale against her winter-sallow skin. "I've got money, babe. You don't need to do that anymore."

She shrugged and smiled. "I like it." More importantly, she wanted money that Stephen had never touched. She wasn't hypocrite enough that dealing bothered her, but Stephen's smiles and generosity made her flesh creep. He was hard and slick as hematite behind the charm, cold as sharkskin.

Jason frowned but nodded. "Okay. I've got some errands to run, if you're going to go out."

"Sure," she said, forcing a smile she didn't feel. "We can hang out tomorrow."

He leaned in and kissed her neck. "We don't have to leave right now."

Her hands slid down the front of his shirt, skin tingling, craving touch. Worn-soft cotton and cracked paint shivered through her fingertips. And below that, flesh, warm and solid.

Rae sidestepped even as her stomach tightened with want. "I really gotta pee." She ducked into the bathroom before Jason could reply, turning the rattling old lock behind her.

After she flushed, she turned the shower as hot as it would go, until steam clouds roiled through the narrow room. Stinging spray pounded the chill from her flesh. Her limbs grew heavy as the last of the mania wore off, joints aching.

Minutes later she heard the front door close again and sighed. Rae scrubbed her long tangled hair and tried to ignore the guilt she felt at that relief.

Liz DREAMED OF a dark forest, of a stone road nearly swallowed by trees and earth. A canopy of branches held the ground in a perpetual twilight that smelled of moss and loam and decay. Weeds cracked the paving stones, and roots thrust them aside. The underbrush was alive with sounds—skittering feet, slithering bodies, huffing breath. Shadows shifted around her and wind hissed through the treetops.

She knew this road, though she hadn't walked it in years. It had never been so dark and overgrown before. If she kept going the forest would end soon, giving way to hills and fields and the city.

"Welcome back, Lizzie."

Liz jumped, throat closing. She looked up to see a girl sitting on a tree limb, feet dangling. Her striped stockings were torn, and mud and leaf-litter clung to the soles of her patent leather Mary Janes. Water dripped from her skirts, a puddle spreading across the cracked stones below.

"It's been a long time," Alice said. A thread of water ran between her bloodless lips, splashing her already-soaked pinafore.

Liz shuddered but didn't look away. She'd never seen Alice after she died; the casket had been closed. Her friend's puffy white face and bruised-violet eyelids were her own invention. "You don't belong here," she whispered.

"That isn't very nice. You used to tell me all about your dreams. You said you wished I could see them too. I remember your stories— the stairs, the city of cats."

"What are you doing here?" Liz said.

"I was going to ask you the same thing. Trying to save someone else?" The dead girl smiled. Her eyes were black wells. "Maybe you'll have better luck this time."

"Alice—" Her voice broke.

Alice shook her head, flinging water. "I'm sorry. That wasn't fair. I know you tried. But you're down the rabbit hole now. Beware the King."

"Don't you mean the Queen?"

But the dream slipped out from under her. Wakefulness returned in layers: cold, stale air; the vibration of engines; a dizzying sensation of movement. A hand on her arm, a gentle shake. She blinked and lifted her head from Alex's bony shoulder, rubbing the pebbled, cable-knit imprint his sweater left in her cheek.

"We're landing," he said, pulling off his headphones. He sat folded like a marionette, knees brushing the tray table in front of him despite the airline's alleged six inches of extra leg-room. Over ten hours in transit had left his hair lank and tangled, and a film of oil and dried sweat clung to Liz's skin and itched at the nape of her neck.

The day after she'd made her decision and bought plane tickets, Liz had slept, deep and dark and dreamless. She'd known it wouldn't last, but Alice's white face hanging behind her eyes made her stomach clench.

The plane banked and turned with a rumble. Leaning across Alex's lap, she saw the last violet and apricot glow fading in the west, and airport lights bright against the black water of the Pacific. She stretched, kneading a knot in her neck.

Alex adjusted his glasses, glancing at her out of the corner of one eye. "Do you feel better now that we're here?"

"No," she said, her voice nearly lost in the low hum of the plane. Action may have bought her a night of rest, but had done nothing to dislodge the feeling of *wrong* that stuck like a bone in her throat. "But thank you for coming with me."

He shrugged. "I've already turned, in my lesson plans for the spring. And it's better than going home to see my parents." His fingers tightened around hers, belying the lightness of his words. Liz held his hand as the *Fasten Seatbelt* light blinked on and they spiraled down and down.

*   *   *

THE SKY HUNG low across Vancouver, spitting rain and veiling the night in grey haze. Liz's eyelids sagged as Alex drove the rental car downtown. She stared through her reflection in the window and tried not to think about how tired and lost she looked.

Fog clung to the streets, turning wet asphalt and trees into something distant and otherworldly. Christmas lights glowed through the brume, muted shades of red and gold and eerie underwater blue. Fairy lights to lead travelers astray—where would they take her if she followed them? But the road carried them safely through, to Granville Island and the glass-and-steel forest of downtown. The mist swallowed skyscrapers, softened sharp-angled condos and bled halos of street lamps and jeweled neon. The brightness of clubs and coffee shops faded as they turned onto the quieter side street that led to their hotel.

A crowd gathered on the sidewalk in front of the lobby, a glistening half circle of umbrellas and raincoats. A man shouted to the onlookers in a deep preacher's voice.

"I have seen the King! He is coming for all of you. Aldebaran is his star, and its light will burn your eyes out."

Liz's hands tightened on the handle of her suitcase. Icy drizzle stung her face as she moved closer, snaked frozen fingers under her collar—she hadn't thought to pack an umbrella. Between the shoulders of the crowd she glimpsed a seamed, chill reddened face and tangled iron grey hair.

"I have seen the yellow sign!"

A pair of police officers pushed through the crowd. "I've seen a sign," one of them said. "It says No Loitering."

The old man tried to pull away. "I have to warn them!"

"Warn them after you've slept it off, Yves." The audience broke apart as the police flanked the preacher.

"You'll see him," Yves yelled as they led him away. "You'll all see him." For an instant Liz met his wild eyes. "Le roi jaune vient!"

Alex caught her shoulder, steering her gently toward the lobby doors. "Come on. I'm sure there's something more entertaining on cable."

*   *   *

SLEEP WAS A long time coming that night. Liz lay still on starch-stiff hotel sheets, listening to the rhythm of Alex's breath and trying not to toss. Wind sighed past the balcony, rattling the windows with spatters of rain. Citylight fell in a pale stripe across the foot of the bed.

She was amazed sometimes how comforting the warmth of another body beside hers could be. She'd spent years thinking she would sleep alone for the rest of her life, after she outgrew childhood slumber parties and realized that the heat of lust and sex that drove the world was something she would never experience. To have found someone willing to look past that, to settle for the negotiation and compromise of a relationship without the haze of pheromones, felt like a dream from which she was constantly afraid of waking.

But no amount of comfort or companionship could soothe her tonight.

Patterns and correlations. Coincidence and hindsight. She wanted to believe that. Wanted to believe that there was nothing she could do, could ever have done. If her dreams and anxiety were only that then she couldn't have done anything to prevent Blake's ominous silence. Couldn't have stopped Alice from lying back in a bathtub with a belly full of pills. Couldn't have kept her parents from getting on a plane destined to fall out of the sky.

What was better—to be helpless and therefore blameless, or to have had the chance to change events and failed?

Sleep stole over her before she found an answer.

3
NEGATIVE SPACE

"So," Alex said the next morning, propping his feet on the coffee table. "Tell me everything you know since Blake moved to Vancouver. He met Alain online, didn't he?"

Sunlight streamed through the balcony door, catching sparks of gold and brass in his damp hair. With the clouds burned away, the city seemed less like something trapped in a snow globe. Mountains rose in the north, soaring snow-veined peaks that might have sprung up overnight. Wind rattled the windows, sharp as a razor despite the morning's brightness.

Liz sat curled in one corner of the couch, still wearing her pajamas, a second cup of coffee cradled in both hands. It wasn't helping; fatigue weighed on her, dragging at eyes and limbs. She'd dreamt no more portents last night, but fitful sleep took its toll.

"In an art forum. A year later Alain came to New York for a week. Blake and I took a train to the city to meet him. You were in London that summer. He was—" She raised a hand, groping for words to describe someone she'd only met once. "Sarcastic, irreverent, sweet. A month later Blake visited Vancouver."

"And decided to stay."

She nodded. It had been no surprise by then, not after seeing the two of them together. Hearing the way Blake's voice brightened every time he answered the phone. There had been no warning dreams, only the bittersweet happiness of a friend leaving. She'd known Blake liked to run—she knew about the nightmare that had been his family, and his escape from home at seventeen. She'd watched him run from half a dozen other situations—some better, some not—before they moved in together. But when he left for Vancouver, she thought he was running *to*, not *from*.

"He wrote at first. Emailed. Called a few times. He talked about the city, about the gallery that showed Alain's work. Everything seemed like it was going well. He sounded... strained the last time I talked to him, but he said it was stress about a show, money, his visa. And then—" She shrugged.

Alex's eyes narrowed. "And then you had the dream."

Liz nodded again, staring into the depths of her cup. The room's powdered creamer left an unappetizing skin across the surface. She'd called again this morning but reached nothing but voicemail. She hadn't left another message.

"Liz." The tone of his voice drew her head up. "If something has happened—*if*—you can't blame yourself for it."

"Of course not." But she was never any good at lying, not even to herself. "I didn't call as often as I should have. I stopped writing—"

"You have a life. So does he. You can't be there all the time. Nor should you." His voice softened. "I know about Alice—"

She recoiled—head turning, arms crossing, one knee pulling toward her chest. *I don't have to ask how it makes you feel,* Dr. Matson's voice echoed in her head. *Your posture tells me that.*

"I'm sorry," Alex said.

"No." She forced herself to unknot, to face him. "Don't be." She never should have told him if she didn't want it mentioned. "Blake isn't Alice."

"No. Of course not." He leaned forward, feet sliding to the floor. "You wrote each other—you have his address. That's the best place to start."

THEY CAUGHT A bus across town, within a block of the address Blake had given her. The apartment was a narrow building above a Korean grocery and a palmist's shop, grimy brick walls and rusting wrought-iron balconies.

A dark corridor lined in mailboxes ran past Madame Cecile's, thick with the scent of kimchi and patchouli. An *Out of Order* sign on the elevator sent them up three flights of creaking stairs. Graffiti hieroglyphs tagged the walls, and green and amber bottles were piled in the corners—someone trying to stay warm.

The fourth floor hallway smelled of musty central heating and damp carpet, cooking spices and trash that should have been taken out a day ago. One overhead light buzzed in a low locust drone. A TV blared at the far end, dramatic music and impassioned voices.

They walked the length of the hall twice, somehow missing the right door both times. The stuttering light set her pulse throbbing queasily in her temples. The air was heavy, and she unbuttoned the collar of her coat. Alex tugged his long striped scarf away from his neck, one hand slipping into the pocket where he kept his inhaler.

"What the hell?" he muttered.

Liz began another pass down the corridor, counting every door under her breath. 425, 423, 421, 417... She pulled up too fast and nearly stumbled, but Alex's hand closed on her elbow, hauling her back to the disappearing door. 419. She pressed a hand against the wood veneer, half expecting it to dissolve at her touch.

She knocked, gloved knuckles muffled against hollow-core, but no one stirred. The door rattled softly under the pressure of her hand; the handle was scratched near the lock plate, as though someone had tried to force it. She rapped again with no better luck.

"You feel it too, don't you?" Liz said, rubbing her aching head.

Alex glared at the door. "I feel something, all right, and I don't like it. You're sure this is the right address?"

She pulled an envelope out of her coat pocket, brandishing it like a warrant. Alex nodded and reached for his wallet. He took out a card—a university copy card, the same size and thickness as a credit card—and held it up in a mirroring gesture. "How badly do you want to look inside?"

Her eyebrows rose. "Will that work?"

"It does in films." He glanced both ways, but the hall was empty.

The television soundtrack swelled to a crescendo. "Nothing like a little B and E to enliven a vacation."

The card slipped between door and sill, scraping against metal. Alex cursed softly, then leaned on the handle. The door swung open with a creak. Liz flinched, expecting shouts, accusations, a sudden blare of sirens. Only silence greeted them, and a draft of cold, stale air that smelled faintly of Chinese food and art supply stores. It was the smell that let her take the first cautious step over the threshold.

Alex shut the door quietly behind them and reached for the light switch, but it clicked back and forth uselessly. Wan daylight seeped through a window across the room. Posters watched them from the walls: Tom Waits, Peter Murphy, a *City of Lost Children* print. Ikea furniture, a threadbare red velvet couch. Art supplies lay scattered across the room, a familiar controlled chaos that made her chest tighten.

"This is it." She spoke in a whisper, but it was still too loud for the silent room. "This is the right apartment."

"It would have been embarrassing if it weren't," Alex said dryly. His voice was thin and strained, his lips pinched pale. His chest swelled as he took a hit of his inhaler and deflated again with his sigh. "I'm fine," he said before Liz could ask, waving her toward the room. The strange pressure and nausea faded as she stepped away from the door.

Newspapers and books covered the folding table in the dining nook. The window opened onto a fire escape and a view of another dirty brick wall. Dishes filled the kitchen sink and white paper cartons littered the counter. Liz's nose wrinkled at the sour tang of old lo mein noodles and sesame chicken. At least it was too cold for flies.

"This has been here for days, at least," Alex said, risking a closer look at the cartons and retreating quickly.

If the apartment had been broken into, she couldn't tell at a glance. The TV and stereo were still there, and it was impossible to tell if anything was out of place amid the mess. Except...

Sketchbooks were strewn across the scuffed wooden floor, pages bent. Despite the chaos, Blake had always been careful with his supplies. Alex knelt, smoothing creases in heavy paper, and handed her a sketchpad.

Liz recognized Blake's work; even simple pencil and charcoal sketches had a powerful economy, a grace of line and form. Disembodied features and anatomical studies covered the pages—the curve of a jaw, hands stripped of skin, a slender back with spine and muscles bared. Over and over she saw the same eyes, dark and narrow beneath a sweep of lashes. At the back of the book she found another pair—pale eyes and arching brows, hints of nose and cheek. Not Alain. Pages had been ripped out, tattered edges caught in the spiral binding. Liz closed the book carefully and set it on the couch.

"What do you think, Watson?" Alex asked, picking up a stack of mail from the coffee table.

Liz tried to raise one eyebrow, but suspected she was only squinting. "What makes you think you're Holmes?"

"Justifiable arrogance and a predilection for pharmaceuticals. And you'd look silly in a deerstalker."

"So would you." She leaned over his elbow to look at the mail. Bills, junk mail, something to Alain Ngo from the University of British Columbia.

"He never wore one in the books, you know. That's—"

"A cinematic invention that became part of the folk process," Liz finished, rolling her eyes. "I know."

"I heard that eye roll," he said, not looking up from the mail. "What was the gallery Blake told you about?"

She frowned. "I'm not sure—it's in an email. Something with an M, I think."

"The Morgenstern Gallery?" He pulled flyers out of the stack and handed them to her with a flourish.

"That sounds right." She stared at glossy paper. *Carving Spirals: sculpture and paintings by Gemma Pagan. The Seduction of Gravity: photographs by Robert Files. Black Dogs and Blue Girls: photography by Alain Ngo.* "This must be it."

Alex arched an eyebrow. "What do you think, Watson? Shall we investigate?"

* * *

THE MORGENSTERN GALLERY was three stories of red brick, wedged into a row of art and music stores along Granville Street. On the sign above the glass double-doors, a faceless angel lifted a star. Its halo was black, an absence of light, and golden wings dissolved into smoke and flame. A poster in the window advertised the newest exhibit.

Deaths and Entrances: Transitions in photography, sculpture, and oils. Open to the public December 20ⁿᵈ through January 25ᵗʰ. Private showing December 19ᵗʰ @8:00 PM.

The gallery was closed, but lights were on inside. Pressing her face against the glass, Liz saw movement. She rubbed the oily nose-smudge off the door—then, before she could stop herself, she knocked.

At first the figures inside ignored her, but after the third knock a dark-haired woman emerged from the shadows. Her sigh was audible even before she threw the bolt and pushed the door open a few inches.

"We're closed," she said, a German accent sharpening consonants already crisp with annoyance. She was tall to begin with, and the doorstep gave her another few inches of imperious height. "The next exhibit opens—"

"I'm sorry," Liz interrupted, voice cracking. Anxiety clenched cold fingers around her throat and stomach. Her cheeks burned with nerves and her tongue felt three sizes too big. *For Blake,* she reminded herself when she wanted to turn and run. "I'm sorry to bother you. My name is Elizabeth Drake, and this is Alex McLure. We're friends of Blake Enderly's. I can't get in touch with him, and I was hoping maybe someone here could help."

The final syllable came out a squeak, the last of her courage run dry. The woman's eyes widened and she leaned back, dragging the door open another inch. "Oh."

A man stepped up behind her, filling the gap in the doorway. "What is it?"

The woman glanced at him. "They're friends of Blake's."

"Oh." He blinked in a nearly identical double-take. His eyes were unnervingly pale in the shadows. "Then you know about the accident?" His *eths* were *zees,* like the woman's.

"We don't know anything," Liz said, her voice rising in frustration. "Only that something's wrong and we can't reach him. What accident?"

The man sighed and dragged a hand through his short brown hair. "It's... not a long story, perhaps, but an unhappy one. There's a café just down the street—would you like to get some coffee and hear it?"

AND SO THEY ended up two blocks away at Café Al Azrad. Red awnings cracked in the breeze and light glowed from the windows—only early afternoon, but clouds rolled off the sea and the day greyed and dimmed. Warm air gusted over them as Rainer—Rainer Morgenstern, the gallery's owner—held the door for them. Liz sighed as she breathed in coffee and cinnamon, and Alex's shoulders straightened from a pained hunch.

As they stepped inside, a picture caught Liz's eye—a framed print dark against the sandstone wall. She moved closer and froze, even when Alex collided with her shoulder.

A man's face floated in black water, his dark skin tinged green. Half-lidded eyes rolled sightlessly back, creased by lines of pain and laughter. More lines connected the flare of broad nostrils to the corners of his full-lipped mouth. A hand and foot and part of an arm floated around him.

Liz's mouth dried. She knew the title before she looked at the plaque: *Osiris*, by Blake Enderly.

"What is it?" Alex asked, only to answer himself on the same breath. "Oh."

They turned to find Rainer watching them, pale eyes narrowed. Alex frowned.

"Was this a test?" he said. "To see if we really know Blake?"

Rainer tilted his head in a shrug. "Yes. And you passed. So let's get something to drink, and talk."

THEY COLLECTED DRINKS and desserts and settled into a maroon leather booth. Liz picked apart layers of baklava as an awkward silence settled with them, full of the hum of machinery and whispering wind. Portishead crooned softly on the radio: *Please could you stay a while to share my grief, for it's such a lovely day to have to always feel this way.*

"Where is Blake?" she asked at last. Memories rose, leaking implacably through her careful walls: muffled voices in another room; her aunt framed in her bedroom door, her face slack and strange; Alis's voice through a bad connection, tinny and flat with distance and pain. All the different guises bad news wore.

The woman—Antja—glanced aside, long dark eyes unreadable. Rainer swallowed and a muscle leapt in his jaw.

"In the hospital. Lions Gate. He's... in a coma."

Liz flinched, slopping cappuccino foam against the side of her cup. Alex leaned forward. "A *coma?*"

"There was a storm. Someone found him washed up on the shore of Carroll Cove the next day."

Drowned. An electric shock washed through Liz; blood roared in her ears, and for an instant everything else was grey and far away. "What happened?" Her voice could have been a stranger's.

"They don't know. Alain was with him." Only a heartbeat's hesitation, but enough to hear the worst in that indrawn breath. "He died."

The grey roar worsened. Under the table, Alex's hand settled on her knee, warm and steady. She straightened, blinking until her vision focused; she could fall apart later. "What's going to happen?"

"I don't know." Rainer's blunt, manicured fingers tapped the side of his demitasse cup. A yellow stone gleamed on his right ring finger. "No one knows." He paused, eyebrows arching. Familiar eyebrows—now she knew whom the second set of eyes in Blake's sketchbook belonged to. "You came all the way from Connecticut?"

"He's a good friend."

"But how did you know?"

"I... didn't, exactly. I had a feeling something was wrong."

She braced for skepticism, but instead he smiled. He wasn't precisely handsome—too little chin, a hairline that promised to recede early—but his smile was charming. Compelling. The pull of it unsettled and warmed her in equal measure.

"I'm glad you did," he said. "Blake will be glad, too. Had you spoken to him recently?"

Was the question a little too casual? Or was that her own guilt talking? She forced down a bite of baklava, washed away the sticky sweetness with her cooling coffee. "Not for a few months."

Their eyes met and she shivered at the intensity of his pale stare. Magnetic, electric. She wanted to lean closer, but was afraid she'd shock herself if she did. Then it was gone, replaced with polite interest.

"What about Alain?" Alex asked. "Will there be a service?"

"Yes. This Saturday at Capilano View." Rainer dragged a hand over his face and his magnetism faded into weary pallor.

Antja glanced up, lovely and inscrutable as a sphinx. She had picked her *pain au chocolat* into tiny slivers, but didn't seem to have eaten any of it. She set down her fork and laid a hand on his arm. "We should be getting back."

Rainer glanced at his watch. "We should. Please excuse us," he said. He reached into an inside jacket pocket and pulled out a business card. "A new exhibit opens on Friday. Blake and Alain's work will be on display. I'd like you both to come." He handed the card to Liz, including Alex with a glance.

Their fingers brushed as she took the card. Instead of the electric shock she'd feared, only a faint shiver passed between them. It left a tenderness in her chest as it faded, like a nearly-healed bruise.

"The show is at eight," Rainer continued. "I hope to see you there." He collected his coat and umbrella and offered Antja a hand out of the booth. Light rippled across the door as they stepped outside, and then they vanished into the gathering dusk.

Liz and Alex exchanged a glance and she swallowed the urge to say *I told you so*. He acknowledged it all the same, a wry tilt of his head.

"Well," he said, snaking out an arm to claim the last of her baklava. "This is an interesting development."

4

DEATH BY WATER

It was only a hospital.

Liz had visited them often enough: her own childhood tumbles, her aunt's hysterectomy and grandmother's bypass, Alex's bout of pneumonia two years ago. Nothing dramatic. Nothing traumatic. Lions Gate was no worse than any of those. But the smell of air freshener and plastic and cafeteria coffee still set her nerves on edge.

It was a hospital, she told herself. Not a morgue.

Liz looked straight ahead as she followed Dr. Haddad down the beige-and-sepia hallway, boots squicking softly on the tiles. She concentrated on the sway of the woman's black braid against her burgundy scrubs and kept her eyes away from open doorways; she needed all her resolve for Blake.

"Mr. Morgenstern called," Dr. Haddad had said when she met them in the lobby. "He told me to expect you. You're Mr. Enderly's sister?" Her eyebrow had quirked when she said it, as if she knew it for a lie. But Liz had nodded, dry-mouthed, and the doctor had accepted her answer.

She was no good at lying, but for Blake she was willing to try.

"You can't stay long, I'm afraid," the doctor said when they reached the room. "His condition is still guarded."

"We understand," Liz said. "We appreciate anything you can do."

The room was silent except for the noise of machines and the faint buzz of the lights. The other beds were empty, their privacy curtains pushed back. Liz nearly stopped in the doorway, but she forced herself to keep moving.

Coma. She'd repeated the word over and over in her head until it became a meaningless collection of sounds. She had braced herself, she'd thought. She was prepared.

She hadn't. She wasn't. Her chest tightened as she focused on the solitary form in the bed. She couldn't get enough breath.

He'd cut his hair. Amidst the mechanical spider web of tubes and wires, the beep and hum of monitors, that struck her hardest of all. It had been the thing she'd noticed first six years ago—a skinny teenage boy sitting cross-legged on the hood of a rust-mottled car, elbow-length chestnut hair falling in front of his face as he hunched over a sketchbook. Now it was a tangled brown shock, sea wrack washed against the pillow.

Other details filtered through more slowly: bruised and sunken eyes, cheekbones too sharp, shadows pooled in the hollow of his throat. Blake had always been thin, but now he was whittled down to bone and sinew. A tube wormed across his cheek and into his nose—her throat convulsed at the sight.

Liz swallowed sour spit and reached for his right hand—another tube was taped into his left. She flinched at the touch: too cold, veins too stark. Tendons and metacarpals stood out through flesh like sticks in a rice paper fan.

"Blake." She choked on his name. "I'm here."

No response, not even a flicker of eyelids. She'd never seen his face so empty before; even in sleep there had been some furrowing of his brow, some movement of his lips. Never this awful repose.

What were you hoping for? she asked herself bitterly. *A miracle?* Of course she was. That she would walk in and he'd wake up, happy as a fairy tale. Pressure swelled in her sinuses, prickling behind her eyes. She knew fairy tales better than that.

"What happened to him, exactly?" Alex asked. Liz was grateful for his calm detachment. She didn't think she could speak around the lump in her throat.

"We don't know," Dr. Haddad said. "He and his friend washed

up on the shore of Carroll Cove after a storm. It's a miracle he didn't die of hypothermia. His oxygen saturation is within normal values and there's no apparent brain damage. He had a few abrasions, most likely from debris in the water, but nothing to indicate assault."

"That's all?"

Dr. Haddad's lips pursed. "His blood alcohol content was point-oh-six. Toxicology also turned up trace amounts of a psychoactive. A dissociative—not one I've seen before."

Alex's eyebrow rose. "Could that have caused the coma?"

"That's difficult to say."

"What's the official diagnosis, then?"

"Hypoxic insult secondary to near-drowning."

Where are you? The rhythm of Blake's heart blipped past on the monitor, faint but steady; his chest rose and fell beneath the white sheet. But the hand Liz held might have belonged to a doll.

"We should be going," Dr. Haddad said after a moment. "We'll alert you if there's any change."

"Thank you," Alex said, touching Liz gently on the shoulder.

"Could we have a minute alone with him?" she asked.

The doctor's smile creased one plump brown cheek, but her eyes were sad. "You can have five. I'll wait outside." The door closed softly behind her.

Liz bit her lip, warmth and pressure leaking out of her eyes. She scrubbed away the glaze of tears one-handed, not letting go of Blake's fingers. Familiar dark crescents still stained his fingernails, ink or charcoal, and pencil calluses roughened thumb and forefinger. She wondered how long it would take them to fade.

But they won't, she told herself fiercely, *because he'll wake up.*

Alex peered into the closet where Blake's clothes lay neatly folded: sweater, t-shirt, jeans, a pair of boots that hadn't taken well to water. No answers. No miracles.

Alex caught her elbow as she turned away from the bed, a steadying pressure. "You can't blame yourself," he said softly.

It did nothing to help the sick, empty feeling in her chest. She didn't reply, only followed him back to the car.

She wiped her eyes with a tissue as she tugged on her seatbelt, staring sightlessly through the windshield, trying to find a way out of the Möbius loop of grief and guilt. A minute later she realized they weren't moving, that Alex had a map open across the steering wheel.

"What are you doing?" she finally asked.

His eyebrows rose as he glanced up. "What do you think we're doing? We're going to Carroll Cove."

THEY DROVE NORTH and east into the indigo shadow of the mountains, where the city gave way to towering firs and blue drifts of snow. No Trespassing signs warned them away from the narrow road to the cove, but no one challenged them as they turned in. At the end of a long, twisting lane, the trees thinned and Liz saw the water.

Glaciated hills rose on either side of a narrow cove, thick with fir and hemlock and cedar. A dirt road circled the shore, connecting the few well-spaced cabins that stood by the water's edge. No cars, no chimney smoke, no sign of habitation. Alex pulled onto the shoulder and killed the ignition; silence rushed in to fill the car, broken only by the engine's fading ticks.

Warmth rushed out as Liz opened her door; yellow grass crunched underfoot. The water was a sheet of grey glass, mirroring the silver-clouded sky. Liz imagined the scent of pine and salt, but all she smelled was winter.

"What are we looking for?" she asked softly. Her voice cracked, and she realized she hadn't spoken since they left the hospital.

"I'm not sure." Alex's voice was hushed as well. The stillness was nearly palpable. "Clues. Though I don't know what might be left to find."

Storm-wrack littered the road—scattered branches, drifts of pine needles, even a few uprooted trees near the edge of the forest. Snow dusted the cracked and frozen ground. The distant cries of gulls scattered across the water.

Something sleek and dark surfaced with a splash. Liz jumped, but it was only an otter. Shining black eyes watched them for an instant before it dove again.

"You're bloody edgy," Alex said.

"Maybe you're too bloody calm." The words came out harsher than she intended and she shot him an apologetic glance, crossing her arms against the cold.

His sigh hung in the air between them. "You were right," he said slowly. "I admit it. But being a bundle of nerves won't help either of you. You'll only wear yourself out."

"Easy for you to say." She kicked a stone, sending it skittering down the road ahead of them. It echoed like a landslide. "Something is wrong. Still wrong. *More* wrong. Don't you feel it?"

"Of course something's wrong. But I believe in unconscious cues, preconscious perception—I never claimed to be psychic."

She never had either. Not out loud. But coincidence and preconsciousness weren't enough to explain her dreams.

They both tensed as they passed the first house, waiting for someone to emerge and accuse them of trespassing. The cabin was dark and shuttered, though, and they heard nothing but gulls and their own footsteps.

A breeze ruffled the surface of the cove. Liz tugged her stocking cap over her ears and Alex wound his scarf tighter. Her lungs burned with every breath—what was the water like? A miracle, the doctor had said, and she couldn't argue with that.

They passed more cabins, all dark and empty. Summer cottages, like the ones in Cape Cod. Expensive for starving artists, even in the off season.

"What was Blake doing out here?" Alex said, voicing her own question. Liz only shrugged.

Alex frowned, shoulders hunching until his chest was a narrow concavity. "Blake and Alain were just out for a romantic stroll and fell in the water?"

Liz rubbed the tip of her tongue against her teeth. "That doesn't make sense, but I'm not sure why."

"Because he didn't have a coat. There wasn't one at the hospital, at any rate. Unconscious clues, remember?"

Liz rolled her eyes, but couldn't stop a smile. It felt strange on her face. "So they were in one of the houses. But which one?"

They followed the path until it ended in a tangle of fern and lichen-green boulders. Beyond that lay the greater water of Indian Arm. Waves glittered like chisel strokes in grey granite. Liz blew on her gloved hands, watching her breath drift away on the breeze. The sky was too heavy—it would crush her if it fell.

They turned back, but Alex's frown deepened as they neared the car. She recognized that frown; he wore it when confronted with a puzzle or an elusive bit of research. "How many houses are on this side of the cove?"

Liz blinked and glanced over her shoulder. "Four."

The frown became a scowl. "That's what I keep thinking too. But there are five."

They turned in unison, as if they might surprise the elusive house. One, two, three, four... and yes, five. But as soon as her eyes moved, the certainty evaporated. Alex stalked back down the path, shoulders hunching like a disgruntled heron.

As they drew closer, Liz blinked against a wave of dizziness. Her temples began to throb. She drew up, but Alex pressed on, and after a moment she stumbled after him. Glass sparkled amid the gravel, crunching under their boots. Something else crunched, too—tar paper. She looked up to see shattered windows, shingles ripped from the roof.

"How did we not notice this?" Liz asked as she caught up. Alex only shook his head. "The storm shutters weren't closed," she continued. "Someone might have been here."

Finally, when they climbed the steps and stood in front of the door, the pain in her head eased and her eyes stopped blurring. From Alex's rasping sigh, he felt it too. The front door was locked, much too secure for a credit card. But with so many broken windows that was hardly a problem.

Liz circled the house, ignoring Alex's strained, "Be careful."

"Help me up," she said, clearing shards of glass from a windowsill on the far side. "What?" she said when his eyebrows rose. "You're the one who started this."

He sighed. "In for a penny..."

In for two to ten. She decided not to say that out loud.

He knelt, and Liz stepped into his cupped hands, trying to ignore his grunt as he took her weight. He boosted her until she had a grip on the inside frame and could haul herself over the ledge. She grabbed his arm and pulled as he scrambled in after her.

They had crawled into a bedroom. The curtain rod hung askew, ripped half free of the wall, and pale light slanted across a neatly made bed. A lamp lay broken on the floor beside the nightstand. Through the cold she smelled damp and insidious mildew.

The whistle of Alex's breath stopped her as she started to leave the room. He sank to the floor, face slick and pale, and tugged the scarf away from his throat while he fumbled in his coat pocket for his inhaler. His hands trembled as he took a hit.

Liz dropped to her knees beside him, her chest tightening in sympathy. "Are you all right?"

He nodded, sucking in a long breath. "I will be," he said on the exhalation. His breath was bittersweet with chemicals. "So much for my career as a cat burglar." He smiled, but the corners of his mouth pinched white.

"Are you sure?" His glasses slid down his long nose, and her reflection floated in the striated blue of his irises.

"Yes. Just let me rest a moment." The lingering wheeze in his breath wasn't convincing. He lowered his head, dusty blond hair drifting around his face. "Go on. I'll catch up. I mean it," he said when she hesitated. "I'll be fine."

She frowned, but finally stood. It was no use trying to fuss over him; he'd never admit to all the pain. She'd appreciated his cool reserve when they first met—a grounding counterpoint to her own nerves and dread—but sometimes she wanted to tear down his walls with a sledgehammer, if that was what it took to get an unqualified answer from him.

Instead she opened the closet door, but found nothing but spare blankets and a bland print of loons on the water that might have come with the cabin. The bedroom door opened into a dim hallway; the opposite room was just as empty.

What had she expected to find? A bloody coat? A body in the closet? *Yeah, me and Nancy Drew.*

The hall led to the living room, where a sliding glass door lay in shining fragments across the floor, Venetian blinds ripped apart and scattered. Beyond the jagged doorframe was the broken remnant of a deck. An easel leaned against the far wall, its wooden legs warped out of true—Liz's pulse sped at the sight.

Despite the breeze rattling the torn blinds, the room held a strange, layered smell. Damp and salt, but also something raw and metallic, a hint of animal musk, a sharp chemical stink like turpentine. Liz shook her head against a sneeze and the miasma faded, until she wasn't sure if she'd only imagined it. Beneath the weight of coat and sweater, her skin crawled.

"Find anything yet, Watson?" Alex asked, pausing in the doorway.

"I'd rather be Nancy Drew," she said, clinging to jokes to hold her unease at bay. "Does that make you Bess or George?"

"Either is better than Ned. At least Watson had a gun."

"Actually—" Even forced humor died as she stared at the floor by her feet. "I think I may have found something."

Red-brown stains spotted the floorboards, nearly hidden beneath a Persian rug. She crouched and eased a sliver of glass free of the tangled fringe. It glittered like a rusty diamond.

"What does this look like to you?"

Alex knelt and took the fragment from her. "Just what it looks like to you, I assume. But we shouldn't jump to conclusions." The interest in his eyes belied the caution.

"What conclusions aren't you jumping to?"

He held the bloody shard to the light, then peeled the rug up to reveal more smeared stains. "You'd think Dr. Haddad would have mentioned a wound that bled so much. So if this isn't Blake or Alain's blood, whose is it?"

He dropped the shard with a grimace and rose, eyes narrowing as he studied the wall beside the broken door. Liz followed his gaze: more dark stains on the white plaster. A spray of thick ruddy drops inches above her head. She wished she remembered more about blood spatter from their undergraduate forensics class.

"How could the police have missed all this?" Alex muttered.

"Maybe they had trouble counting five houses too."

Liz turned toward the water and the wreckage of the deck. The clouds were already darkening, blue twilight leaking out of the mountains' shadow. The cove shone dark as mercury. As she looked down, a glint of silver in the water caught her eye. Boards creaked as she stepped out.

"What are you doing?" Alex asked.

"I see something." She crouched and crawled forward, splinters snagging on her gloves and jeans. A silver chain glittered just under the water, tangled on a broken plank. "I think I can reach it."

"I don't want to drive straight back to the hospital." The deck shivered under his weight.

She tugged her glove off with her teeth and reached down, hissing as the water closed around her fingers. Boards bit into her ribs as she wriggled forward.

"Liz, be careful." A second later Alex's hands closed on her ankles.

"Almost—" she mumbled around a mouthful of leather. She stretched until her arm ached and tendons stood taut in her hand. The icy water numbed her flesh.

Ripples scattered her reflection. The image reformed, but now the pale face floating below her wasn't her own but Blake's. Reaching for her, sinking just out of reach—

She gasped and her glove slipped from her mouth, splashing into the cove and breaking the illusion. Wood groaned and a board slipped. She would have shouted, but the sudden pressure of Alex's hands closing on her coat and yanking her back drove the breath out of her. They staggered into the safety of the cabin as a plank collapsed into the water. The sound carried like a gunshot.

"What happened?" Alex asked, one arm tight around her. His chest rose and fell too quickly against her back; her pulse sped to match his.

"I—" She swallowed. "I slipped."

"Christ," he whispered. His arm tightened convulsively and then fell away. "That was a year of my life. Did you find something?"

She pried open fingers blanched grey as paste. Silver gleamed in her palm. The delicate links of the chain had broken near the clasp, one end tangled around a ring. Liz's chest hitched when she saw the design engraved on the heavy band: an intricate triskelion, its coils dark with tarnish.

Her breath left with a whimper and she bit her lip to hold it back. "This was Blake's."

"You're certain?"

"I gave it to him." It had been her grandfather's, and too big for her to wear. Blake had joked about commitment when she'd given it to him, but he kept it. He wore it on a chain while he painted.

She dried her gloveless hand on her jeans and shoved it into her pocket, the ring still pressed tight against her palm. The temperature was fading with the light, and her teeth began to chatter. Her coat sleeve was damp nearly to the elbow.

"We should go," she said, but when she tried to do just that her knees wobbled.

"In a moment," Alex said, steering her toward the sofa. "You should sit down, and I want to have one last look around."

Cold leather crackled as she sat. The weather hadn't been kind to the furniture. Doors and drawers rattled as Alex prowled the narrow kitchen. Cradling her half-frozen arm against her chest, she stared at the broken door, the glass and blood. The door had shattered inward, but Blake had gone out. Into the cold, into the water.

Alex returned, breaking her view of the gloaming sky and distracting her from increasingly morbid thoughts. His mouth stretched in a thin, humorless smile as he held something out to her.

A checkbook. The checks were all gone, leaving nothing but dusty ragged edges and carbon copy duplicates. All from the account of Rainer Morgenstern.

LIZ RODE BACK to the hotel in a daze, turning the ring over and over between her fingers. She felt numb through, deeper than the blasting heater could ever touch. She surfaced from her fugue when traffic congested and slowed across Lions Gate Bridge. Brake lights blazed Christmas-bright, reflecting in every raindrop scattered across the windshield.

"Oh, for fuck's sake," Alex muttered.

She couldn't see any police cars or ambulances, but all three lanes had trickled to a halt. Car doors stood open in front of them, and a group of people clustered around the far railing.

"Bloody vultures," Alex said. "All they need are bread and circuses. What are you doing?" he asked as she reached for the door handle.

She shook her head and stepped into the icy wind. Frozen grey slush crunched and slipped under her feet. Sleet stung her face as the wind ripped her breath away. The air was too heavy, charged and prickling. Liz's hand tightened around the ring.

"You could have told me you wanted hypothermia for Christmas," Alex muttered as he followed her out.

Liz moved closer, sidling between the spectators pressed against the concrete divider between the northbound lane and the pedestrian walkway, all angling for a better look. "What's happening?" she asked the closest person. The wind moaned around them; steel and concrete creaked and her stomach lurched with the bridge's sway.

"A jumper," the woman said.

"We'll be here for hours," someone else complained, voice high and thin beneath the selfishness.

Liz saw the man then, over the heads of the crowd. He crouched on the icy railing, balancing against the gusting wind, shirtless and barefoot. His skin was already a sickly blue-grey. Long toes curled against the green-painted rail. Matted grey hair whipped away from his face and Liz sucked in a breath.

The street preacher. Yves.

"I have seen the black moons," he shouted. "I have seen the towers of the lost city."

Liz leaned against the divider, drawn by the power of his voice, the horror of the scene. A few onlookers had crossed the barrier and gathered by the rail, hands outstretched and helpless. Someone reached toward the old man; another man shouted him back. A woman knelt beside the railing, trying earnestly to get Yves' attention. A siren wailed in the distance.

"He is coming, and the stars will burn your eyes out! *Mais mon âme, c'est le mien!*"

An onlooker lunged, but Yves had already arched back into the wind, arms spread wide. For a breathless instant he hung there, cruciform against the wide grey sky, and Liz wondered if he might fly. Then he fell, backwards toward the dark waiting water. The crowd rushed forward to lean over the edge. Most turned away quickly.

Someone sobbed once. Someone cursed. The siren wailed again, closer now, but still too late.

In his dreams he drowned.

Blake had never admitted it, not even to Liz or Alain, but he'd always hated the ocean. Its endless pull and alien landscapes. The way it clutched and caressed like hands you couldn't stop. It reduced, devoured. It would always be bigger and stronger than him.

He tried to swim, tried to move at all, but he wasn't sure his limbs were there to answer him. Only the aching cold and relentless current dragging him down. He wanted so badly to breathe, but there was only water burning his eyes and lips and nose.

No light, no warmth—just whispering voices and darkness that tasted of blood and turpentine. Was this what Osiris felt, or Orpheus? Drifting, drowning, numb.

Memories unfurled like anemones behind his eyes, flashes of color and sound: a picture; a door; screams and blood; oil-slick shadows rushing all around him. A storm that split the world open and let all the monsters in. The monsters were with him still, curling inside him, their claws in his brain.

If he drifted long enough the sea would take him apart, reduce him to coral and salt and pearl, and he wouldn't need to think about monsters anymore. That would be a mercy, at least.

I'm sorry, but mercy is not an option. Not yet.

The voice rolled through his head, a rush of warmth amidst so much cold. The sudden uninvited intimacy would have made him cringe, if he'd had muscle to flinch and flesh to crawl. But it was something to cling to, a spar in the storm.

Who are you?

I can be a guide, if you'll let me. There may be a way out, though it won't be easy. You have to remember. You have to rebuild the door.

I don't want to. The childishness of the words drew another mental cringe. But the darkness and cold were a balm, soothing half-healed hurts. Maybe numb wasn't such a bad way to be.

Then you'll be trapped here forever, the voice said, gentle and relentless. Dark as bronze, rich and heavy as velvet. Despite himself, Blake wanted to wrap it around him until he was warm again. **You can set yourself free, if you rebuild the door. The way out is through. But first you must go down.**

The idea should terrify him; he knew that much. But the endless black brine numbed his fear as it did his flesh. And what else did he have to do?

The current pulled him down, and he let memories wash over him.

5

STARS AND OMENS

THAT NIGHT LIZ walked through crowded market streets, listening to vendors hawk their wares. Butterscotch light slanted through low clouds, gilding minarets and rooftop gardens, and the wind smelled of fish and spices and autumn. Wine-colored leaves hung translucent from dark branches, piled in drifts along the cobbled streets. Cats prowled the bazaar, twining around her bare feet and slinking past stalls, snatching any treats that fell. The merchants were resigned to this, and most tossed food to the sleek-furred hordes.

The city was the same patchwork construction she'd always known—red brick and cobbles alongside marble towers and onion domes, ivy and roses growing beside tropical orchids and mango trees. The people were much the same, pale skinned and brown and aubergine-black, scarred and tattooed and veiled. A dozen cultures she might have recognized and more she couldn't. And some furred and scaled, inhuman shapes swathed in silk and muslin robes. All going about their shopping, picking their way through clutters of cats.

Liz shivered as the afternoon chill leached through her pajamas and the soles of her feet. The streets were quieter than she remembered, the shadows more threatening. Last time she dreamed this place it had been sunlit and warm. Last time she hadn't been alone. She turned, even though she knew better, searching the crowd for familiar faces. Waited for someone to call her name.

Nothing. Dreamtime had flowed on without her, washing away all her childhood friends, leaving a city full of strangers who barely glanced at her as they went about their business. Everyone she'd known was gone, and no amount of dreaming could bring them back.

Her life in dreams had been more vivid and rich than her waking world, from the time her parents died until she left high school. When she slept she didn't have to worry about navigating the cruel and alien cliques amongst her peers, or the boys whose desires she couldn't reciprocate, about placating the counselors who thought her too withdrawn, and the guilt in her aunt's eyes whenever she found time for her shy and awkward niece. Then came Alice's suicide, and the rounds of therapy and antidepressants, and Liz wished she could sleep and dream forever.

But she grew up, and college was better, and night by night, week by week, year by year, she remembered her dreams less and less, and her dreamland friends grew old without her. Four years, she realized—four years had passed since she last came back and found them gone.

Wake up, she told herself, but the dream held her. A marmalade cat butted his head against her ankle, mewing in sympathy. Or maybe only for a snack. She scratched his ears, but he wandered off when he saw her hands were empty.

As she straightened a wary mutter rippled between the shoppers, and the crowd parted at the far end of the market. The wind shifted and she smelled wet. She flinched, afraid for a moment that the shade of Alice had found her again, but the figure stumbling down the street was someone else.

The old man hugged his arms against his bony chest. Water ran from his tangled hair, pooled around his feet with every step. Cats followed at a safe distance, sniffing his trail. The locals eyed him with more suspicion; no one stopped to help when he tripped and fell to his knees. Liz's eyes widened as she recognized him.

"Are you all right?" she asked, crouching beside him. Which was, she realized, a stupid question.

Yves looked at her with wide, wild eyes. The Vancouver chill still clung to him, radiating from his grey-tinged flesh. "The water was very cold. It's been so long since I felt warm. So long... I didn't know if I'd ever find this place again."

She smiled ruefully. "It's an easy place to find." Even when you meant to stay away. She offered him a hand and rose. "Go to the temple," she said, nodding toward the ivy-walled tower rising above the rooftops. "The priests can help you."

"*Merci*." His chapped, broken-nailed hands enfolded hers, colder than the stones beneath her feet. Even icy and wan as he was, his flesh seemed more substantial than hers—this was his home now, and she was only visiting.

"The King came for me, you see," he said with a mad grin. "He wanted my soul. He showed me so many beautiful things... I saw the towers rise above the lost city. But I ran." He bowed over her hand, dripping cold salt water onto her wrist. "Thank you for your kindness. Be careful—I see His shadow on you. I'll pray for you and your friend at the temple."

He walked away before Liz could ask him what he meant. She wiped her hand on her T-shirt and chafed her fingers, trying to decide if she should go after him. Before she could make up her mind, a man beside her spoke.

"You have a kind heart to speak so gently to strangers." Tall and broad-shouldered, with skin the color of polished mahogany. He wore robes of white linen and his head was shaved. He studied her with heavy-lidded black eyes. "These dark times make men forget courtesy."

"I knew him from the waking world," she said, trying to keep her composure under the weight of his gaze.

"Ah." His lips curled. "Not a stranger, then, but I think you have a kind heart nonetheless." His voice was deep and rich, carefully measured as a stage actor's.

"What do you mean, these dark times?"

He shrugged, and a golden brooch flashed on his breast. "Travelers bring rumors of monsters on the roads, rumors of slavers. Caravans from Carcosa ride through towns and people vanish in the night."

"Carcosa?" It wasn't a name she'd heard before, dreaming or awake.

"The city of Carcosa. Lost Carcosa, some call it. The roads that lead there have long been sealed, but there are always ways around such obstacles."

Liz hugged herself. "Why does a lost city need slaves? And who is this King everyone keeps talking about?" And what did any of it have to do with Blake?

"He is a very old power," the man said, "whose star is rising again. His shadow is darkest here in the land of dreams, but your world is not untouched by it."

"Who are you? A priest?" He looked the part, but none of the priests she'd met smiled like that, so sleek and knowing and dangerous.

"Not exactly. You may call me Seker."

Her eyebrows rose. "Are you a god?"

Pearl-black eyes narrowed in amusement. "Conventional wisdom encourages me to say yes, doesn't it? But I'm only borrowing the name."

"Do you guide souls through the underworld?"

"I prefer to guide the living. The priests of the Ancients may offer comfort, but stronger measures will be needed as the shadow grows." His gaze held hers, and she felt her heart being weighed and measured. "What about you, dreamer? Will you fight for what you hold dear?"

She swallowed, her mouth gone dry. Her reflection in his eyes was so small. A little rabbit of a girl. "If I have to."

With that the dream dissolved around her, and she opened her eyes to the hotel ceiling and watery light rippling down the walls.

"If you have to what?" Alex asked. Liz turned her head to see him leaning against the doorway, holding a damp paper bag. "I brought breakfast."

RAIN WASHED THE windows while they ate. Liz spread cream cheese across a bagel and watched water sluice past the balcony. Clouds hung low, enfolding the city in grey wings. Through the mist and sifting rain Vancouver was as unreal as any dream city, and less familiar.

"What would you like to do today?" Alex asked.

She turned the idea over in her head. She ought to think of something distracting, a movie or a museum to take her mind off Blake. But even if the weather had been less bleak, the thought of sightseeing made her neck muscles tighten. It's not as though she would enjoy it anyway.

"I want to go back to the hospital."

Alex nodded, but his lips thinned. She couldn't blame him—grief wasn't a spectator sport. "You don't have to go with me."

He took his glasses off to clean them, frowning down at the frames. The sideways light gilded the tips of his eyelashes, turned his irises pale and silvery as water. "I should find something to wear to this gallery opening. Other than that, I wouldn't mind staying in today."

Liz nodded. She'd heard the strain in his breathing as she fell asleep the night before, and his voice was rough around the edges. "Of course."

He looked up and smiled, lenses flashing as he slid his glasses back on. "Don't worry. This is still better than being home for the holidays."

LIZ'S VOICE HELD through the first two chapters of the novel she'd picked up in the gift shop—a time traveling romance, full of questionable anatomy and even more dubious historical accuracy, on the off chance she could annoy Blake into waking up—but a lump kept forming in her throat. If he would just open his eyes, make a joke about Geneva conventions...

She finally let the book fall shut, breathing in the comforting scent of new paper and ink. It couldn't ease the helplessness gnawing at her stomach.

At least she wasn't making anyone else suffer; Blake had been moved to a private room. Was Rainer paying for that? She doubted the province would be so generous to a wayward American indigent.

For all its privacy, the room wasn't much cheerier than the ICU. It smelled the same: plastic, bleach, floor polish, something sour and organic she couldn't identify. At least it had a window. She'd dragged the single chair next to the bed, out of the square of weak sunlight.

She took Blake's cold hand in hers, abandoning the book. Had the staff guessed which hand was dominant? Had they looked at the calluses and ink stains? He could sketch left-handed, too, had taught himself after his father broke his right wrist when he was fifteen.

She tried to take comfort in the steady rhythm of the heart monitor, its constant peaks and valleys, but the hum and whine of machinery set her teeth on edge. His skin was grey as paste, crawling with blue-green veins.

There had to be something she could do, no matter what Alex said. Anything. Why the dreams, if she couldn't use them?

"I won't sit here and watch you waste away." A childish promise—what choice did she have? If she'd come sooner, would it have made a difference? She forced her thoughts away from that thorny path.

Liz scrubbed her clammy palms on her jeans; the ring slid loose on her right thumb. She brushed a strand of oily hair out of Blake's face. His earrings were gone, a row of empty indentations along the curve of his ear. It made her think of all the strangers who must touch him here, how much he'd hate it if he knew.

Where was the spirit while the flesh lay still? His eyes twitched softly beneath closed lids—did he dream? The thought didn't comfort her much.

"I'd kiss you awake, but I'm not qualified. Where's a handsome prince when we need one? Or a strapping highlander."

Drowned.

She closed her eyes against the heat of tears, lowering her head to edge of his pillow. Beneath starchy soap and unwashed hair and the sour tang of poor health she smelled his familiar autumn-leaf musk.

Where are you? The ring pinched her finger as she squeezed his hand. If he was dreaming, she could find him. She just had to dream the same dream.

The light dimmed through her closed eyes, like a cloud passing over the sun. The room tilted, vanished, and she was falling—

Into black and icy water. Blake's hand slipped from hers as liquid flooded her mouth and nose, bitter and rank. Salt burned her eyes. Darkness above and darkness below, with no hope of light or air.

For a moment they floated side by side. Then Blake began to sink.

Beneath him, at the heart of the abyss, something waited. Something vast and dark and hungry.

Liz stretched and kicked. The ring glowed incandescent through the murk as she reached for him. Her lungs burned and pressure closed around her, pushing at her eyes, constricting her ribs. No matter how she fought, she couldn't close the distance, and the black thing in the depths grew closer and closer.

This is no place for you, dreamer, a familiar voice whispered inside her head. **Go.**

She ignored it, kicking harder. For an instant she touched Blake's outstretched fingers. His eyes were open, staring sightlessly.

He is beyond your grasp. Go now!

With an awful wrench she was back in the hospital room, clutching Blake's hand hard enough to bruise. The book slid off her lap and thumped to the floor as she recoiled. Her head throbbed; her lungs ached; the coppery taste of blood filled her mouth.

Her hand burned—she slipped the ring off her thumb and stared at the red mark it left on her skin. Liquid rolled down her lip, splattered thick and crimson against her sweater. She leaned back with a shudder, pinching her nose shut.

Bile seared the back of her throat and she choked, swallowing sour spit. The ceiling swam in and out of focus and her heart pounded against her ribs. It was going to eat him. Whatever *it* was.

The doorknob turned and Liz startled again, scraping the chair back as she turned.

"Oh." Antja froze in the doorway and Liz thought she might bolt. "I didn't think anyone was here. I just wanted to see—"

"There—" Liz swallowed the taste of salt and metal, trying to keep her voice from shaking. "There's no change."

"Oh." Antja lingered on the threshold, hands shoved in the pockets of her black leather coat.

"Come in," Liz said, stepping back from the bed. She slipped the ring—cool again now—into her pocket.

Antja eased the door shut behind her, mauve lips pursing. "Your nose..." She pulled a tissue out of her purse and handed it to Liz. Her accent was thicker than Rainer's.

They both looked down at Blake; Antja broke first. "It's terrible, seeing him like that. Almost worse than Alain." She flinched as she said it. Liz knew better—bad as this was, it could be worse.

"I wish I knew what to do," Liz said, words muffled in tissue. If she'd been alone she might have sobbed. Instead she drew a deep breath, waiting for her heart to slow, for her stomach to stop its nauseous sway.

"Me too." Antja's eyes closed, a weight of fear and fatigue visible for an instant beneath her careful poise.

Liz lowered the tissue. The dizziness had passed, but the smell of blood and air freshener threatened her uneasy equilibrium. Something between fear and jealousy settled heavy in her stomach. She didn't want anyone else to see Blake like this, didn't want anyone else to risk that black abyss.

"We can't do much here but worry. Would— Would you like to get some coffee, or something to eat?"

Antja hesitated, dark eyes veiling. Then she smiled. "Yes. I'd like that."

RAIN DRUMMED AGAINST Café Al Azrad's red awnings and fell in shining ribbons to the sidewalk. On the patio, Rae huddled against the wind, but it crept in between the buttons of her coat, through the weave of her scarves, ran icy hands up her legs. But even freezing, she was glad to be out of the apartment.

She shuffled her cards, concentrating on the bright colors of the suits, the flutter of glossy cardstock. The familiar motions soothed her, help clear the lingering cobwebs of paranoia. All week she'd startled at shadows, seen faceless strangers in crowds, felt people staring wherever she went. If she was going to go crazy cooped up in the apartment, she didn't need to be crazy outside, too. But today the only thing giving her goosebumps was the cold.

Shuffling kept her fingers warm, but she'd long given up on making any money today. No one wanted their fortune told in this weather. Even the inside of the café was nearly empty. The owner let her give readings on the patio, and sometimes Rabia or Noor gave her free coffee and baklava. The idea of something hot and sweet was tempting now, but her appetite still hadn't returned.

Cards slapped cold and slick between her fingers. The Tower and the Hanged Man surfaced every time she paused, but she couldn't make sense of either of them.

No one would tell her what happened at the cabin that night, only that Alain was dead and Blake was in the hospital and someone had warded their apartment to keep people from snooping. Something was spinning around her, circling in, but she didn't know what it was. She glanced up, eastward, but saw only the sharp lines of skyscrapers and condos blurring in the haze.

The door opened, shaking light across the glass, and a tall, dark-haired woman stepped out. "Tell your fortune?" Rae called, more on principle than out of any real hope. The woman turned and Rae flinched: angry, roiling colors surrounded her, crackling around her hands and jaw. The auras were worse than ever. Stephen was probably cutting the mania.

The colors faded as the woman took a step closer, leaving only a cranky-looking stranger. Rae had seen her before, coming and going, talking to Rabia and Noor, but didn't know her name.

The woman frowned down at the cards. Her hair was cut in a blunt bob around a square jaw, baring the strong lines of her neck. Coat and sweater muffled her shoulders and folded arms, but her hands were hard and scarred. Not pretty, far too strong and arresting for *pretty*, but striking all the same; Rae wished she could ever look that strong.

"Do you really believe in this stuff?" the woman asked, tapping one short, thick nail against the table.

Rae had heard that question often enough. By now it was easy to smile instead of sighing or rolling her eyes. "It's symbolism. You apply the meaning of the cards to your questions, and maybe they help you see things you wouldn't have thought of. It's not real magic."

"No. Real magic is nothing to fuck around with."

Rae had heard that before, too. Either from concerned churchgoers worried about her soul, or from wannabe sorcerers convinced that they knew secrets no one else could fathom. Now she did sigh. "So I hear." She glanced at the window and saw Rabia staring at them from behind the counter.

The woman bared her teeth in what might have been a smile. "But you haven't listened yet. I wouldn't try too hard to look beneath the skin of the world. It's ugly down there." She turned away before Rae finished flinching.

Rae grabbed for her cards like a security blanket, but her hands were shaking and she fumbled the deck. Cards sprayed across the damp table and sidewalk and she cursed. By the time she knelt to retrieve them, the woman had vanished down the sidewalk.

Footsteps clicked on the pavement as she groped under the table for the Five of Cups, paused beside her. "Rae?"

"Antja?" Rae caught her elbow on the metal chair as she straightened. Antja Schäfer always left her feeling awkward and clumsy—too much grace and poise and not enough left for anyone else.

"Hello." Antja paused by the table, a shorter girl beside her, shiny boutique shopping bags hanging from both their arms. For an instant Rae's vision swam and there was a third shape beside Antja, a shadow where no shadow should be, but she blinked and it was gone.

An awkward silence settled between them. "How have you been?" Antja finally asked.

Confused, she wanted to say. *Scared.* She swallowed it for the stranger's sake and settled for "Okay." An unspoken *considering* hung in the air.

"Will you be at the service?"

"Of course."

The other woman shifted her weight and Antja blinked. "Excuse me. Rae, this is Liz. She's a friend of Blake's."

The woman stepped forward, raising a hand in greeting. Her cheeks were red, ash-blonde hair damp and wind-tangled beneath her stocking cap. Her eyes flickered toward the scattered cards and her chapped lips tightened. The Tower and the Hanged Man lay face up again.

"Do you want your fortune told?" Rae asked, trying for a smile. It felt crooked on her face. Their eyes met and she felt that spinning sensation again.

Liz's answering smile looked just as strained. "Maybe some other time."

Antja waved, and the two of them stepped into the warmth and light of the café.

Rae gathered her cards and wrapped them haphazardly in a silk scarf. Clouds scraped the rooftops, thick and swirling. Shadows lengthened. Time to go home. Behind the lowering sky the star was rising; its pull surged sharp in her blood.

As she rose movement drew her eye, a flutter of black in the corner of her vision. Darkness gathered in a doorway across the street, thicker than the afternoon gloom. It flickered as she watched, from a low crouching shape to a tall gaunt figure leaning in the alcove. She couldn't see its face, but she felt its attention.

The deck carved lines in her palm as her hands clenched. She couldn't see its face because it had none: no eyes, no nose, no mouth, just slick blackness. It had no aura, either. Or at least no colors—a nimbus of emptiness surrounded it, devouring any light that got too close.

Rae stared, frozen, unable to move or look away until a cluster of office people emerged from the next building and broke her line of sight. When they passed, the shadow-thing was gone.

She almost bolted for the café, for the safety of light and company. But if she went in, she'd have to come out again, and it would only get darker and colder.

She shoved her cards into her pocket and wound her scarf around her neck. Her umbrella unfolded with a snap. Keep to the light, catch a bus home—she could do that. All of a sudden her stuffy apartment didn't seem so bad.

WITH HIS SARTORIAL obligations fulfilled, Alex lingered in the shelter of a bus stop studying the map. The Museum of Anthropology sounded like a good way to pass a few hours, but Liz's misgivings had started to spread—he couldn't shake the sensation that someone was watching him. A black-coated figure had moved in the corner of his eye one too many times, never mind that half the people he'd seen in Vancouver fit that description.

The darkening sky and lingering ache in his chest made the decision for him. After a detour at a liquor store, he made it back to the hotel with a bank of clouds spitting sleet at his heels. He couldn't feel his hands or feet, but a glass of Chartreuse remedied that. The green fire also chased away the headache that had followed him since yesterday. He nursed a second glass while he waited for Liz, the muted television casting flickering shadows against the walls.

Something was bothering him besides contagious paranoia, but he couldn't decide what it was. No, he decided, he did know: he didn't trust Morgenstern. The man's charisma might work on Liz and hospital staff—and maybe on Blake, to judge from the sketches—but Rainer reminded him of people he'd known years ago, who he'd left behind and tried hard to forget. The magnetism, the attraction that even Alex couldn't dismiss, though it raised his hackles.

Rainer reminded him of Samantha.

His hand closed on the cool plastic of his inhaler. His chest had ached since they'd visited Blake's apartment—the pain reminded him of Samantha, too. Every attack, every albuterol hit, every round of pneumonia. The weakness in his lungs was congenital, but ever since that disastrous night in Boston seven years ago, it had been close to crippling. Or would be, if he let it.

He let go of the inhaler and fished a two dollar coin out of his pocket. It winked in the lamplight as he walked it across his knuckles.

He tried not to think about Samantha, normally, or to think of her only in the simplest terms. Sometimes that worked. He'd been young and stupid, reckless, gotten involved in a relationship that only a seventeen-year-old could have fallen for and ended up hurt. These things happened.

But the other things, the things he remembered in scattered flashes—the chalk circle on the hardwood floor; Samantha's voice rising in an incantation; the writhing, luminous shape that answered... Those things didn't happen. She'd told him they hadn't, after all, when she finally visited him in the hospital. Embarrassed, not meeting his eyes as she invented a story about a gas leak, about mold in the walls. And even then, knowing she was lying, knowing that she'd used him and something had gone wrong, though the details of why and how were lost to him—even then he had wanted to believe her.

He'd been stupid and gotten hurt. So had Blake. Maybe for the same reasons. Alex could sympathize, but that wasn't enough reason to get involved.

But maybe Liz was. And—though he could never admit it to her—the mystery piqued his interest. What the hell had Blake gotten himself mixed up in?

Ice rattled against the windows by the time Liz returned, damp and flushed and weighed down with shopping bags. His second glass was nearly gone.

"I was starting to wonder what happened to you." The bi-metallic coin flashed between his fingers.

"I ran into Antja at the hospital."

"And you had to perform some sort of ritual shopping exercise?"

Liz wrinkled her nose at him as she carried the bags to the bedroom. She returned coatless and barefoot; the dark blue carpet swallowed her footsteps. "Ritual shopping exercises are a good way to learn about someone." She nudged his legs out of the way and sat down on the couch, tucking her feet beneath her. Second-hand chill soaked into him. Her eyes were brighter than they'd been this morning. Maybe it was only the cold putting color in her cheeks, but he felt a futile jealous pang that someone else had managed to cheer her up.

"And?" he asked, pulling himself upright. He flipped the coin one last time and caught it before reaching for his glass.

"I'm not sure," she admitted with a shrug. "She was close to Alain, and I think she feels guilty about whatever happened. Rainer is paying Blake's hospital bills, but she doesn't want to talk about that. I can't exactly tie her to a chair and show her the instruments." Her smile faded quickly. "But she's upset. And scared." A familiar sympathetic frown creased her forehead. "I think I need a drink."

"My sentiments exactly."

She filled both their glasses and settled next to him again. "Now what?"

"We could call the police." It didn't seem a helpful suggestion, especially with their penchant for trespassing, but it needed to be said.

She paused, glass half raised, and chewed her lip. "I don't want Blake in any more trouble than he might already be."

He arched an eyebrow. "What if he did something to warrant it?"

Her jaw tightened, and he cursed his absent tact. She rolled her glass between her palms; the liquor glowed green-gold. "Hurt someone, you mean? Pushed his boyfriend into a lake?"

"Yes."

"He didn't. He wouldn't."

Pressing the subject was a singularly bad idea. But the words welled up when he opened his mouth. "Can you be so certain? A boy is dead, and that's all we really know."

Her agate eyes narrowed. "I know Blake."

There was no arguing with that look on her face. And as much as he wanted to distract her from silence and guilt, he wasn't willing to pick a fight to do it. "Fine," he sighed. "But you might be doing them a disservice by not calling the authorities. What if someone else pushed them into the lake?"

From her sideways glance he thought she knew exactly which someone he meant. "Let's see what happens at the gallery tomorrow. We need more data."

It was hard to argue with that. "Fair enough." Another swallow of Chartreuse lined his throat with warmth. He didn't want to argue. He just wanted to be warm for a while, to not worry. If he drank enough, the gears in his head might stop grinding so furiously. "We can stay up all night worrying about this, or we can watch the monster movie marathon on cable and worry tomorrow."

She gave him a crooked smile and leaned her head against his shoulder. "Monsters it is, then."

He wished he thought she meant it, that more than half of her was in the room with him. But saying anything would only make her feel worse. Sometimes it was better to take what he could get.

6

THRESHOLD

LIZ DRIFTED OFF curled against Alex's side, tipsy and warm, her brain too crowded with rubber-suited monsters to be afraid of what waited for her on the other side of sleep. *Just this,* she pleaded as her thoughts slowed and dimmed and stillness closed over her. *Just tonight.*

But the stillness rolled away again, leaving her standing in a shadowed corridor. Gas lamps hissed along the walls, a ghostly iridescence that gave no warmth. Floorboards creaked as she took a hesitant step. Tulle petticoats rustled against her thighs. She looked down at blue skirts and starched white apron and sighed.

The hall stretched on and on, worn white wainscoting and yellow plaster, the familiar spaces of her boarding school dormitory made infinite and strange. Pictures lined the walls, set in alcoves and shadow boxes and gilded frames. Memories, all of them, people and places faded with time: her mother and father standing in front of a ruined jungle wall; Alice and Alis in their school uniforms; the stuffed patchwork cat she'd slept with for eight years, bleeding stuffing through his worn-thin seams. Liz stared at the points of her boots rather than face them.

Something growled in the distance, a dry coughing sound.

Only a dream. Not even a true dream, only her subconscious's pasteboard knock-up.

"It's more than that."

Alice's voice didn't make her jump this time, but Liz's shoulders tensed as she turned. Water dripped from the dead girl's hair, puddled under her shoes and seeped in dark lines between the floorboards. Her soaked-shiny dress was red instead of blue, but the aprons were the same.

"It's a liminal space, a place between true dreams and the normal kind."

"What are you doing here?"

Alice shrugged. "I'm a liminal thing, aren't I? Trapped between death and memory."

"Are you? Trapped?"

The dead girl grinned. "It's your subconscious. Maybe I'm your power animal."

A whisper carried down the hallway. Too faint to understand, but the voice was familiar.

"Blake?"

Liz turned away from Alice. Blake's ring shone fitfully against the gloom. The metal was cold against her skin.

"What will you do if you find him?" Alice asked as Liz started down the hall; she had no answer.

The corridor ended at a stairwell. Her footsteps echoed as she rushed down. Too fast—this wasn't something she should run toward. But that certainty did nothing to slow her pace. Alice followed, silent as any ghost. The ring grew colder with every step, and an answering chill gathered in her stomach.

The stairs ended in another hall, this one lined in doors. Plain white paint and brass knobs, innocuous and identical. Every one she tried was locked. The ring flared brighter, and her hand cramped with the cold. She worried the inside of her lip until she tasted blood.

The last door was locked, too, but this knob was as cold as the ring. She yelped as she touched it, half expecting to leave a rime of frozen skin and flesh behind.

"What now?" Liz asked, cradling her numbed hand against her chest. "I need a key."

Alice tapped one foot. "You already have a key."

Liz stared at the ring and the angry red skin beneath it. She clenched her hand. When she opened her fingers again, a silver key glittered on her palm, its teeth twisting in triskell coils.

"See? You're getting the hang of it."

The hall shuddered, a stomach-churning sideways lurch. Liz grabbed the doorknob as she swayed. The walls were smoother, more liquid, as if they were about to melt.

"I think this rabbit hole is going to collapse," Alice whispered.

"No!" The floor shivered and firmed again. "I've come this far."

She fumbled the key into the lock. It turned with a click while the threshold ran like ice cream in the sun. The door opened.

Into the abyss.

Darkness vast and hollow as a cathedral vault, a place where daylight could never reach. Bottomless. A single step would carry her across the threshold, but it was too great, too black and heavy and she was much too small to face it.

But it had Blake. He hung in front of her, arms outstretched in a dead man's float. His hair writhed around his face in anemone tendrils.

She looked back at Alice, but the ghost shook her head. "That's not my place. I can't follow you there."

With a gasp, Liz lunged through the door as it dissolved.

The drowning was familiar by now—the breathless crush, the searing cold. She stretched and dove and her hand closed on Blake's. His fingers were limp and icy.

This time they weren't alone. Ghostly shapes writhed all around them, pale as gossamer, luminescent as anglerfish lures. They wailed a discordant siren song, a paean to the hungry presence waiting at the bottom. Already she felt it reaching for them, unfurling a tenebrous arm. They were nothing to it, less than nothing, but it would eat them anyway.

Not you, dreamer. Not yet.

No! She opened her mouth to scream and darkness poured in. Blake's hand slipped from hers as the abyss spat her out. The dream spat her out, and she screamed again as she fell.

* * *

ALEX COULDN'T SLEEP. One drink too many, and now the alcohol in his blood was insomnious instead of soporific. His brain refused to shut off, tumbling questions end over end, dredging up memories. He tossed and turned on the stiff hotel sheets, listening to the keening wind and watching minutes creep into hours.

Liz's hair rustled on the pillow as she shifted in her sleep, smelling of vanilla shampoo and warm girl. She made a soft kitten noise and her hand tightened against the blue bedspread; Blake's ring glinted dully in the dim light.

It wasn't jealousy that twisted behind his sternum—he wasn't that foolish. More of a morbid curiosity, perhaps. If he were the one in trouble, would she be so fierce?

Probably, Alex decided. He didn't understand her altruism, her willingness—her *need*—to help everyone before herself. Everyone but herself. It was so far removed from his other relationships—his parents, Samantha—that sometimes she might have been a space alien.

She stirred again, head tossing, lips shaping a word. A name.

Not jealousy, but jealousy might have been simpler.

He threw back the blankets. Already four in the morning, and sleep was no closer.

He sat at the bar, nursing a glass of tap water and watching city lights shimmer on the clouds—an expressionist blur without his glasses. One hand rose to toy with the medallion around his neck, the silver warm from his skin. He ran a fingernail over the familiar lines of St. Catherine and her wheel; the patron saint of scholars. Samantha had given it to him when he was accepted to Harvard. It was the only gift of hers he'd kept, a reminder and a warning. And because it annoyed the hell out of his father's Protestant sensibilities. Who was the saint of detectives, anyway?

A muffled cry came from the bedroom. Alex dropped the medal and very nearly his glass as he jolted off the barstool.

"No," Liz said, over and over, tossing and clawing at the covers. Tears shimmered down her cheeks, silver in the halflight.

"Liz." She didn't respond, only tossed again. Another broken sound scraped between her lips, too choked to be a scream. He usually let her sleep through her dreams, even if it meant retreating to the couch to avoid stray elbows, but this was worse than he'd ever seen.

"Liz!" He sat on the edge of the bed and touched her shoulder. "Wake up."

She lashed out, clumsy but strong with panic. "No!"

He caught her hands and pinned them at her sides. Her skin was icy and sticky-wet, her pulse beating against his palms like a trapped moth, and she fought so hard he feared he'd bruise her. The air was brackish, bitter with salt and a strange chemical reek. "Liz, wake up. It's me."

Her eyes opened, black in the pallor of her face. The violence of her struggles lessened.

"It's me," he said again. "It's all right. You were dreaming." Letting go of her hands, he reached for the bedside lamp. She flinched away from the light and moaned. "It was just a dream."

She wrapped her arms around his waist with a sob, holding tight enough to hurt his ribs. Her fingers knotted in his shirt. Tears soaked the fabric where she pressed her face against his chest.

"It's all right," he whispered, stroking her damp hair and back. "You're okay." Lies and nonsense—she obviously wasn't. But eventually her sobs eased and her muscles relaxed as she sagged into his lap.

"It ate him," she gasped, breath hitching. "It tried to eat me."

"Nothing's going to hurt you." Her skin warmed slowly. The strange smell had faded, nothing worse than the sour tang of her fear-sweat. Her breathing calmed, but she didn't let go.

"Talk to me," she murmured, breath soft against his thigh.

He shifted surreptitiously, warding off his body's reaction to a warm girl in his lap; it would hardly help matters. "About what?"

"Anything. Nothing. It doesn't matter. Give me something to listen to."

For a moment he couldn't think of anything. He had no voice for lullabies, and fairy tales seemed too cruel.

"Hwæt," he said at last, "wē Gār-Dena in geār-dagum þēod-cyninga þrym gefrūnon, hū ðā aeþelingas ellen fremedon." Liz made a choked little noise that might have been a laugh, but relaxed her death-grip on his shirt.

"Oft Scyld Scēfing—sceaþena þrēatum, monegum mægþum—meo-do-setla oftēah; egsode Eorle, syððan ærest wearð fēasceaft funden..."

By the time Hrothgar built his mead-hall, she was asleep in his arms.

HOURS LATER, RAE sat on her bed, safely enclosed in familiar walls. She tilted the vial, watching lamplight gleam against the curve of the glass and in the golden fluid inside. A little murkier than it should be, like tap water after a storm. What was Stephen cutting it with? Arsenic, maybe, or strychnine—one of the usual poisons.

She needed to slow down, be careful. The side-effects were impossible to ignore. Auras and tracers she could handle, but not these walking, stalking shadows. And if they weren't hallucinations...

She wrapped her arms around her knees, hair falling in long black tendrils around her face. This was too weird, too dangerous. But the stars itched in her blood, calling to her, and it was getting harder and harder to resist.

Her stomach growled, the first hunger pangs she'd felt in days. All they had in the kitchen was ramen, though, and MSG always made her sick.

Chemicals, man—they'll fuck you up. She laughed softly against her knees.

She needed to get out of here, but she wasn't sure which *here* she meant. Away from Jason, maybe, but two years weighed like an albatross around her neck. It wasn't really his fault he didn't make her happy anymore. They wanted different things, but that was a stupid line, and she didn't know what she wanted anyway. She could call her sister, but the thought of going home to Fort Charles was nearly worse than the shadow monsters.

After three AM already: Jason would be home any minute. If she was going to do this she should get on with it. Mania's disassociative effects happened randomly and sometimes not at all. Sitting in the dark talking to colors wasn't what she needed tonight. She needed out. Her body would be safe here in the well-lit room. She'd even dragged a lamp in from the living room to keep the shadows out of the corners. If she could only reach the singing stars, all this would be worth it.

She unscrewed the vial and tilted her head back. Hard not to twitch away from the drops, no matter how many times she did this. Cold and sharp, and she shuddered as they spread across her eyes. Bitter chemical tears beaded on her eyelashes when she blinked.

It started slow: a tingle in her fingers and toes, a shiver creeping under her skin. Then came the warmth, slow and rich, filling her veins with liquid sunlight. The constant winter chill faded and Rae sighed. She lay back, floating, watching the plaster twist across the ceiling. Waiting for the moment when she could slough off her too-heavy flesh and fly.

Instead the world opened beneath her and dropped her into the dark.

Falling. Floating. Drifting in freefall until something caught her and spun her into its gravity.

She stood in a hallway lined with doors, watching a hand that wasn't hers reach for a doorknob.

The door opened and the world exploded.

Light and heat and color, shattering on her skin. The smell of wine and honey and rot-sweet roses. A wild cacophony rose around her, pounding drums and a screaming refrain: *Euan euan eu oi oi oi!* Rae stumbled, but hands held her, bore her up till her feet learned the steps. Round and round they circled, chanting and laughing as she took up the chorus.

Euan euan. Iä iä eu oi oi oi!

Her hair flew as she twirled, skirts whipping her legs. She'd never felt so wild, so alive. A dark-haired woman took her in her arms and kissed her, all wine-sweet lips and sharp, sharp teeth. Rae looked up into a maenad's laughing black eyes.

And fell into the darkness again. The bacchanal vanished, leaving her gasping and dizzy on the bed. Her throat ached as if she'd screamed.

Jason leaned over her, his hair brushing her cheek. "Babe, are you okay?" He sighed when she focused on him, shoulders sagging. "Shit, I thought you were having a seizure."

The fire still burned, too hot for her to speak. She grabbed his neck and pulled him down, kissed him till she tasted blood. For an instant he flinched away, but her hands were under his shirt, nails raking flesh, and soon he kissed her back, knotting his fingers in her hair.

The wild chant of the bacchante echoed over and over in her head.

HE WASN'T ALONE in the abyss. Voices whispered to Blake as he sank. Alien voices, rising in song. Words he couldn't understand, though he thought he might soon. They didn't sing to him, but to something else that shared the darkness with him. Something waiting at the bottom of the bottomless deep.

Other voices were familiar, the ghosts of memory. Rainer's voice, Alain's, distorted echoes of himself.

I don't like the storm.

Do you still want this?

The cruelest word in the world was *want*. But he had said yes. He'd nearly trained himself out of it, once, beaten it down with every betrayal, every loss. But first Liz and then Alain had won their way through his defenses, and he'd relaxed. Weakened.

He thought he heard Liz amid the echoes, calling his name. He'd meant to call her, hadn't he? Before... Before what?

His closest friend for years. The only person before Alain to make him feel safe, even when he'd known better. Life wasn't safe, and no matter how you warded against it, it always won. You always let it win.

He heard her voice again, louder. Not a memory. The sound of his name penetrated his drowning lassitude. A hand closed on his, an electric shock after so much emptiness. He pried his eyes open, remembering Alain with him as the water closed over his head. But it was Liz's pale face hanging beside him now. She opened her mouth, but the abyss swallowed the sound.

Then she was gone, and a different darkness enfolded him, warm and velvet-soft.

Not yet.

Liz! But he had no air to speak. Already the sensation of touch faded, leaving him numb once more.

She's searching for you. Trying to save you. Amusement veined the voice. **But first you have to save yourself.**

How? Where was he, that Liz was trying to rescue him? Where was Alain? He sank faster, down through the endless dark. Toward the heart of the abyss and the vast thing that brooded there.

Hold on, the voice whispered, already fading. **It will be worse than this before the end, but you won't be alone.**

The darkness wrapped Blake in its coils and pulled him down. It swallowed him whole.

7

MASKS

FRIDAY EVENING LIZ stood in front of the mirror, watching the self she recognized slowly disappear. She felt like a child playing in grownup clothes as she zipped herself into her new dress.

The reinforced bodice closed over her ribs and chest like armor, compressing her into a sleek crimson hourglass. Silky lining was cold against her skin. The color was more daring than anything she would have chosen on her own, but it brought out the green in her eyes and made the upswept twist of her hair even paler. Above the strapless neckline, her collarbones flared with unfamiliar elegance. Whatever secrets Antja might be keeping, the woman knew how to shop.

Liz had winced at the price tag, but her credit cards were already bleeding for this trip, so what were a few more drops? Aunt Evie would send a Christmas check soon, anyway, one of the biannual guilt offerings that translated to, *I'm sorry I didn't have time for you*. Her aunt was convinced that her poor parenting had doomed Liz to a life of dusty academic spinsterhood.

Her mother's voice whispered to her as she leaned toward the mirror; Liz could almost see her in the glass, brushing out her long red hair. *"Remember your Chomsky, Elizabeth. Simple and elegant—it works for more than just language."*

Liz swallowed against the tightness in her throat and began to put on her makeup, hiding the bags under her eyes with cream and powder. A stranger's face regarded her when she was finished. No more pale rabbit girl—the reflected Liz was bright and bold and collected, all the cracks hidden beneath a glossy finish. This Liz wasn't crazy with nightmares and helpless worry. This Liz wasn't afraid.

Alex waited for her in the other room. He was half a stranger, too, his usual jeans and dusty peacoat replaced by crisp black and white, his hair pulled back to show off the angles of his face. He watched her as she collected her purse, eyes hidden behind the white reflection on his glasses.

"Is my lipstick smeared?" she asked.

"No." He unfolded himself from the couch and handed over her coat. His dry, spicy cologne tickled her nose. "You look lovely." Now she could see his eyes, and he was just Alex again. The boy who'd traveled across the continent with her, who recited Beowulf to help her sleep. Her cheeks warmed beneath their weight of powder.

"Thank you," she said, trying to fit everything she meant into two syllables. She could read half a dozen languages, trace words back hundreds of years, but so many things were still impossible to express. She stretched to kiss him, and prayed it was enough.

A CROWD MILLED in front of the gallery, cigarette embers winking like orange fireflies. Liz and Alex gave their names and coats to the girl at the door and followed the trickle of guests up the curving iron-railed staircase. Liz felt conspicuous as a bloodstain as her heels clacked on the polished tiles, poppy-red against the stark white walls. But the girl whose face she wore wouldn't mind, she reminded herself, and kept her chin up.

She looked for Rainer or Antja as they reached the landing, but saw only strangers. The flow of the crowd carried her and Alex through an arch into a long narrow room lined with paintings. Guests drifted from picture to picture like flocks of dark-plumed birds; the room hummed with their chatter. The air was thick with perfume and champagne.

"Shall we mingle?" Alex asked, sounding none too enthused with the idea.

"Unless you brought the magnifying glass and fingerprint kit with you."

He made a show of patting his pockets. "Damn. It's in my other coat." One-handed, he scooped two glasses of champagne from a table and passed one to Liz.

Jokes felt brittle on her tongue. The lights were too bright, the room too full of strangers. Even too far away to see the paintings, the colors unsettled her—angry reds, bruised shades of green and yellow and purple, black and dull greys.

The first scene she stopped to study did nothing to ease her misgivings. Maenads danced in the foreground, eyes glazed and wild with fervor. Blood smeared their hands and mouths, bright as pomegranate juice on pale skin. Behind their writhing limbs, a man's body lay torn on the ground. In the background, at the edge of a shadowed wood, a yellow-robed, ivy-crowned man watched the carnage with dispassionate dark eyes.

Not so dispassionate, she decided. A smile played on the edges of his mouth, lush and cruel. Liz could nearly smell the blood. She took a hasty sip of champagne to clear her head.

"Look," Alex said, moving on. "Here's one of Blake's."

The painting was a sickly monochrome, not quite sepia. It showed a homeless man leaning in the mouth of an alley, a wine bottle in one hand, the other raised—in invitation or warning she couldn't decide. His eyes were empty sockets, and the veins in his cheeks snaked black as tar beneath his skin. *The King of Rags.*

The old man was Yves. *The stars will burn your eyes out.* Only the glass in her hand kept Liz from hugging herself.

"Not my favorite of his," Antja said as she stopped beside them, "but it's still lovely. In a morbid sort of way." She shrugged and silver pins flashed amid the dark coils of her hair. Her dress was bronze, liquid and metallic, and amethysts sparkled at her ears and throat.

"That's one word for it," Alex said.

Painted lips curled. "Lovely, or morbid?"

"Take your pick."

Rainer appeared behind her, and Antja stepped aside to make room. She was the taller in her heels.

"Good evening," he said. "I'm glad you could come." The cut of his jacket flattered his shoulders. The purple shirt beneath it matched Antja's amethysts and picked up answering slivers of violet in his eyes. He shook Alex's hand, and reached for Liz's.

And froze as he took it. His pleasant grip tightened and he raised her hand as if he meant to kiss it. Instead he met her eyes, and Blake's ring gleamed between them.

Stupid. Stupid, careless girl.

He squeezed her fingers and let go. The ring felt three times as heavy as her hand fell to her side. It was all she could do to keep her head up, her mask in place.

"Blake has a ring just like that," Rainer said, his voice deceptively light.

Alex stiffened beside her. Her pulse throbbed in her throat and butterflies hatched in her stomach. She thought of lies, some of them even plausible, but discarded them—she didn't need lies when she had her mask.

"This is Blake's."

Rainer's eyes narrowed. "He was wearing it—" He stopped on the brink of admission.

"I found it by the lake."

Rainer's shoulders tensed. Liz caught Antja's blink out of the corner of her eye. "By the lake?"

"Carroll Cove. It was tangled near the shore. He must have lost it when..."

"What else did you find out there?" The full electric force of his stare settled on her, and Liz felt like a very small animal indeed.

"A lot of empty houses," Alex said before she could think of a reply. He tossed back the last of his champagne. "What were Blake and Alain doing there, anyway? We thought it was private property." Liz wanted to kiss him, to reach out and squeeze his hand. She cupped her glass more firmly instead, letting it warm to her skin.

Rainer hesitated. "They were staying at my cabin. They wanted a weekend away."

Liz bit her tongue. Part of the truth, at least. As much as she'd offered. "What happened?"

Rainer shook his head. "I don't know. I lent them the key, and the next thing I heard was the call from the hospital."

"The doctor said something about drugs," Alex said, all innocence. "A hallucinogen?"

"Oh." Rainer's narrow lips thinned further. "That doesn't surprise me, I suppose. Mania, it's called."

Antja laid a hand on Alex's arm and inclined her head toward the far end of the room. "You should see the rest of the exhibit. The best pieces are further in." Alex's eyebrows twitched, but he accepted the change of subject.

"Antja is right," Rainer said. "Let's enjoy the show. It seems the least we can do, under the circumstances."

PARTITIONS SECTIONED THE gallery into a labyrinth of twisting rooms and corridors. Antja and Alex wandered ahead, and after a few turns Liz had lost sight of Alex's head above the crowd. A few more and she wished she'd brought breadcrumbs.

"Where's Ariadne when you need her?" she muttered.

Rainer chuckled. "Abandoned on Naxos."

Liz shot him a startled smile; it was a rare occasion when strangers got her jokes. "I'm sure she would have reminded Theseus to change his sails. Assuming, of course, that his forgetting wasn't contrived to get rid of Aegeus."

He laughed again. "Assuming that, yes. But Ariadne met Dionysus on Naxos. I think she traded up. Blake said you were a student. Are you a classicist?"

"Technically my Masters is in Comparative Linguistics." She pulled out the self-deprecating little smile she used whenever she talked about her degree.

"What will you do with that?"

"I don't really know," she admitted. "Find a Ph.D. Program, I suppose. But grading freshman essays has cured me of any desire to teach, and there isn't much call for mercenary translation these days. Sometimes I wish I'd become an adventurer like my parents."

She was talking too much, but it seemed to go with the face she wore. Rainer had the knack of looking interested and encouraging.

"What do they do?"

"My father was an archeologist, and my mother was a linguistic anthropologist. They did a lot of fieldwork—Indonesia, Micronesia, the Philippines, Sri Lanka. I spent most of my childhood following them around."

His eyebrows rose. "More interesting than most. Have they retired?"

"They died when I was eleven."

"Oh." The chatter around them filled up the pause. "I'm sorry."

She shrugged, a rote response by now. "It was a long time ago." She paused to study the nearest painting, wishing for the glass of champagne she'd abandoned several rooms ago.

A man lay on a sandy seabed, dappled with filtered blue-green light. Dark hair floated in a weed-tangled cloud. One half of his face was handsome and proud, the other eaten to the bone. A pearl gleamed in the empty eye socket. Spidery crab legs left indentations in his flesh as they crawled over his cheek. Razored barnacles crusted one hand.

"'Full fathom five thy father lies'," Liz whispered. "'Of his bones are coral made—'"

Rainer took up the verse. "'These are pearls that were his eyes. Nothing about him that doth fade, but doth suffer a sea-change—'"

Into something rich and strange.

Was that what was happening to Blake, as he sank into the abyss?

Liz took an unsteady step backward and nearly collided with a passing couple.

"Are you all right?" Rainer asked.

"I'm fine." She drew a deep breath, blinking against a sudden disorientation. The painting was only a painting—it wasn't Blake's face there. "I just... I'll be right back." She turned away before he could answer, heels beating a nervous tattoo on the tiles.

In the ladies' room she ran cold water over her wrists, trying to shed some of the heat suffusing her skin. A pair of sleek-gowned women stood by the floor-length mirror behind her, adjusting curls and lipstick and necklines. The sibilance of their voices and the liquid shimmer of the lights made Liz's head swim.

She met her reflection's eyes. The mask was slipping, fear leaking around her eyes. She had to keep it together—scared little mice wouldn't make it through this maze.

As she watched the glass, one of the women tilted her head and dripped clear fluid into her eyes. Her companion caught Liz staring and turned.

"Want some?" she asked, holding up a tiny glass vial. The woman smiled, white and sharp. Beneath a veneer of makeup, her face was sallow and hollow-cheeked, her eyes black and bright as glass. Like the maenads in the painting. Liz's pulse sped. "Wait," the woman said, leaning closer. "I've *seen* you—"

The door opened before she could finish and Antja stepped in. She frowned when she saw the women. At her glare, vials and droppers vanished back into purses and the pair fled.

"Are you enjoying the show?" Antja asked. Her smile was thin and tight, and strain showed in the set of her shoulders. She was fighting to keep her own bright face intact.

Liz nodded, swallowing against the desert in her throat. She ought to say something polite; she ought to ask about the mania. She couldn't find the words for either. Her courage broke and she retreated with a mumbled excuse.

Rainer was waiting for her by the drowned sailor, and she didn't see Alex or Antja again as they spiraled further into the labyrinth.

They passed through a narrow room that was a sculpture of its own. White plaster arches lined the space, joined by sharp-edged vertebrae overhead. A leviathan's ribcage. Crabs and starfish clung to the ribs, and smaller paintings were carefully hung between them. Light fell between the bones in bright stripes. The effect was striking, but Liz had no desire to linger in the belly of the beast. She quickened her pace until Rainer had to hurry to keep up with her.

Her breath slowed when she turned a corner into the safe planes and angles of another room, and she surreptitiously dried her palms on her purse. She'd never spent much time worrying about being swallowed alive before, but after the last few nights' dreams it seemed all too possible. If Rainer noticed her nerves, he was tactful enough not to show it.

She searched for something clever to say, something funny and light, but found nothing. Then they turned another corner and she saw the painting waiting in the heart of the labyrinth, and forgot everything else.

At first it was simple: a picture of a door. Anticlimactic after the rest of the exhibit. But the longer she looked, the more it grew. The door and its wall were stone, or ivory, or bone. Rough-hewn in places, in others polished and carved in elaborate reliefs: vines dripping fruit, cavorting figures; faces transfigured in passion or horror. The more she studied it the more she found, some of it changing when she tilted her head, details emerging from and vanishing into brushstrokes with every glance. Which were real and which pareidolia she couldn't say.

But more unsettling than the changing stone was the space beyond. The door stood ajar—swinging open, not closed; of that she was certain. The view through the handspan gap was dim, out of focus, blurred by clouds or distance. Liz saw a suggestion of towers through the haze, ivory spires against a plum-black sky. Inky waves broke on the shore beneath them. Winged shapes circled in the clouds.

Liz's vision greyed and the room dipped and swayed around her. Static filled her ears as a sour metal taste washed over her tongue. She took a step back and regretted it as her narrow heels wobbled. Her right hand was numb to the wrist.

She was about to faint—the idea left her strangely calm, even as her knees buckled. She waited for the impact of the floor.

It never came. When the fog rolled away she found herself pressed against Rainer, his arm tight around her waist, her hands knotted in his jacket. Her face had gone cold with shock; embarrassment seared it now.

"I'm sorry," she whispered, cutting off his worried questions. She unclenched her hands, putting a few vital inches between them, but he didn't let her go.

"What happened?" he asked. Their faces were unnervingly close, thanks to her heels.

She swallowed, scrambling for an excuse. Dizziness. Too much champagne. But when she opened her mouth, what came out was, "What is that place?" She felt curious stares as other people drifted into the room, but couldn't pull away.

His electric eyes narrowed, calculating. "Carcosa."

She stiffened. Rainer's arm slipped off her waist, but his gaze held her all the same. The cold had spread from her hand through the rest of her limbs. "Blake is there." She'd meant it as a question, but certainty filled her when she said his name.

His hand closed on her elbow, hot as a brand in the chill of the painting's shadow. "How do you know?"

"I dream of him. Every night since your *accident*." She caught whispers from across the room; they were making a scene. For once she didn't care. Her skin tingled, but not just with nerves—she felt her masks peeling away.

Rainer's face sharpened. His grip on her arm tightened, and she braced herself. Then he released her and took a hasty step back, straightening his jacket convulsively. The sudden raw *need* in his face eased into polite curiosity.

They both paused for breath; the air between them tasted of ozone. Rainer's throat worked.

Before either of them could speak, they heard the first scream.

8
TERRIBLE ANGELS

As Alex followed Antja through the gallery, he wished more of the work would catch his interest. He wasn't curmudgeon enough to deny the talent on display, but his knowledge of art dropped sharply after the Gothic, and he didn't think anyone here wanted to talk iconography or Marian devotion. Even worse, they'd wandered into a room dominated by heavy sexual symbolism. If he wanted genitalia in art, he'd crack open an anthropology textbook. He sighed under his breath as they passed a statue of a woman and serpent entwined.

"How much longer do you have?" Antja asked dryly.

Alex looked up from the reflection of the track lighting on his wingtips. "Excuse me?"

"Until you die of boredom. It looks like a terminal case."

He snorted. "Am I that transparent? So much for my dreams of the stage." He was being rude, and it wasn't her fault—under other circumstances he would likely have found her charming company. But his lungs were still unhappy, and talking only made it worse.

Her dark eyes slitted in amusement. Amethysts glittered in wire cages as she cocked her head. "Let me guess. Coming here tonight wasn't your idea?"

"I couldn't make Liz come alone." Though he hadn't seen her in nearly an hour. He looked down at his empty champagne flute.

Was this his third, or fourth? He hadn't eaten since breakfast, and the combination of alcohol and Antja's perfume left him light-headed. A headache tightened slowly around his temples.

Antja's smile faded. "No. I'm not really in the mood for it either. Not after—" She made a vague gesture. "Would you like another drink, at least?"

He swallowed the lingering metallic taste of champagne. "Do you have anything less bubbly? Like scotch?"

"Of course. I'll be right back."

He scanned the crowd for Liz's red dress, but saw nothing. He should find her. They could come back on Monday during the public showing, when there might be fewer people, less brittle laughter and forced witticisms. Instead he found a bench in a corner and slumped, elbows on his knees. The polished tiles threw back the light, and he squinted against the glare. His headache eased when he tugged the elastic band out of his hair, but not enough. What the hell were they looking for, anyway?

The room in front of him was lined with ribs like flying buttresses. Peering over the tops of his glasses, Alex had the unsettling feeling that he'd been swallowed by Jonah's whale.

A woman wandered past, her eyes glassy and unfocused, tongue flickering wet across her lips. Was that mania? Maybe he should ask for a sample. In the interest of informed judgment, of course.

Footsteps and voices approached. Antja and a man, their conversation low and serious.

"—losing his grip, and you know it," the man said. "He's a disaster waiting to happen, whether it's the police or your monsters."

Antja's voice could have cut glass. "You don't need to stay if it worries you so."

"You're the one who should leave. He lost three of his artists in one night, not to mention his protégé. Do you think you'll end up any better?"

They paused at the corner. The man was blond and sleek, his voice veined with smugness under the veneer of concern. Antja stared at him, her face an ice sculpture, a glass of amber liquid in her hand. Neither of them noticed Alex.

"And where would I go, Stephen?" Anger made her accent stronger, deepening her rich contralto.

"I'm sure you could find someone else to appreciate you."

She gave him a disdainful laugh. "Someone like a backbiting street-corner pusher? Or one of your gangster friends?"

Stephen's smile chilled. "At least I wouldn't throw you over for the first pretty boy with a sob story who wanders by."

A second of frozen silence followed, before Antja flung the contents of the glass full in his face. Ice rattled against the floor.

Stephen wiped his eyes with a steady hand. "Sorry. Did I touch a nerve?"

"Get out," she spat. "You can't buy your welcome here any longer."

"Whatever you say. Just remember, when everything's burning down around your ears, that I offered to help." He turned, dripping, and stalked away.

Antja looked up and caught Alex's gaze. She drew a sharp breath, then started to laugh. "I'm sorry," she said, setting the empty glass on the bench. "I seem to have spilled your drink." Her shoulders shook and the stones of her necklace threw off sparks. "It was the cheap stuff, anyway."

Alex arched an eyebrow. "As long as it went to a good cause."

She laughed again, low and rich. "Believe me, that was an excellent cause." She tried to school her expression, but her eyes were bright. "We have better scotch upstairs, if you'd like. I think I could use some too."

It was better than anything else he could think of, besides finding Liz and getting the hell out of there. "Why not?"

Antja led him through an emergency exit in the corner. Winter chill coiled in the stairwell, and darkness puddled beyond the reach of the white LEDs on the landings. Her heels echoed on the concrete steps as she climbed. Her dress left her back bare, and muscles shifted under smooth skin with each step; fabric shimmered with the sway of her hips. Her perfume trailed behind her, poppy and narcissus and bitter myrrh.

Perhaps this was an adventure better had sober.

As they neared the top floor, they heard a soft scratching noise.

Antja stopped, and Alex nearly collided with her. His hand closed over the cold iron railing.

Shadows gathered at the top of the stairs, black and liquid. As he watched, a shape coalesced from the gloom. A man, tall and gaunt. Then it moved, and it wasn't a man at all. Cold air gusted over them as the shadows flared. Alex couldn't move, only stare, trying to make sense of what he saw. Lean limbs, tenebrous wings, a faceless horned head snaking toward him...

Antja screamed and the darkness shattered. Alex clapped his hands over his ears, certain his eardrums would rupture. The thing on the stairs retreated from the onslaught of sound.

She spun, grabbing Alex's arm as she pushed past, dragging him down the stairs. In the aftermath of her shriek, an ocean-rush echoed in his ears. The exit sign writhed like red snakes. The door opened and the flood of light washed his vision white.

Antja released him in her haste, and his head and stomach churned too badly for him to follow. He groped his way down the wall to the bench and sank onto the cool plastic, cradling his head in his hands. If the monster wanted to eat him, it could damn well come and find him.

No, not a monster. A trick of the shadows. Too much to drink—

His vision darkened from white to grey and back to color, and no shadow-creatures appeared. Eventually his ears stopped ringing, and he heard the approach of high-heeled footsteps. He looked up to a crimson blur that resolved itself into Liz when he blinked.

"What happened?" she asked, crouching in front of him.

His eyes burned, a bruised and bloodshot ache. "I'm not sure." He winced at the slur in his words.

Liz frowned. "We should leave."

"That sounds like a wonderful idea." He let her pull him up and throw an arm around his waist. As much as he despised leaning on anyone, he doubted he could make it down the hall without help. The room spun, and Liz was the warm stationary center of the universe. A crowd had gathered, and their whispers rippled behind them.

Rainer intercepted them by the main stairs. "Are you leaving already? Antja had a bit of a fright, but everything is fine." The wild look in his eyes belied the reassurance.

"Alex isn't feeling well," Liz said, cutting off his own less tactful reply. "We need to go." With that, she dragged him down the stairs and into the frozen night.

"WHAT HAPPENED?" Liz asked again when the gallery doors swung shut behind them. All the smokers had fled, and they were alone on the sidewalk.

Alex shook his head, wincing as movement sent pain dancing across his frontal lobe. A car roared by, rattling with bass. Headlights flashed against the inside of his glasses and he winced again. "I don't know."

"How much did you have to drink?" The glow from the windows warmed her pale face and etched the creases of her frown sharp and black.

He tried to glare, but couldn't muster much force behind it. "Not that much." He considered calling a cab, but maybe the biting air would clear his head. He'd be damned if that much cheap champagne would deprive him of his faculties. He started walking, hunched against the cold, eyes on the icy pavement. His ears still rang from Antja's scream, and he felt as though he were about to give birth to Athena.

Wind whistled beneath them as they crossed the bridge. Liz glanced down at the black water and swiftly looked away. Traffic rushed past, spraying slush from tires.

"Antja said something about monsters," Liz said.

Alex shuddered and tried to blame the cold. *Whether it's the police or your monsters*. He'd imagined something much more metaphorical.

"There was... something there. But I don't know what." He shoved his hands deeper into his pockets and clenched his jaw. At least the pain and cold helped strip away the alcohol haze.

One foot slipped on ice and Liz twined her arm through his to steady him. He shortened his stride to match hers, trying not to think of the indignity of it all, or the tightness in his chest.

Wind gusted and something *whooshed* over their heads. Liz froze, fingers digging into his arm. Alex shuddered again and his chest spasmed. They stood frozen for a moment, searching the sky, but whatever it was didn't return.

"A gull," Liz murmured.

"Just a gull." He tried not to think of black wings in the darkness. Friday night partiers crowded Granville Street, swirling in and out of bars and clubs. Music leaked through doorways, drums and pounding bass in sync with the throb in Alex's head. Neon bled across the night, ignis fatuus to guide Hell's revelers.

When they turned onto the hotel's cross street, Alex paused and leaned against a lamp pole. His fingers tightened around his inhaler until plastic creaked. Liz stood close, shielding him from the worst of the wind. "Are you all right?" Her tone was softer this time.

Chemical sweetness filled his mouth as he took a hit, settled heavy in his lungs. Then came the rush of expansion and he sucked in a long cold breath. "I will be."

The alchemy of alcohol and albuterol left him tingling, thrumming with nerves. Paranoia, he thought, when the sensation of being watched slid down his back. But Liz tensed with it, too, eyes narrowing as she peered down the sidewalk.

"What is it?" he asked. Moisture streaked his glasses, filling his vision with shattered rainbows.

"I've seen that person before."

Alex wiped his lenses on his scarf. He slipped them on in time to catch a glimpse of a figure in a long black coat vanishing into the crowd. Something familiar about the cut of that coat, the fall of dark hair—

"Where?"

"When I was out with Antja."

"I've seen him too."

Her chin lifted. "Coincidence? Apophenia?"

"I won't discount it. But three times in as many days makes me wonder, all the same."

The crowd moved past them, a too-bright glitter of sequins and laughter. When they were gone, so was the man. Liz's cold fingers tightened around Alex's.

"Let's get off the street."

He wasn't inclined to argue.

*   *   *

Hours later, after the guests had departed and the last congealing canapés been disposed of, Rainer circled the loft above the gallery one more time. Three in the morning, said the clock on the wall. Three hours since he'd locked the doors and dimmed the lights, all spent searching every inch of the gallery. None of his wards had been disturbed. Nothing had entered his apartment, or the connecting loft, he was certain.

"Are you sure?" he asked again. The floor was cold beneath his bare feet.

"I know what I saw." Antja sat curled on the couch with a blanket around her shoulders. She no longer trembled, but her face was pale and hollow-eyed. Her upswept hair had wilted, long dark coils trailing over her shoulders, still glittering with pins.

He looked in all the corners, switching on lamps to dispel the shadows. Nothing crouched in the narrow kitchen, or lurked behind the screen that separated the bed from the rest of the loft. He brushed his knuckles across the top of the safe that sat beside the bed, concealed by a drape of black silk. The spells of protection that sealed it more surely than any lock thrummed against his skin; the books had not been touched.

But just because nothing had come inside didn't mean nothing had tried. Easy to ward private places, homes, but the gallery below was open to the public—the rules of invitation and consent didn't apply. The monsters could have slipped in downstairs, or through in-between spaces like the stairwells.

They'd entered the cabin easily enough. Had someone let them in? A door or window left ajar by accident? By malice?

Rainer completed his circuit and turned back to Antja. She cradled a coffee mug between her hands, watching him with red-rimmed eyes. He dragged a hand through his tousled hair. Vancouver should have been an end to running, to jumping at shadows.

"What are we going to do?" she asked, and her voice was small and fragile. It had been so long, he realized, since he'd seen her without her careful masks. When had she started wearing them for him?

Leather creaked softly as he sat beside her. He draped an arm around her shoulders. "I don't know, *liebchen*."

She leaned her head against his shoulder. He'd forgotten how comforting her warmth was, how familiar. But it wasn't her face he saw anymore when he closed his eyes. No wonder she wore masks. She deserved better.

Blake deserved better, too. Robert and Gemma had been due more—they hadn't even been buried. God only knew what the jackals did with the bodies they disposed of for their exorbitant fees. At least Alain would have a grave.

"You have to do something," Antja said, pulling away. "Stephen and his friends are watching, waiting for their chance. He wants you out of his way."

He sighed. "I know." Like many younger cities in the new world, Vancouver lacked entrenched magical orders, but had plenty of squabbling young cabals. Rainer had needed allies when he arrived in the city, and fell in with Stephen York's faction. It had turned out to be a poor decision.

Let him try, he wanted to say. He wanted to wash his hands of all of it: the scheming and intrigue and petty hedonism of mages, the wheedling and flattering and grueling finances of the gallery. But it wasn't that simple. He'd invested too much to simply walk away. He'd cut his losses in Berlin and fled, but he knew how lucky he and Antja were to have survived that.

"Do you think—" He paused. The thought had circled in the back of his mind ever since the failed investment, but he hadn't yet spoken it aloud. "Do you think he was responsible?"

Antja frowned into the bottom of her mug as if she could scry the answer there. "No," she said at last, not looking up. "I don't. But that doesn't mean he won't try something else."

"I'll deal with it," he promised. "One way or another."

She began to speak, but her breath caught sharply. Rainer leapt to his feet, *otherwise* senses screaming. The lights went out; porcelain shattered on the floor.

A draft rushed past him, tugging at his untucked shirt. An instant later a tremble like a silent thunderclap shook the room. His guts twisted as the fabric of the world tore open. But his wards were silent; he had invited this.

Rainer dropped to one knee, turning his eyes to the floor. Antja whimpered. The temperature dropped hard and fast and his eardrums popped with the change in pressure. The smell of wine and honey and roses flooded the room.

:**You summoned us**: A polyphonic voice—one high and piping, one the swell and throb of organs, the third shivering inside his skull. The overlap set his teeth on edge.

Three days ago, he thought, even as he shuddered. He bit his tongue. Some things weren't meant to be admonished. His eyes adjusted swiftly to the dark, but he didn't look up. Whether they came as the voice of the King or as his wrath, his messengers were never easy to behold.

Ein jeder Engel ist schrecklich.

"I have questions." His teeth chattered, and his breath frosted in the air.

:**About your failed ritual**: Sinew creaked as its wings extended. Mushroom-colored undersides rippled, mottled with dark veins. The top thumb-joint nearly brushed the rafters.

"Yes." Rainer swallowed, his throat painfully dry. "We were attacked."

The angel paced on crooked legs, clawed feet gouging the floor. Its tail lashed the air with a rattle of bone. Rainer raised his eyes and tried to follow its path, but light and shadow twisted away from its lean frame. It bruised the world with its presence.

:**Beings from the dark places in the lands of dream. They serve our master's enemies**:

"What do they want?"

The creature turned its long head and Rainer couldn't meet its eyes. :**To destroy you**: He didn't think he imagined the chiding note in its voices. :**It is no light matter to summon us, Chosen**:

"What about—" His voice broke on Blake's name. "What about the supplicant? He lives, but his soul isn't with his flesh, and I can't find him." If what Liz had said was true—

:He is with us now. The bargain was interrupted, but the King will complete it:

Rainer's breath left in a rush. "So he's all right? He'll wake up?"

Wings flared, shrug-like. :That remains to be seen. The King will decide if he returns to you or stays with us:

"What do you mean? That wasn't what I intended."

Ivory talons rattled. :That is hardly your concern now. You should be spreading His word, His vision. Already mortals dream of Him, and it is good. He is pleased with you, Chosen. Your offering is insignificant compared to that work:

Insignificant. Blake. His throat tightened around a bitter reply.

"I serve," he said at last. It was the only answer he could give.

:Yes. Unto death, and beyond: The angel turned to him with a scrape and rustle of wings, bathing him in its cold presence. Beneath cloying sweetness its scent was dark and musty. The smell of altars, of tombs. One attenuated hand reached for his face, tilting his head back. Its touch seared, but he didn't pull away.

:One setback does not diminish the service you've given. Know that He values you, and do not despair:

Now he met the angel's eyes, black and full of stars. The void pulled him in, chilled him till his bones would shatter. Then he fell through the other side, into golden light and the presence of his master. Beautiful and terrible, crowned in darkness and robed in flame. The smell of wine and hot blood washed over him, stronger than before, and the distant howls of the choir rang in his ears. *Euan euan eu oi oi oi!* Light poured into him, burning clean all the dark places.

Then the vision was gone and the messenger with it. Rainer knelt on the floor of the loft, shaking and awash in sweat. Antja wept softly behind him.

"Are you all right?" she asked as the lights returned, lowering her hands from her tear-slick face.

He could only nod, trembling and speechless. He swayed and fell to his hands and knees. His flesh felt frozen through, but golden fire still pulsed in his veins.

Antja slid off the sofa and crawled to him, heedless of the broken mug and spilled coffee. The light inside him pulsed hotter as she touched his face. She pulled him close and her heart beat hard and fast against his chest.

He threaded tingling fingers through the weight of her hair, spilling pins across the floor. The smell of her skin dizzied him. Her pulse fluttered under his lips as he kissed her throat. She stiffened, and for an instant he thought she would pull away. Instead she let out a shuddering breath and kissed him.

His hands tightened in her hair as she fumbled with the buttons of his shirt. Thread popped. Her teeth sank into his lower lip and he tasted blood. Her necklace bit at his fingers as he reached for the straps of her dress. He tugged at the chain, and amethysts spilled across the floor in a glittering rush.

She pushed him back onto the unforgiving floor. They would both pay in bruises, but for now nothing mattered but Antja and the fire.

For a moment, it was almost enough.

9

FUNERAL WEATHER

On Saturday, Antja went to meet the devil at the crossroads.

High noon, but already the sky hung low and sunless, swollen with a weight of freezing rain. Only hours left until Alain's funeral. Until she saw the grave she'd put him in.

Mourning black hid her bruised knees and the teethmarks on her throat and shoulders; makeup hid her swollen, red-rimmed eyes. Her hands were steady as a gun-fighter's, her reflection in shop windows straight and poised. Her boot-heels tapped a confident rhythm on the sidewalk. She only shook on the inside.

Rainer had offered to come home with her, to pick her up for the service. She'd refused both out of pride, to prove she wasn't afraid of monsters under the bed. He had enough to worry him. And the monsters would find her anyway.

Rain beaded on her leather coat as she walked aimlessly through the downtown streets, trickling cold across her scalp. Her umbrella was in her purse, but the weather suited her mood. The brittle light dulled the gaudy Christmas decorations, robbed holly and tinsel and wreaths of their warmth and color. The people around her might have been ghosts.

For a moment last night things had been the way they were, when Rainer held her like she was the only thing left in the world. When every night in a new rented room might have been their last.

She'd never thought she would look back fondly on those awful months they spent running across Europe.

The first pretty boy with a sob story who comes along.

If she had known, would she have done anything differently? The answer was still no.

She swallowed a bitter lump of self-pity. It wouldn't serve her. Not with what she was about to face. Her neck and shoulders tightened just thinking about it.

Come on, damn you. Come and talk to me.

She paused at a corner to wait for the light to change. Even though she expected it, she jumped when the dark man appeared beside her. No one else so much as glanced at him.

"Some people ask nicely when they want my attention." His voice was a low rumble, a lion trying to pass as a house cat.

"They'll learn better." *The choice was mine,* she told herself as her fists and stomach clenched. *Mine alone. Mine to live with.* The crosswalk chirped. She might daydream of gunfights, but there would be no showdown today. He led; she followed.

"You called?" he asked when the reached the far sidewalk. He wore a different shape today. She'd seen half a dozen since he first appeared to her at a crossroads in Rouen years ago. Like all his faces, this one was beautiful: dark copper skin, strong bones, long black eyes. He might have stepped straight from an Egyptian tomb painting, never mind the bespoke suit. He burned against the dull grey day, too warm and vivid to be real.

Der Herr ist mein Hirte, nichts wird mir fehlen. The Psalm was a distant memory, the days of attending mass with her family a lifetime past. She could barely remember the words. *Muss ich auch wandern in finsterer Schlucht—*

"*Ich fürchte kein Unheil, denn du bist bei mir.*" His voice rasped over her skin, like velvet against the grain. "Do you really think anyone is listening, my dear?" He gave her an indulgent smile. "And besides, *I'm* with you now."

Her fists knotted in her pockets. "What happened last night? What was that *thing* doing at the gallery?"

"Sit with me." He gestured to a bench by the sidewalk. Rain dripped from the sheltering trees, but the wood was dry. The weather didn't touch him. His otherness was all the more unsettling for the mask of humanity. At least the things Rainer summoned made no pretense of what they were.

"What happened?" She sat. No use in arguing. The cold ate away at her anger. All she wanted was rest. "You promised safety."

He shrugged, adjusting the cuffs of his immaculate suit. A gold and lapis scarab gleamed on his lapel. "You are safe, aren't you? What have I ever done, Fräulein Schäfer, except help you?"

"People died! I did as you asked and people died."

"I only suggested you open a door."

"Damn you. You sent them there, didn't you? You brought the monsters."

He turned to face her, catching her in his obsidian gaze. Her reflection stared back at her, trapped in glass. "Those creatures are nothing to do with me."

She looked away. "Lies. You're the father of lies."

He laugh was as lovely as his voice, warm and rich. "Hardly. Everything I know of deceit and duplicity I learned from your kind. I have no need of lies. I'm no more responsible for the monsters that killed your friends than I am for the creatures your lover calls. They don't do my bidding."

"Whose, then?"

His smile stretched. "Why? Do you think you'd like them any better than me?"

She shuddered. The memories waited whenever she closed her eyes: the demons pouring into the room like ink, razor-edged shadows; the shock on Gemma's face as they laid her open. The blood, the stink, the screams...

"There's so much moving beneath your world that you don't see, above and behind and beside it. Even your lover's Brotherhood, for all their pomp and mysteries, have barely scratched the surface. The Yellow King, the lords of the Abyss, Leviathan in the depths, and so many others, all with their foolish followers. They play long games, and a great many pieces wind up broken. And forgive me, child, but you would scarcely be a pawn on their boards. You may not think so, but you were lucky I'm the one who answered you. And luckier still that I don't draw the curtain back for you."

She looked down at her hands, clenched white-knuckled in her lap. The devil she knew. He was impossible to deal with on a good day, and it had been so long since her days were good.

"You're tired, Antja." One dark hand lifted a stray lock of hair off her neck. She flinched as his scent surrounded her—myrrh and bergamot, sharp and bittersweet. "You should rest."

"Don't say my name," she whispered, her voice too small. His warmth lapped over her, driving away the chill.

"Why not? It's a lovely name, Antja Michaela."

No one called her that, not since her father died. "Don't."

"But it's my name now, isn't it, as much as yours? You gave it to me."

Languorous heat spread from his touch and it was harder than ever not to cry. "I didn't know."

"You knew enough to call me, enough to make the bargain. I never lied to you."

His thumb traced gentle circles on the back of her neck, taking away the pain. The sound of rain on leaves faded, along with the hum and bustle of traffic. Everything was soft and dreamlike, like she'd stepped sideways out of the world. It felt so good not to hurt.

"Don't do this." Her voice caught.

"Why should this be unpleasant? Have I ever failed you? You did what I asked of you. You should rest now, enjoy your safety."

"Safety? We could have died at the cabin. Alain died." There, there was the anger she needed. Her first and best friend since they'd arrived in Vancouver—her only real friend besides Rainer. Her fingers clenched on the edge of the bench, splinters pricking her skin. The pain drove away the distraction of his touch.

"I'm sorry," he said. "I didn't realize he was to be part of our arrangement. I would have been more than happy to renegotiate."

She twisted, one hand flying toward his face. He caught her wrist before the slap struck home, holding her effortlessly. A sliver of wood jutted from her palm, piercing the mount of Apollo. He plucked it out and flicked it aside. Before she could pull free he raised her palm to his lips and kissed away the bright bead of blood.

"I get the impression you no longer want my help." He sounded almost hurt. He lowered her hand, but didn't let go. "Do you think your life would be so much better without me?"

"I'm willing to try it." Her voice was dry, but desperation tightened her throat. Desperation and panic. He had kept them alive. Could she really throw that away?

Men and women passed them on the sidewalk, umbrellas raised, collars upturned against the cold, coffee cups steaming in their hands. Friends and families laughed together. Lovers linked arms. She wanted to scream at them, to make them look. So many terrors waiting for them, in daylight as well the dark. Why couldn't they see?

The devil watched her with heavy-lidded eyes. "It would be unkind of me to continue our relationship against your wishes."

A muscle twitched in her jaw. "Don't toy with me." Too late for that, damn him. She'd called him for answers, but he'd twisted her around and distracted her. She closed her eyes, fighting for composure.

"What would you be willing to do, to end our bargain?"

Tricks. Tricks and lies. She tried to squelch the hope that welled in her chest. The cruelest of all Pandora's devils.

"You won't let me go. I can't afford anything you would ask."

He glanced at her out of the corner of one eye, a smile glinting there that didn't reach his lips. This was what the gazelle must feel when the lion closed in.

"I'm sure you can find something to interest me. Be creative." His voice dropped lower, until she felt it behind her sternum. "Think about it, Antja Michaela."

She expected him to vanish. Instead a sleek black car pulled up to the curb, the driver hidden behind tinted glass. The dark man stood, flicking a stray drop of water off his sleeve, and slid into the backseat.

Antja sat alone on the bench long after the car pulled away, shivering in the freezing rain, with the smell of incense and oranges clinging in her throat.

"WE DON'T HAVE to do this," Alex said, watching Liz's reflection in the clouded bathroom mirror.

She paused, comb slowing through her damp hair. Cosmetics lent color to her cheeks and eased the sunken shadows beneath her eyes, but he could guess from the careful way she moved how badly she needed rest.

"I do," she said at last. "For Blake, I have to go. If nothing else..." She trailed off.

He nodded. And if nothing else, he could go with her, despite the waiting sharp-toothed cold and the pain dragging at him. He couldn't remember when his head hadn't ached. He wished he had Liz's skill with makeup—the artifice of health might have been a useful placebo—but even in his undergrad theatre days, he'd never learned the trick of it.

Her eyes met his through the glass. "You don't have to go."

"Yes, I do." He turned away from the mirror and flipped open his suitcase to find a black shirt. He'd fallen asleep still twitching at shadows. He couldn't admit that to Liz, but neither was he about to leave her alone with Rainer and Antja.

He glanced back as he buttoned his sleeves and found her still watching him, agate eyes unreadable. He gave her a lopsided smile. "At least the weather's fitting."

THE PATHETIC FALLACY was still in effect when they joined the mourners on Capilano View's soggy green lawn. Haze swallowed the mountains, turned pine and cedars and bone-bare maples into towering grey specters. Umbrellas sprouted like black plastic flowers from the sod.

The grave was a scar of dark earth against the wet grass, the headstone nearly lost beneath swags of flowers and mementos. A young woman next to Rainer wept softly; another man looked as if he'd have flung himself onto the turned earth, but the mud would have ruined his coat. Others gathered opposite Rainer's group. Antja stood apart from all of them, wearing her rain-soaked clothes like a penitent's sackcloth. Alex wondered what the factions and divisions meant.

He shifted his grip on the umbrella, the patter of rain on plastic drowning the eulogy. Liz huddled close against him. At least she didn't go in for histrionics—he'd been the one to look after his mother at Great Aunt Kathryn's funeral, and he'd never seen such a case of the vapors. The Priors were more inclined to dramatics; the McLures tended to stoicism and bitter inebriation.

Someone else took a turn extolling Alain's virtues. Alex wished he felt a little grief, if only for Liz and Blake's sakes, but he suspected Alain might still be alive if he'd been more careful in his choice of friends. Unkind, but maybe not untrue.

If he had died in that hospital in Boston, the dry voice of his devil's advocate asked, did that mean he would have deserved it? Would Samantha have paid for his funeral?

He put an arm around Liz's shoulders. He knew better than to use a person as an amulet, but for the moment she was warm and solid and reassuring. "Next time we're going to the Bahamas," he murmured, "or the south of France." She made a disapproving noise, but the corners of her eyes crinkled.

A moment later her gloved hand tightened on his elbow. "Look," she whispered.

He followed her gaze to a shadowed copse of evergreens, and the dark-coated figure half lost in their gloom.

"He should find a new routine," Alex muttered, trying to ignore the unpleasant sensation in his stomach. "Repetition is so dull."

Liz left the shelter of the umbrella, her boots leaving dark prints in the wet lawn as she started for the trees.

"What are you doing?" Alex fell in beside her, skirting the crowd. Everyone else was too focused on the eulogy to notice them.

Her chin lifted, dangerously stubborn. "Looking for answers." But before they had a chance to find any, the man vanished into shadows and mist. Liz's breath hissed through her teeth. "Damn."

Alex caught her arm when she would have kept going. It didn't take clairvoyance to see the danger in following a stranger into a dark wood. The wind gusted, whipping rain under the umbrella.

Antja looked up as they returned to the service. No artistry with waterproof makeup could hide her red, swollen eyes. "Someone you know?" she asked.

"No," Alex said. "We were hoping you might."

She shook her head. "Thank you for coming," she said after a moment. "I'm sorry about last night." Her gaze settled somewhere in the middle distance.

Sorry for what? he wanted to ask. That half-glimpsed black shape still haunted him. He could have written it off as a hallucination, but she had seen it too.

The last eulogy ended and the bereaved began to disperse. Some drifted in ones and twos across the grounds, but others stayed close to Rainer.

"Are you coming back to the gallery with us?" Rainer asked Antja, including Alex and Liz in the invitation with a tilt of his head. Mostly Liz—his eyes lingered on her a heartbeat too long, just enough to get Alex's hackles up.

Antja shook her head. "Maybe later."

Rainer frowned but finally nodded. His conspiracy of bedraggled ravens followed him toward the parking lot. What did you call a plurality of goths, anyway? A draggle? A misery?

"Come with us," Liz said. "Have something to drink and get out of the rain."

Antja's smile was bitter. "I seem to have come down with a case of martyrdom. It's the Catholic upbringing."

"You should consider C of E," Alex said. "We advocate tea and cake with the vicar and appropriate raingear."

She blinked, raindrops glittering on her lashes. Then she laughed—it brought color to her cheeks, but her humor dimmed quickly. "You're probably right. Even so, I'm afraid I'll pass. Thank you all the same." She crossed her arms and glanced toward the grave. "I need a moment alone."

"Not everyone wants to be rescued," Alex murmured as he and Liz started down the dirt path toward the parking lot.

Liz frowned and huddled deeper into her coat. Her skirt slapped against her boots as she walked. "That doesn't mean I shouldn't offer."

He glanced back as they reached the blacktop; through his fogging glasses Antja was a dark shape, nearly lost in the haze. Taillights flared as Rainer and his friends pulled away.

As Liz and Alex neared their car, three people melted out of the deepening gloom. Two men and a woman—no one from the service. One man walked with a pained shuffle like a stroke victim, while the other hunched and hugged himself. Over the rain and earth and wet asphalt, Alex smelled the rank sourness of unwashed flesh, and something else, cloying and sickly sweet.

The woman moved with a disturbing, disjointed grace. Dark hair streamed down her cheeks and shoulders, and her coat hung open over a slinky cocktail dress. Her feet were bare and tar-black with mud. Liz stared at her and stiffened.

"Can we help you?" Alex asked, tightening his grip on the umbrella. Not much of a weapon. Pity he didn't have a steel-lined bowler to match.

"I know you," the woman whispered, her glassy black eyes locked on Liz. "The dreamer, the door-opener. I saw you on the threshold. The King let you in."

Alex slipped his free hand into his pocket for the keys, calculating the distance to the car. He risked a glance over his shoulder, but Antja was lost in the shadows. The rain was falling harder. Where the hell was a Mountie when you needed one?

"I don't want in," Liz said, as if the woman made sense to her. "I just want to get my friend out."

The woman laughed. "Why would anyone want out? Haven't you seen him? You opened the door—open it for me. I need to be there."

Liz shook her head, hands clenching at her sides. Rain darkened her hair, plastered her bangs to her skin. "I can't. It's too much. My friend is drowning in there."

"He's with the King. Where we all should be. The maenads promised I would join their hunt."

She moved closer, stretching out a hand. Alex swallowed his rising gorge at the sight of her bloody, broken fingernails. He took a step toward Liz, but the shuffling man *hissed* and he recoiled.

The woman caught Liz's shoulder. "I can smell it on you. You have to take us there. They promised."

Liz shook her head, scattering rain. "I can't help you."

The woman grinned. "Don't you remember what happened to Orpheus, little girl?"

Alex shook off his stupor, thumbing the umbrella's catch and tugging it closed. Icy needles of rain stung his face and streaked his glasses. "Leave her alone."

The woman laughed. The shuffler lunged with animal speed. Alex swung, and the jolt of plastic against flesh jarred his arm all the way to the shoulder. The man ripped the umbrella out of his hand and knocked him sprawling to the flooded pavement.

Breath left in a painful rush. Over his ringing ears he heard Liz shout, but the world was a wash of rain and movement as his glasses slipped down his nose. He pushed himself up and saw the woman wrestling Liz to the ground. Then the shuffler was on him again, his face a waxen grey blur in the shadow of his hood as he seized Alex by his jacket and hauled him upright. His glasses tumbled to the asphalt. The man hissed again, and through the myopic haze his teeth looked sharper than they should.

Somewhere behind them, Antja shouted. Alex would have let out a grateful breath if he'd had any to spare. The shuffler glanced up, evaluating the new threat, and Alex kicked him. It would have been the euphemistic foul blow, but his aim was off and instead his foot connected with the man's knee. Cartilage crunched, but his attacker didn't let go.

Antja screamed.

He'd thought she was loud the night before, but that was nothing. The shuffler stumbled back, dropping Alex. The man opened his mouth in a moan, but Alex couldn't hear anything; his skull was unraveling at the seams. He would never have imagined her husky contralto could reach such a note, let alone hold it so long.

It stopped abruptly, choked off. Blood throbbed in Alex's ears and the world swayed beneath him. He could only sit, gravel scraping his palms and rain soaking his clothes. The shuffler shook himself like a dog, flinging water. Liz and the woman were still sprawled in a tangle of limbs. So where was the third—

Alex turned, head throbbing, and saw the second man struggling with Antja, his hands locked around her throat. Not as efficacious a rescue as he'd hoped. He staggered up, swallowing bile. The sickly stench of their attackers clung to him, coated his tongue. How could he help anyone when he could barely stand?

Liz yelped in pain and his stomach turned over. He stumbled

toward her, grabbed at the other woman, and took an elbow in the chest for his trouble. Asphalt scored his hand as he caught himself. Useless!

The air was too thick, too wet, and the pain in his head metastasized into something sharp and electric and blinding. Adrenaline coursed through him until he thought his skin would spark.

"Let her go!" The words hurt, like swallowing a too-large mouthful. His head rang with them.

The woman flung herself backwards off Liz, baring bloody teeth in a snarl. A shot cracked and Alex flinched. Well and truly deaf now, he spun toward the sound.

Antja's attacker had fallen. She stumbled away, clutching her throat. Alex knelt, groping for his glasses—not broken, thank god, only scratched and mud-splattered. The world snapped into focus again in time to see the man in the black coat walking toward them, a gun in his hand.

No, he realized. A woman. She held the gun in a steady, two-handed grip. In a film her coat would have billowed dramatically around her, but she was as drenched as the rest of them.

The muzzle flashed once, twice, before Alex could do more than flinch. Liz's attacker—the maenad—slumped to the ground.

"Everyone all right?" the woman asked. Her voice was harsh and distant through Alex's ringing ears.

For a moment he could only stare at the black gun. Then Liz made a soft hysterical sound and he scrambled to her side. Red scratches scored her cheek, dripping pink in the rain, and she cradled her left hand to her chest.

"Are you hurt?" He felt his mouth shape the words, but his voice was queer and not his own.

Liz looked up, her eyes wide and dark. "She bit me."

The maenad stirred, bloody hands scrabbling at the blacktop. Before she could rise, the gunwoman aimed and pulled the trigger again. Chunks of brain spewed like hamburger across the wet asphalt. Liz gasped, high and quick, and Alex choked down stomach acid. But when the corpse fell, baring the ruin of her once-pretty face, he couldn't control his stomach any longer. He stumbled away from Liz to vomit up his lunch.

"For fuck's sake!" He scrubbed sour spit off his mouth as he stood. "Was that necessary?"

The woman's smile was sharp and cold. "You tell me." She gestured toward Antja's attacker.

The man sat up, jerky marionette movements like some obscene Saint Vitus dance. Never mind the hole in his chest, the blood seeping across his shirt.

"What do you think is necessary?" the woman asked. The pistol was trained and steady in her hand, but she didn't fire.

Alex swallowed the foul taste in his mouth. "Call the police. Call an ambulance."

The man rose, a black stain spreading down his shirt and dripping from the hem. He touched the wound and stared at his bloody fingers, then turned and bolted for the trees with that impossible animal speed. The woman let him go.

Alex looked back at the shuffler, but he was down for good; the first shot had struck his head. A bloody halo like a think bubble dissolved in the rain.

Liz rose, shaking, and Alex helped her stand. Beneath mud and blood her face was pasty grey. "Who are you?"

The gun disappeared back into the woman's coat. She crouched and collected her spent shell casings, every motion quick and brutally efficient. "My name is Lailah." When the last flash of brass had vanished into her pockets, she knelt beside Antja. "Are you all right?"

Antja's throat was already bruising, and pink rivulets of blood trailed from a split lip. She drew a breath, but before she could speak Liz let out a startled exclamation.

The maenad was deflating. As they stared, her skin darkened from grey to green to plum-black and began to slough. Fluids oozed from her shattered face. The stench sent Alex staggering back, fighting not to retch again. Hair drifted free of her skull and crumbled; within moments all that remained was a greasy-grey mass deliquescing inside filthy clothes.

The same process was happening to the shuffler. Alex watched the necrotic mess leaking toward the car tires, and wondered how much extra the rental company would charge for that.

Lailah turned her head and spat.

Alex fumbled for his inhaler. "What just happened?" he asked when he could draw a breath again.

"We should get out of here," Lailah said. "Someone will have heard the shots."

Half of Vancouver must have heard the shots—his ears still rang, and sound carried farther in the rain. "And then you'll tell us what the bloody fuck is going on?"

"We'll see." Lailah helped Antja to her feet, catching her when she stumbled. "Do any of you need a doctor?"

Antja shook her head and winced at the motion. "No. No hospitals." The words were an ugly croak.

Alex glanced down at Liz, but she didn't argue. Lailah nodded. "Where do you want to go?"

Antja took a step back. "Why would I go anywhere with you?"

"Come with us," Alex said before Lailah could respond. Antja studied him, perhaps as surprised by the offer as he was. Then she nodded.

ALEX OCCUPIED HIMSELF on the drive back to the hotel by cataloging symptoms of shock. Or acute stress reaction—whatever they were calling it these days. Whatever it was that happened after one was mugged and watched people get shot. People who melted.

Never mind that, he told himself as he led Liz and Antja to the room. And never mind his own icy hands and still-racing heart; they were all three wet to the skin and shaking with cold, but he wasn't injured. He kept himself busy to ignore his own nerves—dragging blankets off the bed, finding Liz a dry sweater and pressing one of his own shirts on Antja.

Lailah let herself in soon after. She'd stayed behind to clean up the remains, a task that didn't bear thinking of. Alex swallowed recriminations when he saw the first aid kit in her hand. For a time there was near-silence as Alex ransacked the kit and Lailah ignored Antja's protests and inspected her throat.

Liz hadn't spoken since they got in the car. Her pupils had shrunk to normal, but she stared at nothing, cradling her injured hand in her lap. Occasionally he caught her mouthing words to herself. *The door. Open the door.*

She understood what the madwoman had said to her. It meant something. What wasn't she telling him?

He couldn't worry about that now, but he could do something about her hand. Her glove was crusted in mud and blood, leather torn around the base of her thumb. She let him take her hand, but yelped and jerked as soon as he began to cut the glove away. She finally focused on him, and the relief was nearly nauseating.

"It will hurt less if you sit still," he said, because it was the easiest thing to say. His voice was beyond calm, nearly flat. Disassociation. Internalization. Intellectualization. Whatever got him through the night.

"Easy for you to say," she muttered, but let him take her hand again.

Dark flakes of blood and mud cracked and drifted to the floor as safety scissors chewed through leather. Liz's throat worked as she watched, and so did his. Grime etched the lines of her palm, and beneath the filth a double crescent of teeth marks sank deep into her heel of her hand. The bleeding had stopped, but the flesh was swollen and hot to the touch.

"Soap and water first," he said. He tossed the ruined glove into the trash bin, wishing for a sterile environment.

Liz nodded and rose, ignoring his attempts to help her off the couch. Stubborn or not, she moved clumsily, limbs jerky and out of sync. The aftermath of adrenaline—he'd shake himself to pieces given the chance. Not now. Not in front of strangers. When he heard water running, Alex poured himself a shot of Chartreuse. Maybe he could drown the reaction before it set in.

Lailah glanced up and cocked one heavy black brow. Alex bit back a snarl. If they were going to play the judgment game, he had a few choice words for people who shot first and asked questions later.

Even if she had saved his life? And Liz's?

He glared into his drink, and Lailah returned to washing Antja's throat. Antja bore it in silence, but her eyes glistened and her hands clenched white-knuckled on the bedspread that draped her shoulders. In spite of the pain, she seemed calm. Shock, he wondered, or had she done things like this before?

Without enough distraction, Alex felt the bruises throbbing down his back. His palms were stiff with drying scabs and the scratch on his glasses flashed white over his right eye whenever he turned his head.

He hadn't been in a fight since his first year in the States, when high school bullies had targeted him for his accent and glasses and precocious erudition. That had only lasted until summer, when he grew six inches in as many painful weeks. He'd despised the helplessness of being bullied then, and it didn't taste any better now. He took another shot of Chartreuse, and nearly regretted it when he heard Liz retching in the bathroom. Let that be delayed reaction, he prayed, and not some fast-moving infection.

She emerged a moment later, splotchy and miserable but steadier. Lailah uncoiled from her crouch and intercepted her; Alex stiffened, but she only took Liz's hand and inspected it.

"Well," Liz said, her voice straining with forced lightness, "will I turn into a zombie?"

Alex winced. It might be a joke, but it didn't stop the images crowding behind his eyes.

Lailah's mouth twisted sideways, a crooked smile. "It doesn't quite work that way." Her voice was low and husky, a hint of accent in her vowels that he couldn't pin down. "But this will turn septic if you don't treat it."

Alex pushed himself away from the bar. "You need medical attention." His own tone made him even angrier. He'd never gone in for jealousy or posturing, but something about Lailah—or her gun— roused atavistic territorial instincts in his amygdala. Liz's mouth tightened, and he wished he had a bucket to drown his lizard brain.

"She needs antibiotics," Lailah said. "Which I have." She rummaged in the first aid kit and produced a brown plastic prescription bottle. "Are you allergic to penicillin?"

When Liz shook her head she tossed her the rattling bottle.

"Are you always prepared for zombies?" Liz asked.

Alex tried not to glare, but suspected he failed. "Could we not use the zed-word, please?"

"Do you have a better one?"

Maenad. He bit back the reply. Somehow it seemed worse. He remembered the painting at Rainer's gallery; the woman's tangled hair and wild glassy eyes were too close a match, her bloody lips and hands. Worry about blood poisoning instead, he told himself, the disgusting state of the human mouth. Liz sat down again and Alex poured hydrogen peroxide onto her hand. It fizzed and bubbled in the bites and she hissed. He flinched at the sound.

"Why should we trust you?" Alex asked Lailah. "You've been stalking us all week."

"And you're lucky I was." She stepped away from Antja and leaned against the wall, a dark stain against creamy wallpaper. She was around Antja's height, but broader through the shoulders and hips, with a square face and scarred, sinewy hands. Her hair clung to her face, drying in frizzing waves. "I didn't imagine you'd get yourself in quite so much trouble so fast."

Alex's chest swelled with an angry response, but he forced himself to deflate. Telling off a trigger-happy stalker might not be the most prudent choice. He helped Liz with ointment and bandages instead. The swelling was already worse.

"You're sure you don't want to go to the hospital?" A reasonable tone, he hoped, for a more than reasonable suggestion.

But her mouth flattened again. "I'm fine."

It was one of the worst lies he'd ever heard. But a hospital would demand explanations and police reports, or clever prevarication. He wasn't sure he had any cleverness left.

He had stubbornness, at least. "Who were those people? And what the hell happened to them? No, wait." He raised a hand before Lailah spoke. "Who are you—then who were they?"

"You're a jackal, aren't you?" Antja whispered. Her voice was an ugly rasp. "I thought you didn't get involved."

Lailah rounded on her, all her earlier solicitude vanishing in one snorted laugh. "We've been involved since we cleaned up your boyfriend's mess. *Messes*, if you count all the maniacs I've been scraping off the streets."

Antja's chin lifted and a muscle worked in her jaw. That was a fascinating line of inquiry, but Alex didn't let himself get distracted.

"What does any of this have to do with Liz or me?"

Lailah's black eyes turned to him, narrow and measuring. "That depends on how fast you get out. My job is to clean up messes, not babysit tourists. And not to give you answers that will only get you into more trouble."

Liz leaned forward, shrugging off Alex's warning hand. "What happened to those people at the cemetery?"

"That's what happens when you take too much mania. One of the things that happens."

Liz stiffened. Her good hand curled against the chair. "Will it happen to Blake?"

A shrug. A flicker of her eyes. "I don't know."

"That's not good enough!" Her voice cracked on the last word. A tremor shook her jaw.

"It's all I have. He's been pretty damned lucky so far."

Antja stood, the blanket sliding off her shoulders. She hadn't fastened all the buttons of her borrowed shirt, and it gaped over the soft curve of her stomach. "I should go." Her voice was painful to hear.

"Just like that?" Lailah said. "If anyone owes an explanation, it's you. Don't you want to tell them about your boyfriend's business, and all the ways it's coming round to bite you?"

"Leave Rainer out of this."

Lailah pushed away from the wall with a laugh, her posture intent and predatory. "It's a little late for that."

Alex was inclined to agree. But Antja had helped them, and without the reassurance of a gun. He rose, pulling his shoulders straight.

"I think everyone's day has been bad enough without an inquisition."

Antja reached for her coat, not quite hiding a flinch as she slipped it on. "I agree." Her hand brushed Alex's arm in passing. "Thank you. For the shirt."

Lailah scowled at the door as it swung shut. "You've picked dangerous company to keep," she said when the latch clicked. "Keep going and you'll become one of the messes I have to mop up."

"All we want to do is help our friend," Liz said.

Lailah's frown softened as she studied them. Pity, Alex decided, was worse than threats. "Go home. That's all you can do—go home while you still can." And she followed Antja out the door.

Alex shot the deadbolt behind her and fastened the chain. The locks offered little comfort.

10

TOUCH

By the time the cab stopped in front of Antja's building, the icy rain was a welcome relief from the blasting heater and the chatter she couldn't reply to. Her throat burned inside and out, limbs stiffening with adrenaline aftermath—she wasn't sure if she shook from nerves or anger or grief or all three. As soon as she was inside, she promised herself, safe in her own condo, then she could collapse. Scream and shake to her heart's content.

She pulled her filthy coat closer as she hurried down the sidewalk. The sky was the color of tarnished pewter and the rain promised to become sleet. It stung her face and dripped cold through her hair, warming by the time it trickled under her collar. She drew glances as she neared the lobby. She knew what she looked like: tangled hair and torn stockings; a swollen lip; a man's shirt. At least the doorman would have something to gossip about.

A tattered curtain of water poured off the awning; she gasped as she stepped through it, and regretted the breath as soon as her throat expanded. When she wiped her eyes, she saw a man leaning against the sheltered wall.

"Excuse me, Miss—"

Drowning out his question, a too-familiar voice filled her head. **Don't let him touch you.**

A perfectly ordinary man, dark-haired and well dressed, the sort she passed a dozen times on the street every day. Black-gloved hands left his pockets, reaching as if to catch her attention. Not leather, those gloves—rubber. Rubber shimmering with moisture. The smell of honey wafted through the air.

Seconds passed between the warning and his touch, but she was too slow and befuddled to react. His hands closed on hers, wrapped around her wrist. Cool, but warmer than her own winter-chilled flesh.

"What—" She jerked away, but he held on.

Warmth seeped through her skin, and a sharp, stinging taste filled her mouth, pungent as raw garlic. She shuddered and might have fallen, but the man caught her elbow and held her up.

"Miss?" She read the word on his lips, but the sound drowned in her rushing pulse. "Are you all right?"

I did warn you.

Poison. Her knees buckled, but the man didn't let go. His hand burned on her bare skin. Heat flooded her, surging in time with her heart. She recognized that liquid fire, like a summer sky in her veins. Mania. *Morpheus.*

She hadn't taken it in years, not since Berlin. Lovely languid warmth, clarity of senses, an intoxicating amplification of her own magic. But it wasn't worth the visions and nightmares that came after. Something was wrong, though. This was too fast, too strong.

Augmented. Not just the drug, but sorcery with it. The fire would scorch her from the inside out, turn her brain to cinders. And the assassin would hold her as she died, his dark eyes wide with concern.

The world sharpened. Rain fell like steel shot against the pavement. Tires shrieked loud as baboons, and her pulse roared in her ears. Colors deepened, shone like sunlit cathedral glass. The wind whipped razors through her flesh, while inside she burned.

The stained glass world shattered and fell away.

Not the assassin before her now but Rainer, his hands in hers, her name on his lips. She wanted to cry, to fall into his arms and let him make everything all right again. But darkness stood behind him, his angel wrought of leather and bone, enfolding him in winding-shroud wings and the stench of tombs.

:He is ours: said the angel, and its eyes were full of stars. :He has always been ours. You can never touch the oaths he has sworn us, or replace us in his heart. He is Chosen, and he can never choose you:

As she watched, Rainer's forget-me-not eyes ran black. Ink spread under his skin, filling every vein. In the darkness that was his eyes, pinpricks of light began to burn. Wings the color of decay unfurled from his shoulders. He was the angel and the angel was him, and they spoke with the same shuddering voice.

:I'm sorry. Nothing you do can change this:

His wings unfolded and carried him away, ripping his hands from hers and leaving her in darkness.

But not alone. Alain stood beside her now, pale and translucent as milk and cobwebs. His eyes were black pits, all light extinguished, and when he spoke his gravelly voice was wet and drowned.

"Everything you've done is for nothing. You can't save him, any more than I could save Blake. I held on—I held on tight, but it was no use. They consume us like moths, without even meaning it. But it's all right—stay with me. Wait with me, and we'll watch it all burn."

But she was falling away from his outstretched hand, into a red-lined darkness that went down forever.

Antja Michaela!

A snap, a wrench, and the world was back. She stood on the sidewalk, untouched by wind or rain, and watched herself slump in a stranger's arms. Raindrops glittered in midair, frozen along with time.

The dark man stood beside her, a frown carving his beautiful face. "I warned you. Now look what's happened."

"You could have warned me earlier." It didn't hurt to speak here, outside of time and flesh. All her aches and bruises were far away, only dying echoes of pain.

"I could have. I could have blinded him, let him stand in the rain long after you were safe inside and you never would have known."

"Then why didn't you?"

"Do you know how many times I've saved you and your beloved? Do you know how many of the Brotherhood's assassins

I led astray after you first called me? How many other random perils I've shielded you from?"

Her mouth opened and closed silently. "You don't," he went on, his voice gentling, "because our arrangement was never about keeping score. It was about your safety, for as long as you wanted it, in exchange for a few eventual favors."

"I don't like your favors," she whispered, hugging herself though she felt no chill.

"No one ever does, after the deal is struck. But you like your life, and your beloved's life. I didn't warn you earlier because I don't want you to take me for granted. And I don't want you to remain blind to problems that are within your power to solve."

"It doesn't look like I'll be solving this one." She stared at herself—mouth open, eyes rolled back, spine arching as if about to fall. She looked awful. Her collar gaped to show the swelling, hand-shaped bruises around her throat, the scratches the maniac's nails had carved. Her cheeks were pale and splotchy, the skin around her eyes fragile as tissue under smeared makeup. So much, she thought wryly, for leaving a good-looking corpse.

"In a few seconds, the spell that's soaked through your skin will reach your brain, and rupture. Not unlike an aneurysm. You'll die quickly and in pain. When your corpse reaches the morgue—don't worry, I think you'll have a bruised, Ophelian sort of beauty about you—the doctors will discover a very high concentration of mania in your blood. And the police will want to know where it came from."

"And they'll go to Rainer." She swallowed. "All this to cause trouble for him?"

He took her hand and squeezed it softly. "Forgive me, my dear, but this is hardly much effort as murders go. One death, quickly accomplished. I'm sure the spell was a tricky bit of work, but that's practically its own reward to a good magician."

"Who—"

She stopped even as the dark man tilted his head chidingly. "I think you can deduce that."

And she could. It was clever: not only might the police trace the mania back to Rainer, but any serious investigation into their finances would stir up even more trouble. And though the police couldn't catch Rainer, his absence would mean that control of mania would fall into the hands of his sometime business partner.

And a bit of revenge for a wasted glass of scotch thrown in for good measure.

She let out a long breath. Outside of her dying body, she could appreciate it. Admiration would fade when the pain of her death set in, she was sure.

"Oh no," the man said. "You're not going to die. That would be breaking our agreement, and I could never have that on my conscience. Look closely."

She followed his pointing hand. If she concentrated she could see the magic moving through her body—not the quiet sparkle of her own craft, but the shining gold of Stephen's spell. It pumped through her blood with the mania, traveling to her heart and lungs before it reached her brain. It was already in her chest—it wouldn't take long from there.

She knew what she had to do. Easy now to step forward and plunge ephemeral fingers into her own flesh, and pluck out the spell.

It shimmered in her hand like a golden pearl, filled her head with the scent of brandy and smoke and Stephen's cologne. She tilted her palm and it fell to the rain-drenched sidewalk. It crunched like a pearl, too, as she brought her boot heel down.

The devil's smile warmed her through, and she hated herself for it. "That's my girl." He leaned down to kiss her brow. "Now take care of this poor dupe."

With that she was back in her wet, bruised flesh, crumpling slowly backward, the taste of garlic and chemicals in her mouth and mania surging through her veins. She caught herself, straightened in the would-be assassin's grip. The smile that stretched her face felt terrible; he flinched from it.

"Miss?" Still following the script, but now his motivation was gone. "Are you all right?"

"I'm fine."

The warmth of the drug eased the pain, flooded her with strength. Easy now to twist her arm free, to catch his wrists in turn and force them upward, toward his face. He realized what was happening, but couldn't tear away from the hooks of fascination her voice sank in him. Gently as a caress, she pressed his own palms to his cheeks, held them till the ensorcelled mania and its absorbing agent sank into his blue-shaven skin.

She leaned close enough to kiss. "Tell Stephen," she whispered, her voice ringing with command, "that the next time he has a clever plan like this, he should come himself."

He stumbled back, eyes widening. Slipped and fell on the pavement. Other pedestrians paused in concern.

"Sir?" Antja called from the shelter of the awning. "Are you all right?"

The man gaped, stammering something incoherent. Another man tried to help him up, but he shrieked and scrambled away. Already lost in the nightmare.

Antja watching him dash through honking traffic and vanish into the twilight gloom. Then she opened the door and stepped into the warmth and light.

Her composure crumbled as soon as she locked her door, and all the hysteria she'd promised herself came rushing in. A terrible noise scraped out of her throat, neither laughter nor a sob. She pressed a hand to her mouth to stifle it, wincing as her cracked lip stung.

She had to call Rainer. Everything was spiraling out of control and she couldn't handle it alone. As she tried to simultaneously strip off her coat and fumble her phone out of her purse, her shoulder clipped a picture frame hanging by the door. Glass sprayed across the floor.

Pressure bloomed inside her sinuses and her eyes began to leak. Call Rainer, let him comfort her and promise to make everything all right: it would be a lie.

Her throat burned with every sob, but she couldn't hold them back. Burying her face in her hands, Antja sank to her knees amid broken glass and wept.

AFTER THE FUNERAL, Rae rode back to the gallery with Rainer and Jason and the others. But when they disappeared into the warmth of the building, she stood on the steps, staring at the gloomy parking lot and the service alley behind it.

"Are you coming up?" Rainer asked, lingering in the doorway.

"In a minute," she lied.

His lips thinned, but he nodded. "Be careful."

She didn't ask what he meant her to be careful of. There were too many possibilities. Instead she nodded, forcing a smile until the door swung shut between them.

She couldn't go inside, couldn't go home. She'd held Jason's hand through the service, but all she'd felt was numb. Her friends were his friends, and she knew she wasn't going to call her sister. There was no one to call. Too much explaining and not enough answers.

Her bones itched and the rhythm of the maenad's dance still tugged at her. Maybe she should just walk and see where she ended up. The vial in her pocket would keep her warm.

Which was, she thought wryly, as far from careful as she could get without a map and a native guide. But it was the only plan she had. And if she wandered in front of a bus or got eaten by a monster, at least she wouldn't have to worry about breaking up with Jason.

The ritual of mania soothed her: the stinging drops that turned to bitter tears leaking down her cheeks. Then came the warmth, driving away her fears and doubts, filling her with starsong strength. The gloom lessened as her eyes sharpened. Colors brightened and gleamed. Restless energy surged through her, and Rae pulled up the hood of her coat and began to walk.

The rain had let up. Now it was a frigid haze, swirling like the breath of ghosts. Streetlight haloes bled through the fog, shimmered on the webs of ice that spidered across the sidewalks. The bacchanal chorus swelled inside her.

Mist ebbed and eddied, turning familiar streets into a twisting dream maze. Dancing shapes flitted around her, whirling and spinning just out of sight. They whispered her name. Her vision wavered, and the towers rising around her weren't brick and glass but ivory and jade, the soaring arches and minarets of a fairy city. Christmas lights became flickering will o' the wisps.

Rae laughed aloud and spun, skirts belling. Laughter answered from the shadows as she staggered to a dizzy halt. The rhythm of dancing feet echoed around her.

She walked blind, full of visions of dancers and angels and bloody-mouthed maenads. The fog smelled of roses and incense and the warmth in her blood burned away the winter chill. She would have danced forever, followed the visions wherever they led.

They led through Gastown, she realized when her eyes finally cleared, to a narrow alley near the docks. A clatter and boom rolled through the haze, echoing like hammers, like giant sour bells. Only container trains loading and unloading, but she couldn't shake the feeling that she'd left Vancouver far behind. She shivered; twilight had given way to true night and the cold was worse than ever.

Light burned at the end of the alley, painting wet bricks orange and gold. She followed the promise of warmth into a dead end, where a fire crackled inside a rusted metal drum. A man crouched beside the barrel, muttering to himself. Hatless and gloveless in the cold, sweatshirt sleeves pushed past his elbows. The flickering light washed his shirt from blood to black and back again.

He looked up as Rae approached, his face a mask of shadow. His aura writhed with black and yellow flames. Paper piled in drifts around him: newsprint, receipts, crumpled napkins. Metal gleamed in his hand.

"They sent you, didn't they?" His voice was rough, wet and bubbling, like he gargled milk and broken glass for breakfast.

She moved closer, into the fire's warmth. "Who is *they*?"

"The twins."

The knife flashed as he drew the blade along his forearm. Steady looping strokes, calligraphy in flesh. She sucked in a breath, waiting for the ruby spill, but he didn't bleed. She smelled blood, though, clotted and sour.

She crouched beside him, folding her arms across her knees as she studied the loops and whorls covering his arms. The same writing covered the scattered paper. "What is that?" The smell was worse here, cloying under the ash and hot rust from the fire. Rot-sweet. Honey-sweet. He was manic too.

"I don't know what it means," he said, "but they keep showing it to me. I have to write it down so I'll remember." Gaunt and sunken-eyed, hair matted with pine needles—she wondered if he'd been sleeping in a park. In the unsteady light the veins in his wrists and neck were black.

"How long have you been here?" she asked, touching his hand. A spark crawled between them.

"I'm not sure. It's so foggy." He took her hand and turned it palm-up. Her veins looked dark, too, threads of licorice under almond-milk skin. "I remember the door opening. You saw it too, didn't you?"

She nodded. His hands were icy despite the fire. "I saw."

"After that... it gets confusing. I was with my friends. We were going to find the door. But something happened. Screaming and thunder..." He stood, pulling Rae to her feet with careless strength. Letting go of her hand, he tugged up his ragged shirt. "Something bad."

Dried blood covered his chest and stomach. More soaked the front of his jeans. She hissed at the neat black puncture below his sternum: so much blood for such a tiny little hole. His skin stretched as he moved and the rusty crust cracked in webs.

"I was scared at first, but then they started talking to me."

"Who? The twins?" She reached out, stopping before she touched his skin. He caught her wrist and pressed her fingers to the wound. Cold meat. Jellied blood.

"Yes."

The women in her visions, the maenads. Rae shivered with the memory of a bloody kiss. "What do they say?"

"They're coming. The sisters and their king. They're coming and we have to wait for them. They'll make us into something more."

He pressed her against the wall. One rough hand brushed her cheek, pushed back her hood to stroke her hair. She shuddered. "I'm glad you're here," he whispered. "I didn't want to wait alone."

Her breath rushed out, shining in the firelight. The fire's warmth rolled over them, but his flesh was cold as the night. She couldn't see his face, only his glowing aura. The knife glowed too as he raised it, light sparking on the edge.

"What—" She choked on the question. Black yarn parted with a rasp as he cut through her sweater. The blade never touched her skin. Sweater, T-shirt, the camisole beneath: he peeled her layer by layer until her chest was bare to the winter night.

"What are you doing?" She ought to be scared, ought to scream or fight. But the tremble in her limbs wasn't fear.

He ran a hand from her sternum to her navel, caressing the curves and hollows of her stomach. Her chest hitched, silver flashing. "Do you feel it?" His breath was cold on her cheek as he leaned close. "Do you feel the stars?"

She felt the maenad's need coursing through her, drowning anything careful. Anything sane. He was dead. Her hand slid beneath the gore-stiff fabric of his shirt. Blood crunched under her nails. "Yes."

He leaned closer, grinding her shoulder blades against the bricks, and she whimpered. His face was in her hair, lips on her ear, her throat. His hand slid up, grazing the underside of her breast; her hips twitched.

"Can you see the towers?"

She closed her eyes and watched black moons wheel over an ivory city. Her back arched, pressing her hips against his; he wasn't that dead, after all. His palm closed over her breast, pinching flesh against metal. She was warm enough for both of them.

He drew back to look at her and she tilted her head. What did dead lips taste like? But he shook himself like a dog and pulled away. Rae whimpered again, trembling for the press of flesh.

"I can't," he said, even as he swayed toward her. "Not yet. I need to write it all down. I can't forget the things she shows me."

The knife kissed her ribs, an ice-feather tickle. She froze, breath caught. "What—"

"It doesn't hurt. You'll see." His other hand cupped her cheek and she fought not to lean into the touch. "She'll show you too."

She gasped as the blade pierced the skin below her ribs. No pain, just cold and pressure, a pop and tug. Easier than any of her piercings. Skin gaped and dark blood oozed down her stomach, thick and sticky as treacle.

"Don't," she whispered.

"I can't forget."

The night shattered into thunder and light and fell around her in razor shards. The dead man jerked, the knife slipping from his fingers as his right temple burst. Blood and brains spilled like pomegranate seeds. Rae let out a startled squeak as they splattered her face. He toppled sideways, colors fading from his aura.

A dog-headed monster stood in front of her, teeth shining in the firelight. It touched her face with burning taloned hands. Now the fear came, washing away desire and leaving Rae cold and shaking. She wanted to scream, but her voice was dead.

"Did he hurt you?" the monster asked, and now it was only a woman, dark-haired and familiar. She looked at Rae's stomach and cursed. The wound stretched with every panicked breath, but only bled a slow molasses trickle.

"Not you too," the woman muttered. Oil-slick metal gleamed in her hand as she stepped back and raised the gun. "I'm sorry."

"Don't." It was the only word she could manage. Rae looked down at the dead man, but he was a blur of red and shadow. She couldn't hear the chanting anymore, couldn't smell the roses. Only wet brick and charred metal and blood. Only the echo of distant trains. The world spun beneath her. The wall tilted and threw her off.

"Don't," she whispered again. Then she slid into the dark.

VOICES REACHED HER as though through deep water, but Rae couldn't open her eyes. Someone held her, strong arms cradling her like a child. She felt another heartbeat through cloth and flesh. The touch was warm and soothing, a sharp contrast to the icy breeze against her face.

"No," a woman said, low and harsh. A familiar voice, but Rae couldn't place it. "You can't bring her here."

"Why not?" This voice belonged to the person holding her. The woman from the alley; her chest swelled with the words.

"She's tainted. The stain runs too deep."

"She's sick. We can help her."

"This isn't an ordinary drug." A third woman speaking now,

and this voice too was familiar. Rae tried to stir, but her limbs hung limp and unresponsive. "You can't lock her up for a week and let it work itself out of her system. The sickness is in her soul."

"We can *help* her," Rae's rescuer said again. "You helped me."

"There's only one way to help her now. You know it, Lailah."

Recognition came at last. The other women were Rabia and Noor, the baristas at Café Al Azrad. Rae had never heard them so grim and cold before. Sticky lashes parted, and through a glaze of tears Rae saw the sisters framed in the light from an open door. They stood shoulder to shoulder, blocking the way. Their shadows streamed down the steps, bent and inhuman.

"You can give her mercy," Rabia said. "Or I can." She offered it as easily as she'd once offered Rae free coffee.

"This will bring you no joy, Lailah bat Raz." Noor's voice was inflectionless, but the words struck Rae like stones. She tilted her head and her eyes flashed red-gold. "And a great deal of pain."

"Damn you both," Lailah spat. She spun, and Rae's stomach rolled with the motion. Rae moaned, and Lailah peered down at her, her pupils shining like an animal's in the darkness. Rae shut her eyes tight against the sight.

SHE OPENED THEM again to the poison-green glow of dashboard lights and headlamps slicing through the foggy night beyond. Glass pressed cold and hard against her cheek and a seatbelt chafed across her collarbone. An engine's purr shivered through her bones. Her mouth tasted like dirty pennies.

"Where are we?" Phlegm crackled in her throat.

"The middle of nowhere." Green light lined the driver's broken-nosed profile. Her aura glowed brighter: plum wine, marbled thorny red and black. Not reassuring colors, but familiar. The woman from the café, who'd warned her about magic. At least she looked human now, no trace of the sharp-toothed second face Rae had glimpsed in the alley.

"Where are we going?" The heater blasted over her, but she was chilled through. She curled her legs clumsily beneath her, wincing as she scuffed the expensive leather.

"Even farther."

"Why? Mercy?"

Lailah's eyes flashed as she glanced sideways. "I could have done that in the alley. Is that what you want?"

Rae touched her face, scraping a dark crust off one cheek. Blood like pomegranate seeds. Her nails bit her palm as her hand clenched. "What happened?" Someday she would say something that wasn't a question.

"After the dead man carved you up? You fainted. Then you started to bleed. Why don't you tell me what happened before that?"

Rae eased a hand under the tattered wool of her sweater, bit back a whimper as she brushed gauze and tape. There was the pain she hadn't felt earlier.

"You'll need stitches," Lailah said.

Rae tugged her ruined top closed, pressing a fist against her mouth to hold back the ugly noise welling in her throat.

"What's your name?" Lailah asked.

"Rae." It took two tries to make the right sound.

"Is that short for something?"

Her mouth twisted. "Raven. No, really," she said when Lailah snorted. "Raven Solstice Morisseau. My mom is a hippy."

"No kidding."

"Lailah means night."

Another sideways flash of eyes. "It does. I guess I can't laugh." She shifted gears and violent red ribbons bled from her hand. Rae flinched. "The solstice—that's tonight. The longest night of the year."

"No kidding," Rae echoed. Her hand tightened in her ruined sweater.

The road curved and sloped and inertia pressed her against the seat. The car growled like something sleek and dangerous. Headlights grazed a wall of trees. Beyond that, a deeper darkness blotted the sky. The mountains.

"So what happened, Rae?"

"I don't know. It's all confused." She brushed a tangled rope of hair out of her face. "Why did you shoot him?"

"His having a knife in you wasn't reason enough?"

She shivered, hunching tighter. "He was—" *Only trying to write it down.*

"Dead?" Lailah said instead. "Yes."

Rae swallowed. "Am I... dying?" She couldn't be dead yet: her pulse beat too hard in her throat.

"No. But something's not right, either. I can still smell the mania in you." Her mouth pinched at the corner.

Rae stifled a sigh at the familiar disapproval. This wasn't quite the same as arguing about smoking pot with straight-edgers. "The taint. Is that what Rabia meant?"

A dark shape flickered in front of the car, skirting the edge of the lights. Lailah swore and tapped the brakes, but when she flipped on the brights the road was empty again. Rae's neck prickled as she clutched the shoulder strap; she knew that liquid darkness. The car slowed, engine quieting. Wings rushed softly overhead.

"Bat country," she whispered.

"They're following us. Hunting."

"Hunting what?" She swallowed hard in Lailah's silence. "Me? Why don't they do something?"

"Traveler's luck. Motion gives you purpose, purpose gives you strength. If we stop, though..." The shape passed them again, light teasing a lithe oil-black body. "Should I give you to them?" It sounded more an honest question than a threat, but wasn't any more reassuring.

Rae's fingers poked through the weave of the yarn. "You saved me in the alley. Doesn't that mean you're responsible for me now?"

Lailah laughed, low and bitter. "I guess it does. All right then— hang on."

She floored the gas.

11

BLACK HORIZONS

ALEX TRIED TO convince Liz to go to bed a dozen times, but sleep was the last thing she wanted. Hours past midnight she still sat curled on the sofa while he paced, picking at a mangy grey gum scar on the blue upholstery and breathing in the faint mustiness left by the dozens of people who'd sat there before her. If she kept her left hand still in her lap, she could almost ignore the pain.

She couldn't ignore the memory of the woman lunging at her, bearing her down. Sharp teeth closing in her flesh. Heat and pain and pooling blood. A dead woman's flesh leaking across wet asphalt.

Open the door.

A shadow passed between her and the lamp and she flinched, but it was only Alex. By the way he looked down at her, one eyebrow cocked, she realized he must have spoken.

"What?"

His lips thinned. "I said, what was that woman talking about? You understood her."

His accent was thicker, the words too precise. She could smell the liquor filtering through his skin. When she didn't answer he started pacing again.

"Dreams," she said at last. "She was talking about my dreams."

He stopped and his mouth opened and shut with a snap. Then he fell into a chair. A coin appeared in his hand and he began walking it across his knuckles. His unoccupied hand clenched against the arm of the chair.

"How?"

"I don't know." She sat up straighter, wincing as her hand shifted.

"Liz—" He shook his head, glasses flashing. "I want to understand this, but you have to give me something to work with."

"Like what?" Her voice cracked, leaking frustration. "I dream of Blake, see him drowning over and over again. There's a door in my head that leads to him, but I can't hold on long enough—"

"To what? Save him? You can't keep doing this, blaming yourself. You're making yourself sick."

"This isn't a delusion! And that woman saw it too."

"That woman was drugged out of her fucking mind." He stopped over-enunciating and the edges of his words softened and slurred. "She saw whatever the hell it is junkies see, and you latched onto it because you can't let this go. Because you care too bloody much."

Her scratched cheek stung with her flush. "It's a hell of a lot better than the alternative."

The coin fell from Alex's fingers, winking as it rolled under the table. He uncoiled from his chair before it stopped moving. His hand closed on her left forearm and she squealed in pain.

"You think I don't care? I care about you. And this"—he shook her arm and she squealed again—"is no dream." His eyes narrowed, red and glossy behind his glasses. "We were lucky. I didn't come here to see you end up in the hospital too. Or worse."

She jerked her arm away, rubbing the red mark his fingers left. The bite throbbed, sharp and nauseating. "I know that," she snapped, fighting back an angrier retort. He was worried, and scared, and that bothered her more than any anger or disbelief.

He yanked his hand back, as if realizing what he'd done. "We can't stay here forever. We have school, jobs. Lives, even if yours isn't as dear to you as it should be."

She swallowed the sour taste of nerves, her stomach roiling. Argument was just as sickening as her swollen hand. "I know," she said softly. "We still have a few more days."

Alex stared at her as if he could read her unspoken thoughts beneath her skin. "Would it be so easy for you to give up everything? To throw your life away to help someone else?"

"Not easy."

He nodded slowly. "But you'll do it anyway."

"Alex, please. You're drunk, and we're both exhausted. Can't we talk about this in the morning?"

A muscle twitched in his jaw. "You're right," he said at last, his diction sharp as a slap. "I am drunk, and I'm going to sleep it off. I'd suggest you do the same, but we know how much good that would do."

Before she could think of a reply, he walked away. He didn't slam the bedroom door, but it echoed in her chest all the same.

ANOTHER HOUR CREPT by, and another. Liz huddled under the scratchy blanket, all the lamps turned off but one. Her eyes ached, dry and raw, but sleep wouldn't come. Beneath the churning growl of the heater, Alex's breath rasped from the other room.

She wanted to go to bed, to curl into his warmth and to hell with dreams, but she couldn't. Not pride—not only pride, at least—but a sick dread. He would leave. If she didn't find Blake soon, didn't do something, he would leave. She couldn't blame him—she was still amazed he'd come with her at all, that she hadn't had to face this alone. But it couldn't last.

Blake couldn't last. Even if the thing in the darkness didn't swallow him, how long could machines keep him alive? How long would the hospital bother?

The curtains swayed in the heater's draft. Wind whistled past the windows and her thoughts chased their tails.

Blake's painting, Carcosa, the King, mania. There was a thread in all of this to lead her though the maze, she just had to find it.

The girl at the café and her scattered tarot cards. The Hanged Man—sacrifice and resurrection—and the Tower.

I have seen the towers of the lost city, Yves said. She saw his face as Blake had painted it, his eyes seared and empty. *Aldebaran is his star.*

Aldebaran. She tried to remember her astronomy class, wishing she had Alex's memory. Part of Taurus, she thought, or maybe the Hyades. And weren't the Hyades the nymphs who watched over the infant Dionysus? She straightened, a tiny burst of endorphins pushing away her fatigue.

Liz stood, wincing as blood tingled back into her feet, and wrapped the blanket around her shoulders. The wind was a razor's kiss as she opened the balcony door, slicing through cloth and flesh. She pulled the blanket tighter and peered up at the sky.

The rain had stopped and a tattered lace of clouds drifted over the sky, stained orange-grey by citylight. Through the gaps Liz found the three bright stars of Orion's belt and followed their line to Taurus and the vermilion gleam of Aldebaran. The bull's eye.

Concrete numbed her bare feet and the blanket snapped in the wind. What did it mean? What did that furnace of hydrogen and helium have to do with Blake?

Her good hand tightened around the ring. *Open the door.*

The star pulsed brighter and she couldn't look away. Aldebaran drowned the lesser lights, drank them down, and she heard the song that echoed in the blazing fusion of its heart.

The world slipped.

Buildings shivered and changed, steel and glass twisting into stone. The railing in front of her vanished and she stood on a narrow ledge, her toes brushing empty air. Her stomach gave a vertiginous lurch as she looked down. It was a long way to fall.

She stood above a twilit city, beneath a bruised and lowering sky. Towers still rose around her, tall as Vancouver's skyscrapers. But scrape was too mild a word for these spires and steeples. Sky-gougers. Sky-renders. Clouds bled darkness where the summits ripped them open. Beyond the buildings, black water stretched to the horizon.

The light brightened by inches. Not a grey or golden dawn, but blood-red and burning. Aldebaran rose, swollen and simmering, and a breathless sound slipped between Liz's teeth. An ancient star, a dying star—it would swallow everything in reach before it spent itself and cooled. Fire-opal brilliance seared away the ocean mist and hot incarnadine light spilled between the city walls. The air was harsh with brine and a sharp chemical tang.

Shouts drew her attention downward, and she raised a hand to shield her streaming eyes. A wild procession leapt through the streets below, cries of *euan euan eu oi oi oi* carrying on the cloying breeze. The wind ripped at her hair as she watched, tugging at the blanket.

The procession wound toward the shore, where black waves lapped against the quay. The tide was rolling in. Two figures, one dark, one light, walked in the center of the panoply, a measured counterpoint to their companions' reckless caper. Leopards and other beasts prowled amongst the dancers, and the footsteps that echoed between the buildings sounded more like hoofbeats.

Euan euan eu oi oi oi! Iä iä oi oi oi!

"You're a long way from home, dreamer."

She startled at the voice and lost her balance. Warm hands caught her and pulled her back from the edge. She clung to Seker until the vertigo passed, each panicked breath carrying the scent of sandalwood and bitter citrus.

"Careful," he admonished softly.

"What are you doing here?" She unclenched her fingers from his robes, biting her lip at the ember of pain pulsing in her hand.

"Watching the parade."

She looked back; the procession was nearly to the quay. "What's happening?" Seker only shrugged.

Steps led down to the water, and the dark figure and the light descended the glistening stair. Women, Liz guessed, from their slender shapes. One wore a white cowl; the other's hair spilled wild, tangled through with ivy.

Waves broke against the seawall, black as obsidian. When they rolled back, a pale shape lay motionless on the stones. The revelers howled and chanted as the women bent and dragged the flotsam away from the water's grasp. Naked limbs sprawled on the steps. Dark hair clung to a narrow white face.

"Blake!"

Seker's hand closed on her arm. "Quietly. You don't want their attention."

The chant swelled, echoing between the towers and across the water. Liz dragged her eyes off Blake for an instant to glare at Seker.

"You stopped me." Hearing his voice again, she was certain. "Twice I reached Blake, and twice you pulled me away."

He nodded, still holding her arm. She couldn't break his grasp. "It wasn't your time."

She looked down; the revelers hefted Blake's limp body and carried him back the way they'd come, the two women leading them. "Where are they taking him?"

Seker steered her around and pointed to a distant tower. More sky-wounding spires, taller than the rest, like carious yellow teeth piercing the clouds. Winged shapes circled their peaks, small with distance. "To the palace of the King." His breath was warm against her cheek.

Liz shuddered. Her hand throbbed in time with her heart. "I have to go there."

"Really?" He released her and she nearly fell. Her head swam. "Do you think you're in any condition to help him?"

"It doesn't matter. I won't leave him." The stone shook beneath her. Or maybe that was just her quaking knees.

"Already the dream tries to cast you out. You're not meant to be here, and you're not strong enough to stay."

She clenched her jaw and met his black gaze. "Then I'll have to be stronger."

His eyes narrowed. "Do you understand exactly what you're attempting? Every time some mad or foolish person finds their way here, the walls weaken. Every contact between Carcosa and your dreamlands—or your waking world—strengthens the King and his retinue that much more."

Liz swallowed. "So even now..."

Seker nodded. "Your presence here unravels the seams, even now."

Ice water filled her stomach. "I can't leave Blake."

"So loyal. So foolish." He smiled ruefully.

Her chin rose. "You can't stop me."

Now he laughed. "Oh, yes I can, dreamer. But I'll only give you three warnings. I won't hinder you again. For now, however, you must return."

"No!"

But he was gone, and Carcosa disintegrated under her feet. Red light burned her eyes and her mouth filled with blood.

She screamed as she fell.

IN SPITE OF his claims, Alex didn't sleep. Insomnia was an old friend. Sleep, like doctors' waiting rooms, was an unavoidable waste of time. He rarely remembered his dreams, save for the occasional anxiety nightmare. If he wanted to relive the awkward contretemps of adolescence he'd watch a teen comedy. Liz's oneiromancy was as alien to him as high school had been.

Which didn't excuse the fact that he'd acted an ass. Even if he was right.

Being right was a hollow sort of consolation if this was the straw that broke their relationship. Liz forgave him any number of faults: his acerbic temper, snobbery, pedantry, and probably others he was less aware of. But the one thing she couldn't forgive was a lack of compassion. Of care. And the fact that he cared for her so much it hurt would never be enough.

His last two relationships had been with people who thought only of themselves. The difference wasn't as amusing as it might have been.

But he didn't get up to apologize and Liz didn't come to bed. In the morning, he decided, he would swallow his pride. For now he could savor the bitter taste of being right, even if it soured his stomach.

When he had memorized the shadowed hotel ceiling, he opened the doors of his memory palace. Sleep might be fickle, but the *ars memoriae* always answered.

The doors swung inward—heavy polished teak, studded with brass and framed in floriated pillars, topped by an intricate lintel. One of dozens of architectural styles that had struck his fancy enough to incorporate into the locus. They opened into a long hallway lined with doors and niches. He'd begun the palace at thirteen, and the early wings were crude. The hall resembled something from primary school, and smelled of chalk and floor polish no matter how he added on.

The niches held books and recitations; he'd since added a library to house his university textbooks and lesson plans. He moved that way now. Perhaps *Summa contra Gentiles* would finally send him to sleep.

He paused at a branching corridor. Of all the rooms and halls in the burgeoning labyrinth, it alone was dark. The breeze that wafted out was cold and dusty. All his memories from Boston, the focus of which had been Samantha's study. He was almost feeling masochistic enough to pick at those scabs.

Before he could decide, a door slammed in the distance, scattering echoes down the hall. A hot wind gusted, reeking of brine and chemicals and the cloying sweetness of funeral roses.

The memory palace crumbled like a sand castle and Alex jerked upright in bed. The same draft whipped through the hotel room and a strange red light filled the doorway. He stumbled up, groping for his glasses on the nightstand.

The balcony doors stood open, rattling on their hinges, curtains flapping. On the ledge, a blanket puddled at her feet, stood Liz. But the view beyond her wasn't Vancouver.

She stood silhouetted against a crimson sky—bloody light and clouds dark as scabs, and twisting alien towers beyond. She leaned against the railing, hands upraised as if to ward off a blow. Against that bleeding sky, the wrought iron barrier seemed fragile as blown glass.

She let out a breathless scream and fell.

Alex lunged with a prayer and saw it answered; she fell back and not forward, crumpling onto the narrow concrete ledge, trapping the blanket beneath her before the wind could claim it.

The red light vanished as he reached her. Alex pulled Liz into his arms, scanning the sky for anything to explain what he'd seen. But there was only the winter night and city lights like a web of stars. The shearing wind smelled only of rain and cold and the bitter blend of exhaust and ocean and wet concrete.

Liz moaned as he dragged her onto his lap, her head lolling. Her skin was scarcely warmer than the air. Moisture dripped warm onto his arm, chilling quickly; her nose was bleeding. Adrenaline spiked and he lifted her, dragging the blanket with them. The room was dark—the lamp's bulb had blown.

Alex made it to the bed before his strength gave out and retractions squeezed his ribs. His hands shook so badly he could barely get the inhaler to his mouth. He counted to sixty and sucked in another dose.

Liz moaned again. Blood trickled down her cheek, staining her hair and the sheets. Alex fumbled for a tissue and pressed it under her nose.

Was this the door the maenad had wanted open?

Her eyes fluttered, black beneath damp lashes, and she murmured something.

"You were sleepwalking," he lied. "Go back to sleep." He wiped away more blood and stroked her tangled hair until she lay still.

No chance of rest now. Adrenaline and albuterol stretched his nerves taut as piano wire, played a jangling jazz progression up and down his spine. Alex sat with his back to the creaking headboard and held Liz's hand until dawn crept cold and blue into the room.

THAT NIGHT, RAINER sat cross-legged on the cold floor of the loft, books scattered on the boards around him. Unwarded, the power contained in their pages crawled over his skin, crackled like static at every touch. They whispered in his head, ugly, seductive secrets. Men had killed for the knowledge they contained; the Brotherhood had tried hard enough to kill him after their theft.

None of their incantations could help him find Blake.

He shut his burning eyes. The passages carved themselves into his brain, Greek and Latin characters leaving simmering tracers long after he looked away. Alien energy seethed under his skin, like and unlike the power of the King. He couldn't use it to recall a lost soul—safely, at least—but he could put it to more practical use.

Stretching out his awareness, he channeled the excess power into the gallery's wards. Sigils on doors and windows flared with dull *otherwise* light as new strength flooded them. Enough to keep the shadow beasts at bay, he hoped.

The nape of his neck prickled as the last magic bled away. Fatigue came in its wake, aching to his bones. He needed rest, but the thought galled.

How could the angel expect him to go on as if nothing had happened? Go back to selling drugs to children, teaching them parlor tricks, turning their thoughts to the King. He had buried a friend today, and tomorrow he would host a party like nothing had happened, would coddle and cajole his backers into parting with more money, woo them with free food and wine. It left a sour taste in his mouth.

Blake was worth more than that.

Rainer had known all the ways it could go wrong, of course—the drug and the oath. He'd seen the disasters in Berlin. Acolytes who burned their minds out with visions until their bodies died of shock. But the alchemy was strong enough to keep soul bound to flesh even after death, to keep the shell animate.

His joints popped as he straightened; a book slid off his lap with a spark and scuff of leather. He'd seen all the horrible things, all the accidents and abuses, but he'd been so certain he could avoid the Brotherhood's mistakes. He was better, after all—the one the King had chosen out of all of them, the first Morgenstern in generations to mean the vows he swore.

He snorted at his own foolishness. He'd repeated all the mistakes and made more of his own. Now Robert and Gemma and Alain were dead, and Blake was lost somewhere beyond his reach. Antja had grown distant and unhappy, and the rest of his allies were turning away out of fear or greed.

He had to put things right—with Antja, with the others. He had to bring Blake back. He was sworn to serve, but sometimes the best service was given by ignoring orders.

The floorboards chilled his feet as he unlocked the door and left the loft; the concrete steps in the stairwell were even colder. Goosebumps roughened his bare chest. The emergency exits were locked when the gallery was closed, but the door responded to his hand and will as if to a key. A witchlight floated over his head, bathing the gallery in eerie yellow light. Shadows crawled across the floor and paintings writhed on the walls. His padding steps carried through the silence as he followed the winding partitions toward the center of the labyrinth.

The painting had changed. He had suspected it on the night of the opening, but now he was certain. The door opened wider. Just a fraction of an inch, enough to make him doubt his eyes. But when Blake had first painted it, only a hint of the farther world had been visible, only a suggestion of shape and shadow. Now the outline of a tower was clear, and the black horizon beyond.

Blake had slipped through that door and now he was with the King. Rainer was Chosen—shouldn't the door open for him as well?

The globe of witchlight lowered, spinning in front of his eyes. Bright tendrils lashed out, until a sigil of golden flame hung before him like a misshapen triskelion.

It wasn't, as his uncle thought, a forgotten rune, an alchemical relic. It was a name. The true name of the King, perhaps, that Rainer couldn't yet understand.

Something stirred in his blood in response to the burning sign. A chill uncoiled in the pit of his stomach, crawling through his limbs. This power had nothing to do with his own magecraft; this was the King's gift.

His heart slowed, and his blood thickened and chilled. He closed his eyes as the veins in his hands blackened. The sight still turned his stomach after all these years.

He opened his eyes and fixed them on the door. Blake had passed through—he had to follow. He held Blake's face in his mind, wrapped the thought of him around himself like armor. The door filled his vision, carvings writhing across the marble. Rainer gathered all his power, all the alien strength inside him, and pushed.

The door opened.

Laughter reached him through the void. A woman's laugh, soft and mocking. He smelled leather and musk and bitter cloves, the viney green scent of sap. "A brave little bird to fly so far. But this isn't your place, not yet. And if you've come for your offering, don't worry—I'll take good care of him. Go home, Chosen, and wait for us."

The taste of bitter almonds filled his mouth. Then a wave of darkness poured through the open door, and crushed him beneath its weight.

12

BAT COUNTRY

Rae woke to sunlight and warm sheets. And bound hands.

Steel cuffs circled her wrists, holding them above her head; a chain scraped the headboard as she moved. The metal was warm from her skin, from the watery sunshine spilling across the bed. The flesh beneath the cuffs was tender, as though she'd struggled. She had no memory of it if she had. Beneath the rumpled sheet, she was naked except for her underwear.

Rae tugged against the restraints and gasped as dull fire blazed through her shoulders. Wiggling her fingers brought them from numbness to stinging pins and needles. Her left calf cramped and the pain made her eyes water. Her stomach was empty, her bladder too full.

"Is this how you usually treat guests?" she asked, because it was better than crying.

Lailah stirred, unfolding from a chair at the foot of the bed. Her palm left a red crease across her cheek. Her dark eyes were shadowed and her hair fell in coffee-colored tangles around her face. "Guests who won't quit thrashing, yes. You nearly ripped your stitches out. Not to mention my face." She turned her head to show the angry pink scratches down her other cheek.

Rae remembered the night before in flashes: the alley; the dizzying drive north; a cold, silent house. Light splintering off a needle as Lailah stitched the slash in her side.

Lailah stood and rolled her neck with a crackle of vertebrae. Muscles bunched and uncoiled in her shoulders as she stretched. "How do you feel?"

"Like shit."

"Hold still," the woman said, leaning over her to unlock the cuffs. Rae held her breath against the pain as her arms fell against the pillow, heavy and useless as dead meat. Lailah stepped back and Rae saw the black gun holstered at the small of her back.

"How long have I been out?" She worked a dry tongue against the roof of her mouth. From the light she guessed it was already afternoon.

"Twelve hours, give or take." Lailah sank back into her chair. "You were raving in your sleep. About the twins, the king."

"I don't remember." It was nearly true. Only fragments lingered, flashes of dark-eyed women and writhing dancers. Rae propped herself up and glanced around the room: plain and nearly bare, as devoid of personality as a hotel. Outside the window, bare branches swayed against a cold white sky. "Bathroom?" she asked when she could move her fingers and toes again.

"Down the hall."

Her legs trembled as she slipped out of bed, and she clung to the frame until she was sure they'd hold her. She paused as she passed the window. Winter seeped through the glass, sending goosebumps rippling down her limbs and tightening her breasts until they ached.

Outside, water glittered mirror-bright, framed by trees and distant mountains. Thin, striated clouds streaked the sky, stained orange in the west. Snow lay in drifts beneath the trees, milk blue and untouched by feet or tires.

"Where are we?" Rae asked. Her breath fogged the glass.

"Carroll Cove. Where your friend drowned." Lailah's eyes tightened. "You really don't know, do you?"

"No!" Irritation overcame her fear. "I don't know anything! Not why Alain drowned, or why Blake is in the hospital, or why monsters are following me. And I don't know who you are or what you want." Her tone softened. Shouting in her underwear seemed more ridiculous than righteously angry. "Why? Why bring me here?"

"It's out of the way, in case there's trouble."

"In case you need to shoot anyone, you mean?"

"That's part of it, yes. And there's a certain balance in coming back to the scene of the crime."

"What crime? What happened that night?"

"I don't know," Lailah admitted. "And I think we need to figure that out before we can stop it."

Rae wondered who she meant by *we*. She was about to ask, when movement caught her eye through the window. A shadow fluttered outside, a scrap of darkness at the treeline. Lithe, winged darkness. "Oh." She raised a hand to the glass, half in wonder and half in fear. "Is that... something from beneath the skin of the world?"

"Yes." Lailah joined her at the window, a line of warmth down her back. "Something that's slipped through the cracks from the dark places. Don't worry—they can't come in unless they're invited."

Rae's eyebrows twitched. "Like vampires?"

The taller woman chuckled. "Actually, it doesn't work on vampires. Only things that were never human."

Rae hugged herself tighter. "Good to know."

Lailah shrugged. "This is as safe a place as any." She reached out and tugged the curtain shut, leaving only a narrow stripe of light.

"What now?" Rae asked, her voice fading to a whisper.

"First, get cleaned up. I'll find you something to wear. Then you can tell me a story."

RAE'S BLOOD ITCHED.

She paced the living room of the cabin, this cottage by the sea with its bland, expensive furniture, so clean and unscuffed it could have been new. Borrowed clothes hung heavy on her limbs. Lailah's clothes—a black sweater that fell to her thighs, its sleeves rolled in fat coils above her wrists. The pants were too long as well, hems folded thick, and sagged off her hips. Everything clean, but Lailah's scent lingered, metallic and bittersweet in the folds.

Above the expanse of black water, snowlight paled the sky.

Night had come on while she distracted herself with a shower and tea. It had taken even longer to get through her story. The bones of it, at least: her friendship with Alain and subsequent introduction to Rainer and the gallery; Rainer's magic; Jason's growing involvement with Stephen York; the shapes she glimpsed in shadows.

"You should rest," Lailah said as Rae reached the end of the room and started back. It was the first time she'd spoken since Rae finished talking. She leaned back on the sofa, legs outstretched. Lazy as a lounging panther, and just as dangerous.

"I've rested long enough. I feel better." She did, mostly. The wound on her side had bled a little after her shower, leaking red and sticky between the stitches, but now it was only a line of warmth across her ribs. The warmest thing in the chilly, empty house.

What would it have said, Rae wondered, if the dead man had finished what he started?

Her circuit took her past the sliding glass patio door, and she paused to stare at the grey world beyond. The sky was the color of a mourning dove's belly, and fat flakes of snow spun past the edge of the porch light, turning the trees into spun-sugar fairy castles. How long had it been since she'd seen a sky unstained by streetlights? Since she'd tasted clean snow?

"Don't," Lailah said as Rae reached for the door.

"Why not?" The wind that whistled past the eaves sounded like starsong.

"An open door is an invitation."

"Oh." She peeled her hand off the cold metal handle. She saw nothing but snow and trees and water outside, but who knew what waited in the farther darkness.

"What's happened to me?" she asked, settling onto the far end of the couch. What was still happening? She lifted her left hand, studying the map of veins beneath the skin. Only blue lines now, that would run red if she opened them.

Lailah reached out and took her hand, callused fingers nestling cool against her pulse. Rae shivered. "I don't know," the other woman said. "But you're lucky. We've been keeping an eye on mania for a while now. This isn't the first place it's shown up. It used to be just another drug, not much worse than smack or meth. It might have let people see things they weren't meant to, but who believes a junkie?"

Rae bit back a reply. She didn't have much use for what she was and wasn't meant to do. "Used to be?" she asked instead.

Lailah shrugged and let go of Rae's hand. "At the beginning of the month something happened. Something changed. We felt ripples of it all through the city, weird shivers we didn't understand." She grimaced. "Magic is full of weird shit I don't understand. But whatever it was, it affected the maniacs most of all. Drove them crazy. Drove them... wrong. Killed them, sometimes—sometimes it didn't."

"Like the man in the alley," Rae whispered.

"Yes. We'd seen those shadow things before—nightgaunts, some of my people call them—but now they're worse. They're hunting something. Maniacs, as far as I can tell." For an instant her dark eyes were soft with sympathy, before she drew on her cool mask again. "You're the one who's been taking this stuff. What do you think changed?"

"I don't know." Rae rubbed her arms. Lailah was right: something had happened at the beginning of December. That was when the stars had begun to call her. "There was... a door. A door opening."

"I know Morgenstern did something at his cabin, weeks ago. It went wrong and people died."

"Alain—" She turned sharply. "What do you mean, people? Blake is still alive." Wasn't he?

"Gemma Pagan. Robert Files. Didn't you know them?"

Rae's mouth dropped open and snapped shut again wordlessly. "But they..." Had vanished, hadn't they? She hadn't seen them since Halloween. Which wasn't strange, because they weren't the sort of people she hung out with—artists who weren't starving. "I told you, I wasn't there that night. I don't know what happened." Jason had complained when he'd learned something happened without them, trying hard to hide the sullenness that would only have proved Rainer right to exclude them. If they had gone, would they be missing too?

"They died. Died badly. I think the gaunts got them. Morgenstern called in my people to clean up the mess."

"Your people? Rabia and Noor?"

"They're part of it. They don't usually do the heavy lifting, though."

"You're... what? Cleaners? Hitmen?"

"Sometimes."

Silence settled between them, like an awkward date who didn't know what to do with his arms. Rae stared at the toes of her boots, yellow-eyed daisies painted on scuffed black leather—the only thing of hers to survive the alley.

Behind the feather-soft sky, the stars wheeled closer to dawn. Her blood tingled with their tides. She glanced up to find Lailah watching her sideways. There was less space between them on the couch, and she wasn't sure who had moved.

Rae tilted her head to study the other woman. She reached out, slow and careful, and touched Lailah's scratched cheek. "Sorry about that."

Beneath the nail wounds lay older scars: a rough indention the size of a dime on her left cheekbone; a crescent tracing the curve of her chin, pink and pale against deep olive skin. A shade darker than Rae's own winter-sallow tones, skin that had seen the sun. Fine lines fanned from the corners of Lailah's dark eyes. More tiny scars scattered across her temple, half hidden by her hair.

"What happened?" Rae asked.

Lailah caught her hand and pulled it down. This time she didn't let go. "An IED." Her eyes were darker than ever, black as the maenad's eyes in Rae's dreams. She smelled of musk and metal, warm skin and, incongruously, sweet shampoo.

"You were a soldier?"

"I've been a lot of things." Their eyes met, and again Rae saw a luminous orange flash in the depths of Lailah's pupils.

"Are you—" The word caught in her throat. "Human?"

"I was once. Lately I'm not so sure." Lailah's pulse leapt in her throat. "Rae—"

She read the shape of her name; she couldn't hear the sound over the bacchanal cry echoing in her ears. Her veins were full of stars.

Lailah tried to speak again, but Rae kissed her before she could.

Blood and flesh, a voice sang in her head. *Yours for the asking. Take it, take her. The way opens and we are coming.*

Her mouth on Lailah's neck, salt musk on her tongue. Her fingers tangled in Lailah's hair; Lailah's hands slid beneath her sweater, tightening on her hips. Rae's teeth sank into the join of the Lailah's neck and the other woman moaned and arched against her. The taut resistance of skin and muscle, the give of flesh and the heat of salt and copper. Lailah's thigh ground against Rae's pubic bone as they moved and she whimpered.

Take it.

"No!"

Rae threw herself back, out of Lailah's arms, and sprawled hard on the floor. The fall knocked the wind out of her. She lay trembling and gasping, blood pounding under her skin. Through the tangled ribbons of her hair she saw her hand clawing at the carpet, veins black as molasses in sallow flesh.

Then the pain came, the dull ache of jarred limbs and a hot knife twisting in her side. Her pulse beat in her lips and the taste of blood and skin filled her mouth. Lailah crouched beside her, calling her name. Rae's lip quivered at her touch, and it was all she could to fight back tears.

"Hush." Lailah's arms circled her, lifting her carefully back to the couch. "It's all right." Blood feathered across the skin of her throat, seeping into her collar.

"I'm sorry—"

"It's all right." She touched the bite and stared at the red stain on her fingers; her throat worked. "What happened? Besides—" She broke off, a flush rising in her cheeks.

"I don't know. The way is opening. The door. They're coming." She stared at her hands, knotted in her lap: normal now, and trembling.

"Who is?"

"The twins. The king." Rae shuddered, trying to untangle the images in her head. "The door is opening." The star-tide still moved in her blood.

Dark eyes narrowed. "Can you help me find it? This door?"

She hesitated, listening for distant music, feeling the ebb and tug inside her. "I think so."

Lailah grinned, sharp enough to remind her of the maenads again. "Then get your coat on. We're going hunting."

13

POISON GIFTS

SUNDAY CAME WITH a heavy smothering sky, perpetual twilit grey. Liz welcomed it. She would have wrapped the gloom around her like a blanket if she could—anything to hide the stars. To hide *from* them.

Chills and fever rode her in turns, and she wasn't sure if they were the work of her hand—a sickening pulse of pain, the bandage spotted with rosettes of rust and yellow—or of what she'd seen. Where she'd been. Her head felt soft and swollen, like something overripe and rotting inside. Blood stained her pillow, crusted in the fine hair above her ear and itched inside her nostrils. She wanted to scrub herself clean down to the bones, but the urge to remain small and silent and unnoticed held her.

Alex came and went, not quite in sync with her clarity. She'd expected recriminations, lectures and hospitals, but there was no trace of last night's argument in his face today. She almost preferred it to the sick worry that had taken its place. His long face was thinner than usual, hollow cheeked and hollow eyed.

She swallowed the chalky antibiotics when he pressed them on her, but couldn't stand the thought or smell of food. He spoke, and she wanted to answer, to reassure him, but the words were lost, drowned deeper than her voice could reach.

She was alone in the bedroom when her phone rang. The buzz and rattle stripped away the layers of fog and cored into the chewy, pain-filled center of her skull. She waited for it to stop, but it kept on, shaking itself across the nightstand in its impatience. Finally she thrashed free of the blankets to reach it.

Unknown caller, the screen read. But she thought she knew, even as she pressed the button. "Hello?" Her voice cracked and she had to repeat the word. Unthinking, she brushed sweaty bangs off her forehead left-handed and swallowed against a spike of nausea.

"Liz?" Rainer's voice was nearly as ugly as hers. She hadn't given him her number, but that was insignificant compared to all the other things she had to ask him. A long pause followed, until she thought the line had gone dead. "I need to talk to you," he said at last. He sounded as bad as she felt. "About Blake. Please."

Something sick and desperate in that *please*. Something helpless. She looked down at her bandaged hand, wiggled stiff and swollen fingers. It was dangerous, and stupid, and she didn't want to face the darkness or the stars. But he'd said the magic word. "When?"

"Tonight, after seven. There's a party at the gallery." His breath echoed through the connection. "Thank you."

She was still staring at the phone when Alex returned, a brown paper Tim Hortons bag tucked under one arm and a cup in each hand. He opened his mouth when he saw her, but what came out was a cough.

"How do you feel?" he asked when the spasm passed.

"Better." It wasn't exactly true, but it seemed the safest answer. How bad did she look, to warrant the concern on his face? She took the cup of tea and bagel he offered to make it more convincing. She breathed in peppermint steam until her stomach calmed.

She concentrated on the food to avoid Alex's expression. Caution and pedantry she was used to; anger and condemnation she could withstand—but there was nothing she could do against his naked concern. She couldn't promise the things he wanted to hear.

"I'm going back to the gallery tonight." She said it fast, like ripping off a band-aid. She set aside her half-eaten bagel. "Rainer wants to talk to me. You don't have to come."

Alex frowned and coughed again. He glanced toward the window, quick and distrustful, as if he feared the sky as much as she did. Then he crouched in front of her, laying a hand on her knee.

"I don't think party separation is wise, under the circumstances."

Relief pushed the air out of her lungs. She couldn't find the words to tell him how much she needed that quiet phlegmatism right now. Instead she smiled, threading her fingers through his. "Thank you."

Then she stood, forcing her legs to hold her, and stumbled toward the bathroom. She had to find another mask to wear.

THINK OF IT *as another faculty party,* Alex told himself as they climbed the gallery's marble stair. The landing was warm with body heat, the air heavy with brittle laughter and the smell of alcohol. If the university's history department were filled with drug dealers and cultists, the resemblance would be uncanny.

And now that he thought of it, could he really be sure it wasn't? Cultists couldn't be any worse than Oxfordians.

"What is the plan, exactly?" he asked Liz as they faced the crowd. Her good hand was cool in his, but he could feel her trembling.

"I'm going to find Rainer. You can mingle, if you like."

Her voice was light, carefully nonchalant, and he wanted to grab her by the shoulders and shake her until she acknowledged the gravity of the situation. His free hand tightened and he shoved his fist into his pocket.

"We can't trust them, you know." He lowered his voice, though the chatter drowned them out. "We can't trust anyone here."

Her smile vanished, eyes becoming cool and unreadable as agates. "I know. I'll be careful."

Before he could think of a response, Antja slunk through the press to greet them. Her maquillage was even more cunning than Liz's; one wouldn't imagine she did anything but host parties, let alone that she'd nearly been killed the day before. The high neck of her burgundy sweater hid her throat.

"Quite a crowd," Alex said, a sacrificial offering of small talk. As if this were nothing but another social function.

Antja rolled her eyes. "They're here for the free food." Her face might be flawless, but her voice was still husky and strained. "Rainer planned this party months ago. Before..." She lifted one hand in a shrug.

"Where is Rainer?" Liz asked.

Antja shrugged, dark hair sliding like a veil across her shoulders. "Hiding somewhere. Probably in his office." She gestured toward a hallway on the other side of the stairs. A man greeted her in passing and she turned to smile at him, a dazzling expression that vanished as soon as she looked away. "I have to keep mingling. If you want out of this mess, you can go upstairs."

Because that had worked so well last time. Alex rolled his shoulders against a creeping chill.

"Let me talk to Rainer," Liz said after Antja was gone. She squeezed his hand. "Then we can leave."

He looked down at her hazel eyes, searching for something to say, searching for his Liz beneath her brittle veneer. But he didn't find either, and then she was gone, swallowed by the crowd. Alex stared after her, a hollow feeling in the pit of his stomach. When she was out of sight, he went looking for a drink.

Armed with a glass of Chardonnay, he retreated to a dim corner to watch the festivities. If he didn't concentrate, the noise washed over him, bright and meaningless as birdsong. Most of the guests passed him by without a glance. The wine, while nothing to rave about, was a notch above the Chateau Screwcap usually served at university functions. If Liz didn't come back soon, he might have a second glass.

He watched Antja work the crowd, playing hostess. She should have been a politician. He would have believed her brilliant smiles, but for the ease with which she discarded them. Her shoulders slumped when she thought no one was looking.

The crowd seemed ordinary enough—broken into cliques and clusters, swirling currents of conversation. Doubtless full of the same name-dropping and backstabbing and bed hopping as any other group. And maybe some of them enjoyed chemical diversions and gruesome art. Maybe some of them were jealous or vicious enough to shove two men into a freezing lake. But none of that explained the monsters in the shadows, melting corpses and that terrible red sky. Nothing explained any of it, except madness, or the walls of reality shifting around him. And no matter how he might wish otherwise, Alex felt all too sane.

He was on his third glass of wine when Antja passed him again. She nearly walked on as obliviously as the rest, but stopped with a double-take.

"I didn't expect you to come back tonight." Hard to tell through her cool facade, but she didn't sound unhappy about it.

He shrugged and looked down at his glass. "I'm here with Liz. She and Rainer are having a tête-à-tête."

She frowned, nostrils flaring. Alex drained his glass and marshaled his nerve. "I think we need to know what the hell is going on around here."

Her lips tightened and she didn't meet his eye. For a moment he thought she would refuse. "All right," she said instead. "That's only fair."

She caught another woman's arm and pressed her into service as a backup hostess. When she turned back she was smiling again. Her armor, he realized, as much as Liz's altruism and his own causticity. Or his drinking. He grimaced and set his empty glass aside.

"Follow me," Antja said, beckoning him down the hallway. "I still owe you a drink, anyway."

If it was armor, he might as well be properly fortified. He followed.

LIZ LEFT THE crowd behind, and the noise receded until the only sound was the tap of her boots on the tile and the nearly subliminal hum of the lights. She tugged at the hem of her sweater, but stopped when she imagined security cameras capturing her nerves. She missed the red dress and the poise it lent her.

Rainer's muted voice answered her knock, and she eased the door open to find him sitting behind a desk, elbows propped and fingers steepled. His eyes were shadowed, cheeks dark with stubble. Nice to know she wasn't the only one losing sleep.

"You wanted to talk to me?"

"Yes." He half rose and beckoned her inside. "Thank you for coming."

The door clicked shut behind her as she stepped into shadows and lamplight. She kept her beringed and bandaged hands in her coat pockets despite the room's warmth. Her head was foggy with painkillers, but at least the sickening pain in her hand had dulled.

"I'm being a terrible host tonight." Rainer shoved a stack of papers across the polished desktop and set an open bottle of wine in their place. "Antja will skin me when I finally show my face."

Liz shook her head when he offered her a glass. She wondered how much he'd already had—his accent was deeper than usual, his gaze less focused. The change from two nights ago was unnerving. He'd been so collected at the opening, cool and assured. Now he looked as bad as she felt. She quashed an upswell of sympathy.

"You wanted to talk about Blake." Her throat was dry and she wished for wine after all, but it was contraindicated by both her medicine and her common sense. She couldn't play at small talk, not after last night.

"Yes." Rainer stared at his glass, then drained it in a single gulp. "You said you dreamt of Blake. Of Carcosa. What did you see? Please," he said when she hesitated. "What do you see?"

She couldn't trust him, but his eyes were so tired and shadowed and desperate. She swallowed. "I saw him drowning. Then he washed up on the shores of Carcosa. He's there now, in the city. In the palace of the king." She glanced in the direction of the maze, and the painting waiting at its heart.

Rainer stood, dark brows knitting, and circled the desk, leaning against the near side. "Can you find him? Can you bring him back?"

His gaze was focused now, tipsiness vanished. It pinned her like an insect on a card. "I... I don't know."

He pushed off the desk, stopped again as if caught by a leash. Tension tightened his neck and shoulders. "I need you to try."

"I have tried!" Too loud, and she flushed. "I am trying. It's not easy."

He exhaled and retreated a few inches. "No. I'm sorry. I just don't know what else to do."

"Neither do I." She folded her arms under her chest, pressing sweaty palms against her coat. "But I'll do what I can. What I have to."

Rainer sighed. "You love him."

"Of course." And belatedly she parsed his intensity, the catch in his voice when he said Blake's name. "You do too."

His shoulders sagged and he turned away. "God help me. I do."

Love or limerence? Care or desire? She didn't understand where other people drew those lines. And in the end, did it matter? The absence of lust had never seemed to make her own relationships less complicated. "Does he know?"

He laughed once, raw and humorless. "I've never said anything, if that's what you mean."

She remembered Blake's sketchbook, Rainer's electric eyes captured in harsh pencil strokes. She clenched her right hand until the ring dug into her flesh. This wasn't the time for distractions. "What the hell is going on? You were at the cabin that night, weren't you? I saw the blood. I've seen what happens to people on mania. I've seen a lot of things I don't understand—Carcosa, the king. What happened to Blake?"

He slumped against the desk again. "I don't know anymore. I thought I did, but... Blake opened a door. Then everything went to hell. It wasn't supposed to be like this."

"What was it supposed to be?"

"Something beautiful. I only wanted—" He dragged a hand across his face. So tired. Tired and aching and helpless as she was. It was a trap and she was rushing headlong into it. She didn't know what else to do.

"What do you want from me?" The words came out harsher than she'd thought herself capable of. Rainer flinched.

"I've tried every way I know to find him, to call him back, but nothing works. I tried to open the door myself, but I was... turned away." His shoulders hunched with the words, then squared again. He stepped closer and his need crept like static over her skin. "But you can reach him."

"I'm not strong enough." The admission stung, but it had to be said. "Carcosa is... not a dream I can control."

"What if there was a way to make you stronger?"

She couldn't break away from his gaze. "You're talking about mania."

He waved the word aside. "Morpheus. That's its real name. The king of dreams." He pulled a narrow glass vial from his pocket.

Curiosity drew her across the room in spite of herself. Such a tiny thing, but it weighed heavy on her palm. The liquid inside gleamed opalescent.

Drink me, she thought, and swallowed a wild laugh.

"It drives people insane," she said, looking up at Rainer. "Turns them into monsters."

"How—" His expression was nearly comical.

"I told you, I've seen it."

Rainer scowled. "It was never meant to be like this."

"Of course not." Her fingers closed around the vial.

"It expands vision. Expands talents. With gifts like yours, it makes them stronger."

"What do you mean, gifts like mine?"

"You're a dreamer, aren't you? A true dreamer. The things you see in sleep are as real as anywhere in the waking world." He cocked a questioning eyebrow. Liz could only nod, her cheeks tingling with shock, her tongue numb. She had kept that part of her life a secret for so long, ever since her childhood realization that no one else would understand. To hear it laid out so simply, as someone might notice that she was blonde, or a Pisces...

Rainer grinned, a quick flash of his earlier charm. "I've heard of people like you, read books, but I've never met one before. Is there really a cavern of flame at the bottom of seventy steps?"

"Yes." She shook her head, shook away the questions crowding her head. All but the only one that mattered. "This will help me find Blake?" She lifted the vial, clenching her hand tighter to hide her trembling.

Rainer's delight drained away. "I can't think of any other way." He laid a hand on her shoulder, holding her eyes. "If I could do this myself, I would."

She wanted to disbelieve, but his sincerity washed over her. "What's the price?"

He blinked, and she used that heartbeat's lessening of his magnetism to pull back. "What do you mean?"

"The price. What does this drug take from me in exchange for awesome psychic powers?"

He ran a hand through his hair. "It's... not without risk, I admit."

"So I could still end up a vegetable, or a walking corpse?"

"Not from a single dose. I hope. I can't think of another way," he said again, closing his hand around hers. "I can't reach Carcosa, but you can. I need you. Blake needs you."

"I have to think about it." A lie—delaying tactics. She knew what her answer would be. But she needed to catch her breath and regroup, and she couldn't do that with him staring at her.

With a sigh, Rainer let go of her hand. "Of course." He held the wine bottle to the light, sloshing the last ruby-black drops back and forth. "I suppose this means I should check on the party."

No monsters waited for them in the stairwell tonight, and Antja led Alex into a loft on the third floor. His skin tingled as he crossed the threshold, reminding him of the cabin, and Blake's apartment. Could this door hide itself as well?

Antja turned into the kitchenette while Alex eyed the corners for creeping horrors. Glass clinked, and he looked back to see her pouring whisky. Lagavulin, sixteen year. Not the cheap stuff. And not, thank god, on the rocks. He took the glass from her, inhaling the sharp aroma of smoke and peat. He'd come for answers, but now he couldn't find the right questions. There was nothing he could think to say that didn't sound mad.

No, there was one thing. And now he was embarrassed to have not said it sooner.

"Thank you." He sipped the scotch to ease his dry tongue. "For helping us yesterday. You didn't have to."

She shrugged, looking almost as discomfited as he felt. "For all the good it did." One hand brushed the thick folds of her sweater's cowl.

Which was true, but even Alex would be hard pressed to be so ungracious. "Be that as it may. Thank you."

"You're welcome." She glanced away, and now it seemed that her smooth veneer downstairs had only been an illusion. Her face was wan and drawn, eyes bruised darker than makeup could hide. Her shoulders slumped and she held herself with the stiffness of the old or infirm. He studied his drink to hide his disconcertment.

Antja turned back to the bar to pour herself a glass of wine. When she returned she'd drawn on a smile. "But you came here for answers, didn't you?"

He frowned. Holmes would have already solved the case from a stray piece of lint on her sweater and Bond would simply take her to bed. So would Harry Palmer, for that matter, but at least he'd make breakfast. Alex imagined he was better off asking questions.

"Is it true, what Lailah said? Is this all Rainer's doing?"

Her lips thinned. "Not all of it."

"But some?"

"Some," she admitted. "Is that really what you want to know?"

Alex straightened at the challenge in her tone and cursed himself for it. "All I care about is making sure Liz doesn't end up in the hospital with Blake."

"No, it's not." She set her glass down and waved away his denial. "Not all." Her lips shimmered in the wake of a tongue-trace and color rose in her cheeks. She took a step forward, fragility vanished as if it had never been. "You've seen things. Amazing things. Impossible things." The clack of her heels punctuated each word. "You tell yourself they can't be real, but you can't forget them. And now you have to know the truth." Her eyes met his through a veil of lashes, their darkness shot through with gold. "That's how it always starts."

She stopped within arm's length and it was all he could do not to reach for her. Only his white-knuckled grip on his glass kept him from touching her cheek. Her perfume dizzied him, and he could almost taste her wine and lipstick. Another few inches and he would.

No, he thought, even as his pulse sped. This was wrong. Never mind the ethics of it, or the wisdom—this wasn't him. It was external, forced upon him. He'd felt it before, he realized, though it had been easy to mistake for adolescent lust at the time.

"No!" He jerked away, sloshing whisky over his fingers. It chilled his skin as it evaporated.

For an instant the world sharpened into crystalline focus and he saw it. A shimmering allure lay over Antja like a veil, reaching for him with warm opium-scented tendrils, ready to sink like fishhooks into his skin. Then he shook his head and it fell away, leaving only the woman in front of him, her eyes widening in surprise.

"Don't," he rasped, stumbling back another step. He might have fled, but she stood between him and the door. Instead he downed a swallow of whisky and staggered back.

"I'm sorry," Antja whispered, one hand pressing her mouth. Pale and shaken again, and no lovelier than she ought to be. "This isn't the first time, is it?" she said as he sank heavily onto the couch. "You've seen something like this before."

Fractured memories glittered behind his eyes: a chalk circle and voices, an electric blue twist of light, mocking laughter. It hadn't happened, he tried to tell himself, the response worn soft and familiar with years of rote use. But it had—whatever *it* was—as surely as this was happening now. He drained the rest of his glass, coughing as smoky warmth seared his sinuses.

"Nothing quite like this," he managed, his dry tone ruined by a cough. "What we saw in the stairwell... That was real." He meant it as a question, but it didn't come out that way.

"Yes." Antja sank into the chair across from him. Alex was glad of the distance and coffee table between them. "They're real." Her masks stripped away, and he saw in her eyes a fatigue so deep it swallowed fear. Or was that only another mask itself?

"What are they?"

"I don't know. I think... I think they're after Rainer."

"He's not the safest person to be around, is he?" He meant it to sting, but still winced at the sorrow that crossed her face.

"No."

It wasn't any of his concern and he had no reason to care, but he couldn't stop the question. "Then why do you stay?"

Her voice cracked. "He needs me." She shook her head, but not before he saw the sudden glaze of moisture beneath her lashes.

"I'm sorry," they said simultaneously. Antja chuckled, wiping carefully at her eyes, and Alex fumbled a tissue out of his pocket.

"I didn't mean to upset you," he said, even though he had.

"And I didn't mean to fall apart." Her fingers brushed his. "I am sorry, about—" She made a vague gesture. "Before."

"What was that, exactly?"

One shoulder rose and fell. "A simple trick. A fascination. I'm not very good at this, really," she admitted with a rueful twist of her mouth. "Not compared to some. But I know a few things." She drew a deep breath and raised a hand to her face.

When she lowered it, Liz sat in front of him.

No, he realized, even as he leaned in, breath catching. Not Liz. The ragged ash-blonde bob was right, and the pale oval of her face, but the cheekbones were too high, eyes too green and wide-set. An idealized Liz, without the imperfections and asymmetries. "I could teach you." The voice was perfect, soft and rough, with just a hint of hesitation. But Liz had never leaned toward him in just that way, eyes darkening, warmth rising in her cheeks. "If you want to learn."

He did, so badly it made him shudder like a fly-stung horse. Too much.

"I don't think that's wise," he said, his own voice gone husky.

The false Liz melted and he closed his eyes against the sight. He opened them again to Antja's raised eyebrows. "You won't walk away now. No one does. You'll have to find someone."

He frowned; it galled to be told what he thought, even if she was right. "I pride myself on auto-didacticism."

She laughed. "Even so." She rose and turned to the bar, scribbling something on the back of a card. He felt the sudden distance between them like a severed cord. "If you change your mind," she said, holding the pale rectangle between two fingers.

He wanted to refuse, but instead he rose and took the card—and her number—and shoved it into his pocket. He rubbed his palms on his thighs. "I should find Liz." He never should have left her alone for so long.

"Of course." Antja's face was smiling and immaculate again. He wondered if he could see through her illusions now, but didn't try. He didn't want to know what lay under them.

* * *

NEITHER OF THEM spoke as he followed Antja back to the crowded gallery. He was trying to muster the wherewithal for a polite goodbye when they turned a corner and nearly collided with someone.

The man from the opening, Stephen. Still blond and sleek, but his smug smile was nowhere to be found as he stared at Antja.

"Stephen." She drew herself up, a chilly transformation that had more to do with anger than illusion. Her smile could have cut glass. "Did you get my message?"

"I did." Stephen's throat worked above his shirt collar. "Antja—"

"It was a clever idea. Pity it didn't work out."

"It was a mistake." He glanced at Alex and looked away again in dismissal. "You didn't tell Rainer."

Her smile stretched even thinner. "I don't need him to protect me. You've got a lot of nerve coming here tonight. But you always do, don't you?"

The tension thickened and Alex edged away. He couldn't tell if the intimacy between them was born of desire or anger or both. Their voices were low, but the palpable intensity began to draw glances. Time to slip off quietly and find Liz.

"If you want to kill me," Antja said, and his attention snapped back, "now would be the time to try."

Stephen's expression grew pained. "I said it was a mistake. I underestimated you. I'm sorry." His eyes flickered to Alex again, and toward the people trying to eavesdrop behind them. "This isn't the place for this discussion."

"Isn't it?" Her eyes narrowed. "You weren't invited tonight."

Alex swallowed the taste of ozone. His skin crawled and stung and the hair on his arms stood on end. Conversations faltered and died as more people clustered at the end of the hall to watch. So much for slipping away unnoticed.

"Antja—" Alex reached for her arm, hoping to forestall whatever confrontation was in the making. A spark arced between them and he jerked back with a hiss. Overhead, one of the lightbulbs shattered with a pop and the shivery tinkle of falling glass. He retreated, brushing crystalline dust off his sleeve. The dizziness returned, worse than ever, and his chest ached.

He didn't realize how quiet the room had grown until footsteps broke the stillness. The crowd parted as Rainer strode toward them. Liz followed at his heels, and Alex drew a sharp breath of relief.

Rainer's ring flashed as he gestured toward the crowd. The last scraps of conversation died. "What's going on?" His voice was soft and ugly.

The sound of rain filled the silence that followed, and a low rhythmic rush rose below that. Breath, Alex realized. All the guests stood slack-jawed and vacant, breathing in unison. Mannequins, but for the rise and fall of their chests. It was, he thought wildly, the most effective installation he'd seen in the gallery.

Liz edged away from Rainer and caught Alex's hand. Her palm was cold and damp, but her touch grounded him, eased the electric sting of the air and the disorientation of alcohol and adrenaline.

Stephen looked from Antja to Rainer and turned slowly. Glass crunched under his feet. "Nothing."

Rainer's face seemed to thin as they watched, cheeks sinking and draining sallow. "Are you here to challenge me, Stephen?" His glacial eyes darkened, threads of black spreading from his pupils to eclipse iris and sclera alike. The same darkness crept under his skin, filling veins and capillaries. Alex's hand tightened on Liz's until bone ground through flesh.

A muscle worked in Stephen's jaw. "No."

"Then get the hell out." Rainer's voice was too deep, shivering at the edges; the sound made Alex's teeth ache.

Stephen straightened his jacket in a poor attempt at nonchalance. Then he turned and retreated down the stairs with the measured steps of a man trying not to run.

Rainer turned toward Alex and Liz, and they both flinched. The shadow under his skin rolled back like a wave, leaving his usual face pale and drawn. "I'm sorry you had to see that," he said.

The crowd drew one more collective breath and slowly returned to life. Guests blinked at one another in confusion. A gust of wind shook the windows and someone squealed, followed by a nervous giggle. One by one conversations picked up where they'd been abandoned as if nothing had happened.

Rainer took Antja's arm, and Liz tugged Alex away. Hand in hand they fled down the stairs and into the icy night.

14
HOOKS

Late that night, well into the next morning, Antja sat in the candle-pierced darkness of the loft. Rainer slept at last, snoring softly while rain battered the walls.

She hugged her arms around her knees, as if she could hold herself together so easily. The seams were unraveling, threads slipping through her fingers. The gallery, their lives in Vancouver, the fragile veneer of normalcy she'd built for herself—soon it would all be gone. She'd nearly cut the last thread herself tonight, nearly lost control in a way she couldn't afford. Anger and careless magic were a deadly combination, no matter how intoxicating they might be in the moment. She'd been nothing but reckless tonight, first with Alex and then with Stephen. She couldn't let it happen again.

They could run, she and Rainer. The idea was all too tempting—pack a bag and vanish in the night, as they had from Berlin. This time they wouldn't have the Brotherhood's thugs on their trail. Run and start over someplace new. Someplace warm.

But where would that leave Blake, or Alex, or Liz, or anyone who'd been caught up in her and Rainer's troubles. Alain's death, and all the others, would mean nothing.

And anyway, Rainer wouldn't leave Blake.

They consume us like moths, Alain had said, *without even meaning it.* Had it really been him, or simply her guilt and unspoken fears wearing his face?

He needs me, she'd said to Alex, but was that true? She couldn't tell love from cowardice anymore. Another thought circled, implacable as any shark: she could ask for help. She could bargain.

She would never forget that night, had relieved it in dreams more often than she could count. The sight of the Brotherhood's agent standing under the window of their rented room. The cold rush of panic when she realized their luck had run out. But trained killer or not, the man was still distracted by a smile and a song, by the swirl of her skirt around her knees. Easy enough to join him in the shadowed alley, to lean in close enough to kiss. Close enough to use the wicked little knife in her pocket. But even as she stood over his crumpled body, watching his blood run black into the gutter, she knew she and Rainer wouldn't make it off the continent. With that fear in her gut and the memory of blood sticky on her hands, it had been easy to find the incantations in Rainer's stolen books, to speak them to the dark and make the devil's bargain.

The candle on the table guttered, rippling shadows across the walls. Rainer stirred with a sigh and rustle of sheets, then stilled once more. Antja closed her eyes, burning with sleeplessness and misery, and lowered her head to her knees. "What am I going to do?"

"Yes. What are you going to do?"

Her chair scraped the floor as she started. The dark man stepped out of the shadows behind her, the candle flame washing his black eyes to liquid gold. Rainer slept on.

"What are you doing here?" Her bare feet slipped to the floor and her fingers tightened on the arms of the chair.

"You're distressed. You needn't torment yourself this way." He laid a warm hand on her shoulder and she jerked away, twisting out of the chair.

"Not when you're here to torment me instead."

He chuckled. "That wasn't my intention. Not entirely. I might ease your suffering, if you'd let me."

"With what? More death? Your gifts are poison."

He tilted his head, and the light kissed the curves of his cheek and brow. "You bargained for your safety, and his." One mahogany hand gestured toward Rainer. "And you're both safe. I can keep you free from harm, but not from pain and doubt and fear. Well, I could," he amended. "But I think you're too attached to your humanity for that."

She shuddered and dragged a hand over her face. "What do you want from me?"

"Only your occasional service, as per the terms of our agreement. Some help me willingly, you know. Have you ever considered that?"

She had, if only in the dark watches of the night when she couldn't lie to herself, but she would die before she admitted it to him. "Some people are fools."

His lips pursed. "So very many. All right, Antja Michaela. I can release you, if that's what you wish, but not for free. What do I gain if I strike your name from my book?"

She turned away, hugging herself. Still Rainer slept.

"Would you give me another name to replace yours?"

That drew her around again. "Another name?"

"A trade. But who?" He flicked dismissive fingers at Rainer. "He's already spoken for. Another of his flock, perhaps?"

Don't even think of it. But it was too late. "You would trade a name for a name? No tricks, no lies?"

He shrugged and straightened the flawless line of one sleeve. "If it were a fair trade. Someone talented, someone interesting. Someone who means something to you." He cocked his head. "Why? Do you have someone in mind?"

"I can't," she whispered. "I won't."

"Ah. Well, if you think of something else, do let me know." He closed the space between them and cupped her chin gently. "You look so tired, my dear. You should rest."

Then he was gone, leaving her shivering in the guttering candlelight.

THE STORM RAGED through the night like it meant to end the world, a deluge fit for Deucalion and Utnapishtim. Alex's mood was fey enough for eschatology, even in the comfortable darkness of the bedroom.

Liz lay soft and warm in his arms—except for her inexplicably icy feet, which were tucked against his shins—too still to be sleeping. He wished he could concentrate on the shape of her hip under his hand, the smell of rain clinging in her hair. He could install her image in the galleries of his memory palace, could remember the shades of her hair, the pattern of her freckles and the agatine flecks of her eyes. But the feel and scent of her, the rasp of her breath— could he hold onto those, or would they wither in time like flesh from bone?

But even this moment of sensation did nothing to hold the images at bay: Antja's shimmering glamour; Rainer's eyes gone black. A room full of people turned to dolls with a gesture. Alex wished he could cling to his horror so easily, but Antja was right. The more his shock faded, the more he wanted to understand what he'd seen. The same way he'd felt when he first watched a stage magician make a coin disappear, when he'd first seen an illuminated manuscript written in characters he couldn't read. But this was more than that—something had been taken from him, and he had to get it back.

"What are we going to do?" He didn't realize he'd spoken aloud until Liz stirred.

"I don't know."

She rolled over, touching his chest lightly with her bandaged hand. Her fingertips traced the dips and hollows of his ribs and sternum as if she meant to memorize them, and he shivered. He still responded to her touch, for all he'd tried to train himself not to. On rare occasions she invited—*permitted,* a scathing voice corrected, *endured*—physical intimacy, but now was hardly a time for it. Not with Antja's false face waiting behind his eyes.

"Thank you," Liz said after a moment. If she noticed his shudder, she had the grace to ignore it. "For coming with me. It helps."

"This is too much for us," he said, as gently as he could. "We can't help Blake this way."

She stiffened, and he thought she would pull away. Instead she sighed, warm across his throat and went limp again. "I know."

He'd come to dread those words, so gentle and agreeable and utterly intractable. He wanted to hold her closer, but her wounded hand lay between them and clinging would only drive her further away. He slid his palm over the soft flesh of her upper arm, tracing the familiar constellation of moles there. "Liz—"

"Shh." She touched the corner of his mouth, soft as a kiss. "It's all right. We'll think of something. In the morning."

He prayed that she was right. He didn't know what else to do.

THE SEA SPIT him out but Blake still drifted. Hands buoyed him, clutching too tight. Voices surrounded him, wild and cacophonous, every chant and shriek a spike of pain through his skull. He tried to open his eyes, but hot crimson light slivered between his lids and he screwed them shut again. The revelers bore him on, relentless as any tide, and he sank once more.

He resurfaced blind and bound, strapped tight to a cold, hard surface. More hands touched him, but these were cool and clinical, except for an occasional taunting caress. He tried to fight, to struggle, to move at all, but straps and clamps held him fast, and his limbs were heavy and weak.

After the hands came the blades. Skin split under cold steel, peeled away layer by layer to bare flesh and sinew. No pain, but he felt every centimeter of the incision as they husked him like fruit. He couldn't scream: metal and leather filled his mouth, trapped his tongue and any sound he could make.

"Show us where it hurts," a woman said, soft and mocking. The scalpel stopped below his navel, tracing ticklish, feather-light patterns but not breaking the skin. "It will never heal if you don't share."

Tears leaked hot down his cheeks and mucus clogged his nose. He was glad he couldn't whimper.

Different hands wiped away the tears and stroked his hair. "You have to show us what hurts you, if you want to be free of it." This voice was gentle, veined with distant pity.

Fingers sifted through his intestines, lifting wet coils and letting them fall. The reek of blood and waste filled the air, and something worse, something black and stale and rotting. *It's just meat,* he told himself, an all-too-familiar refrain. *They can't hurt me. It's just meat.*

"So much misery," the first woman marveled. He hated her already. Her hands moved higher, caressing his lungs, stroking the quivering muscle of his heart. "How do you fit it all inside?"

Ignore it. They can't hurt me. Fists and stones could break his bones, bruise flesh and tear skin, but that would heal. He could retreat from pain, hide behind the walls in his head.

A different voice called to him, a whisper from the darkness. A pale spark of presence that smelled of vanilla shampoo.

Liz?

No, he couldn't trust it. He curled tighter within himself, trying to block the sound.

Blake! The fear in her voice seared him like lightning, but he didn't dare reach out.

"You're not listening." A hand slapped his face, light and teasing. The touch lingered, then cool flesh was replaced with cold metal. She held it against his cheek, letting him feel the shape of it. A hook, long and thin and sharply curved. "You have to show us, Blake."

The hook slid into his nostril, a cold pressure against his sinuses. Only fragile whorls of bone lay between his brain and the steel. He choked on tears and the stench of his own fear.

The spark brightened. *Blake, it's me. I'm here.*

"If you won't share, we'll pull it out." One hand adjusted its grip on the hook while the other stroked his jaw.

Justmeatitsjustmeatitsjustmeat—

The hook shattered his skull, shattered his walls, and dragged the first scream out of him.

AFTER THE NIGHTMARE, Liz curled limp and shaking against the slick fiberglass curve of the tub. Her stomach ached from vomiting herself empty; her jaw ached from muffling her sobs. Scalding water stung her skin, but her hands were still cold and tingling. No matter how she scrubbed, she couldn't rid herself of the memory of hands and metal and mocking laughter.

She tried to talk herself through the panic, but none of her rote reassurances could help her now. Blake was trapped, trapped and suffering, and she was too weak to stop the dream from forcing her out, helpless and useless. She couldn't even stay with him through the pain.

Her hiccupping sobs slowed and died and tears and snot sluiced away. Her bandage unraveled in the spray and rusty pus oozed from the bite; the sight made her tender stomach churn all over again. She didn't know how long she sat there; her fingers and toes were wrinkled, but the water was still hot. Her own water heater would never have tolerated hysterics for so long. Finally she shut off the tap and stood, trembling until she thought she would shatter. Tendrils of steam snaked through the door when she opened it. Beads of condensation peeled down the mirror, baring her reflection in stripes.

Rain hissed down outside and Alex still slept. Liz watched him from the bathroom doorway, sticky and shivering. All she wanted was to crawl under the covers with him and sleep for a hundred years, sleep and never dream. But she couldn't—wouldn't—leave Blake in that nightmare city, and he was running out of time.

Her T-shirt and underwear clung to her skin as she pulled them on, and her hair dripped down her shoulders. Four in the morning, the clock said—hours yet till dawn. If she meant to act, she had to do it before Alex woke up.

She left a trail of damp footprints as she crossed the room. Alex slept deeply, a pillow cradled to his chest. The blanket pooled around his hips, baring the long line of his back and the aliform curve of his shoulder blades.

Would he forgive her if she killed herself in some foolish experiment? Would he forgive her if she didn't? She had no choice that didn't hurt.

She had no choice at all.

She leaned down and pressed a soft kiss against his shoulder. "I'm sorry." His skin roughened at her touch, but he didn't stir.

Her coat lay where she'd tossed it over the back of the couch, still damp from the storm. The vial was intact in the pocket. The liquid inside was clear as water in the dim lamplight, with only a faint golden shimmer to betray it.

Morpheus. The king of dreams. Would it open the ivory gate or the horn?

Liz nearly laughed—she didn't even know how to take the stuff. The women in the gallery had dripped it into their eyes; the thought made her flesh crawl. Her knees buckled and she sank onto the couch.

She could call Rainer. But all she could think of was his black eyes, a room full of people with their will stolen. And he'd already said he couldn't do this. She was on her own.

Her fingers trembled as she unscrewed the cap. She expected bitter chemicals, but a smell like raw honey floated through the air. Fluid glistened on the dropper, shivered but didn't fall. Please, she prayed to whoever might listen, and tilted her head back.

The drops stung like ice. She flinched, catching a breath between her teeth. Moisture clung to her lashes and bled down her cheeks when she blinked. She raised the second half of the vial to her lips.

Drink me.

It was bitter as tears after all, bitter as hearts. She swallowed it down.

15
DOWN THE RABBIT HOLE

ALEX WOKE TO cold sheets and the sound of rain, to dreams clinging thick as cobwebs behind his eyes. Dreams of being young and lost, of searching frantically for a woman who wasn't his mother, a woman who wouldn't turn and show him her face.

He sighed into the pillow; his subconscious was such a waste of good processing power.

He tugged the covers closer and dozed again, waiting for Liz to return. The alarm clock on the bedside table was a green-and-black blur until he snaked out an arm and found his glasses. Eleven o'clock. Minutes rolled by with no sign of Liz. The room was so still he could hear the electric hum of the clock. Finally he surrendered his hard-won warmth and rolled out of bed. The movement triggered a sticky cough deep in his chest.

He found Liz in the curtained gloom of the living room, asleep on the couch. Her hair trailed across the cushions and one foot dangled against the floor. He sighed to see her sleeping so peacefully. Then he saw the glitter of glass in her palm.

"Liz?"

Her breath was shallow, pale lips parted. An unsettling sweet scent clung to her skin. She didn't stir as he pried open her cold fingers. He stared at the vial, at the last drop of fluid clinging to the glass, and the tightness in his chest had nothing to do with asthma.

No amount of shaking or pinching or calling her name could rouse her. Her pulse was steady but weak, her breath even, but she was insensible as... as a coma patient. As Blake.

Maybe they could share a hospital room.

"You idiot," he whispered, and wasn't sure who he meant. He should have known. He should have seen it coming. He stopped himself as he reached for the phone, clenched his fist and nearly punched a wall. She wouldn't want him to call the hospital.

If he'd listened to her earlier, if he'd shared the things he'd seen—

That was a pointless line of thought. He could excoriate himself later.

He wrapped her in a blanket and sat beside her, stroking her tangled hair. An hour passed with no change. If anything, Liz was paler than ever, the shadows around her eyes deeper. It wasn't until Alex's fingertips began to ache that he realized he was rubbing the medallion at his throat. He couldn't sit here helpless—there had to be something he could do.

He swallowed an unpleasant taste. There was something, an alternative to a hospital, loath as he was to use it. But what choice did he have?

He left Liz inert on the sofa and went to retrieve Antja's number.

SHE ARRIVED HALF an hour later, damp from the unceasing rain. Alex blinked when he opened the door; her face was scrubbed clean, no cosmetics to hide her chewed lips or bruised eyes. No masks.

"What— Oh." Her eyes slid past him to Liz and she stepped inside. He bolted the door behind her.

"How long has she been this way?" she asked, kneeling beside the couch.

"I found her an hour and a half ago, but she might have been like this for hours before that." Alex folded his arms, forcing himself to give her room when he wanted to hover.

Antja ran careful fingers over Liz's brow, her dark eyes unfocusing. She pulled her hand back with a frown, fists clenching against her thighs.

"Can you do anything?" Alex asked.

She shook her head, her ponytail arcing across her shoulders. "I don't know."

He pulled the vial from his pocket and tossed it to her. "She got this from Rainer, didn't she?" The words were harsh and ugly; fear and fury were a jagged lump in his throat.

Antja caught the glass tube and stared at it. Her already pale lips pinched white as eggshells, and a crease formed between her brows. "Yes."

He took a step toward her. "Blake and Alain weren't enough for him? How many more people is he going to kill?"

Antja's chin lifted. "He's done everything he can for Blake. And this was Liz's decision."

The truth of that meant nothing to his rage. He closed the distance between them and grabbed her arm. The vial fell from her hand as he shook her. "I'm tried of tricks and excuses and lies. Bring her back!"

Dark eyes widened; flesh dented under his fingers. His anger drained away, leaving nausea in its place. Antja let out a rush of breath that was nearly a laugh as he jerked away.

His legs buckled and he collapsed into a chair. He'd laid hands on two people in the past few days, and no amount of anger or desperation could excuse that. He tried to apologize, but the words wouldn't come. Antja settled lightly on the arm of the couch by Liz's feet, studying him. If he'd frightened her, she gave no sign; he wasn't sure if that made it better or worse.

"What is this poison, anyway?" he finally managed. He chafed his hands on his thighs, trying to forget the feeling of yielding flesh.

Antja stared past him as if the answers were written in the swirls of the wallpaper. "It was called Morpheus before it was mania," she said at last, "and probably a dozen other names besides. It was created by a group called die Brüderschaft des gelben Zeichens."

Alex rolled the words around in his head. "The brotherhood of the yellow... symbol?"

"Sign—I think that would be the better word. But yes. They're... magicians. Sorcerers." She arched her eyebrows as if daring him to scoff, but they'd come too far for that.

"Like the Golden Dawn?"

"Something like that. Or the Thule-Gesellschaft, before the Nazis. They like to act respectable, but they're vicious bastards. Morpheus was designed to grant visions, to strengthen magic. Someone eventually found a more lucrative use for it."

"Were you part of this Brotherhood?" he asked.

She laughed humorlessly. "They wouldn't have much use for me. But Rainer's family has a long history with them."

Alex drew a breath to say something caustic, but the words died as he glanced at Liz. Her nose was bleeding. A thick line of crimson ran down her upper lip, pooling in the corner of her mouth before dripping into her hair. Antja hissed in dismay as Alex scrambled for a tissue.

"What the hell does Rainer want, anyway?" Liz didn't even twitch as he wiped away the blood.

"He wants Blake back." Her voice was soft and miserable.

"And he's willing to kill Liz to do it?" But Antja was right: Liz was more than willing to kill herself.

He rose, the crumpled tissue lying on Liz's chest like a blood-spotted flower. "Please." The word caught in his throat like fishhooks. "There must be something we can do. Anything. Whatever you want—" He broke off. He would beg if he had to, but what did he have to offer?

Antja's face drained to a pasty grey. "Do you mean that?"

"Yes, damn it! Of course I do."

"What if—" But she closed her mouth tight against the question, and before he could press her she turned on her heel and fled to the bathroom.

ANTJA LEANED AGAINST the locked bathroom door as if she could barricade herself from the thought that drove her there.

A name for a name. This was her chance.

Alex waited on the other side of the door—a clever young man, already drawn to the illusory ghostlight promises of magic, defenseless now in his desperation to help someone he loved. Desperate enough to take the devil's bargain.

She turned on the tap and splashed her burning cheeks, watching the water swirl around the drain. It would be easy. She sucked in a deep breath and waited for the nausea to pass. She would be free.

"Is this your decision, then? One of them?"

The smell of incense and ozone filled the little room and her stomach churned anew. Her hands tightened on the edge of the marbled counter.

"The girl? The dreamer?" The devil's hands closed on her upper arms, soothing the ache Alex's fingers had left. "No, her young man." His warmth soaked into her rigid spine, but when she looked up she saw only her own tired and damp reflection.

Maybe Alex would make better bargains than she had. Maybe it wouldn't be so bad for him.

"I can't," she whispered. The words washed away with the swirling water.

"It's nothing dramatic." He reached past her to shut off the water. "Look." Gently, he turned her around and opened the door, leading her across the threshold and into the perfect stillness of frozen time.

Rain hung like diamonds beyond the windows, the curtains belling softly in the heater's draft. Alex knelt beside Liz, his hand raised to touch her face. His ditchwater hair was uncombed, clothes rumpled. Stubble glinted along the long line of his jaw. His eyes were shut in misery; the grey light was unkind to the shadows beneath them.

"All you have to do is introduce us," the dark man said. "He's in pain. I can help him."

Do it, she told herself viciously. Alex was nothing to her, just a chance-met acquaintance. Never mind how much she sympathized. Never mind that she had meant it when she offered to teach him. Never mind that she'd wanted to kiss him. Without that spark of interest, it wasn't a bargain the devil would take. And what was one more piece of guilt compared to her freedom?

She could say the words, and spare him this pain. He might even thank her for it.

"The decision is his," the man said, "just as it was yours. All you would do is provide the opportunity."

She tried to summon the cold she'd felt when she reached for her knife all those years ago, the chill in her veins that stripped away doubt. But all she could remember was the hot rush of blood. Blood on her hands, blood in the gutter, blood on the floor of the cabin.

Say it. Say it and end this.

The devil was silent, tracing circles on her stiff shoulders with his thumbs. "You'd rather continue our relationship, then?" he said at last. "I don't mind, of course, if that's what you want."

"We don't have a relationship."

"You'll hurt my feelings with talk like that. Haven't I always been there for you? Who else can you say the same of?"

She'd found the cold after all. It spread from her stomach, chilling her limbs and finally coating her tongue. "You can take your feelings back to hell. I won't help you any more."

The caressing hands stilled. "Do I understand you correctly? Do you no longer require my protection?"

He was calm and gracious as ever, but the words rang with weight. *Take it back, take it back,* the frantic voice in her mind implored her, but she stood on the brink of a roaring chasm and there was no way to go but forward.

"That's right." Her voice didn't crack; she was proud of that.

"As you wish, my dear. We'll see how well you do on your own. If you change your mind, you know how to reach me."

She spun, but he was gone. Time resumed with the hiss of rain and the rumble of the heater. A warm draft blew across her face and she shuddered. She very nearly ran, but her legs were shaking too badly. Instead she turned, bracing herself to face Alex, and her consequences.

ALEX GLANCED UP to see Antja standing behind the couch and nearly flinched—he hadn't heard the door open again. But he was too tired for surprise. He wiped another drop of blood from Liz's cheek, staring at the smear of rust-red across white skin. His head throbbed and his hands trembled.

"If there's nothing you can do, I have to call the hospital." He could have made it a threat, but he was too tired for that, too.

The crease deepened between Antja's eyebrows. She hugged herself as if her own hands were all that kept her together.

"I can call Rainer," she said. "Maybe he can do something." She didn't sound very hopeful.

Alex's hand clenched around the bloody tissue. "Rainer is the last person I want to see right now." Even as he said it, a worm of doubt stirred. Which would be worse—dealing with Rainer, or explaining to the paramedics and police that his girlfriend had overdosed on a strange drug because she was trying to rescue a friend from a nightmare?

The room darkened and Antja started. Alex looked up, but saw nothing but grey sky and rain-streaked glass. He stood, stiff joints popping, and dragged a hand through his tangled hair. "There must be another option. Don't you know any other sorcerers?" His lip curled on the word. His sneer died as Samantha's face rose in his mind.

No. No, anything but that.

He paced an angry circuit in front of the balcony door, bare feet silent on the worn blue carpet. There had to be an answer; he refused to accept the alternative.

The light dimmed again and Antja let out a choked sound. "We have to go." Her voice was strained and clipped.

He paused mid stride. "What? I'm not leaving—"

The window rattled. He looked up to see a sleek black shape slide past the balcony. Adrenaline swept through him in a scalding rush, left his hands icy and shaking.

"We have to go now!" Antja grabbed his wrist and tugged him toward the door.

"I can't leave Liz." He jerked his hand free, but momentum pulled him in her wake. "I thought you said they were after Rainer."

"I don't know anymore." And, more softly, "Damn him."

The balcony door swung inward with a rush of wind and rain. The monster crouched on the threshold, silhouetted against the storm-silver sky. Shadow wings flared, blotting the light.

"Run!" Antja flung the door open and Alex was hard on her heels, even as he cursed himself for a coward. She ran down the corridor and threw her weight against the emergency exit. *Alarm will sound,* the sign read; *Door will open in thirty seconds.* Sure enough, a shrill whine filled the air, reverberating through his skull.

He had to go back, gather his scattered wits and do something. He had to protect Liz. But the monster didn't seem interested in her. It stepped into the hall, head snaking back and forth on its sinewy neck. No eyes, no ears, no features at all to mar the slick black curve of its skull, but it turned unerringly toward them. Alex's vision flickered—one instant it was a man, lean and tenebrous, a long coat flapping around his legs; the next it slunk on all fours, wings furled to fit the hallway. Sickle claws sank into the faded carpet, and it was too easy to imagine them meeting flesh.

Someone called out in confusion and concern down the hall. The emergency door opened with a groan and spilled them onto a rain-slick fire escape. Antja staggered against the rusted railing, and Alex stumbled into her in turn. Raindrops spun toward the pavement below. Icy metal dented the soles of his feet and he remembered his shoes, abandoned along with Liz in the room. Their footsteps rang as they plunged down the iron steps.

"How do we stop them?" he gasped as they reached the next landing. Six more to go.

"Fire works."

Rain fogged his glasses and trickled down his collar—he nearly laughed. Five more flights. The clatter of their descent echoed between the narrow alley walls, a faint and distant sound over the roar of his pulse. Four.

He felt the crack of wings an instant before the creature struck. Black talons whistled past his face and closed on Antja's shoulder. Alex grabbed her arm and pulled her free, only to lose his balance and send them both tumbling down the stairs in a tangle of limbs and wet cloth.

Grey sky and black iron and wet brick kaleidoscoped around him, until his head cracked against the railing and everything washed red. Antja landed on him, driving the last of the air from his lungs. Sobbing, she rose and hauled him down the rest of the steps.

He fell again when they reached the alley floor, bruising his knees on rain-drenched concrete. His glasses slipped off his face, and the world washed grey and featureless. Pain was a hammer on the back of his skull, his lungs filled with molten lead. He slapped at his pockets, knowing it was futile—his inhaler, like his shoes, was still upstairs.

"We can't stop moving," Antja said, tugging at him. Alex wasn't sure he could start. A quick death by claws, or slow asphyxiation. Choices, choices. Only contrariness let him stumble to his feet.

The alley mouth was blocked. The creature crouched like a gargoyle, its horned head trained on them. Oilslick haunches rippled as it started toward them. Even half-blind Alex could see the grace of its movements, its sinuous, Gigeresque lines.

"It's herding us," he said, glancing at the cavernous mouth of the parking garage behind them. Black wings spanned the alley and they fell back. There was no way to go but down.

Wind funneled down the slope of the driveway, slicing through wet cloth and flesh. Sodium lamps cast yellow pools on the slick floor, but shadows filled the corners. The monsters—two of them now—slunk down the ramp, sometimes on two legs and sometimes on four, silent save for the scrape of claws on concrete.

Antja raised a hand and light crackled incandescent around her fingers, shuddering across windows and windshields and glazing the oily puddles at their feet. The glow cast her shadow and Alex's huge and grotesque against the walls; the creatures cast none. They balked at the sudden brilliance, whip-sharp tails lashing, but didn't stop.

The light showed the lines of strain carved on Antja's face. "How long can you keep that up?" Alex asked. His voice was a thin wheeze, his chest cramping with want of air. Drowning on dry land.

"Not very." Her voice was soft and grim; the light wavered. Broken glass glittered on the ground; his feet were bleeding, the pain a distant warmth. He wondered if he could hotwire a car.

He might not last much longer than her light. The drone of the lamps echoed in his skull, and his vision tunneled. He felt the adrenaline-scald of panic moving through him, but it too was distant. At least unconsciousness meant he would stop hurting.

He didn't realize he'd stumbled until Antja reached to steady him. Her light died with the movement. A blister wept on her right palm where the fire had been. Her good hand lingered on his arm.

He ought to say something noble, like "Save yourself," but he didn't have breath to spare.

Antja shook her head as though she'd heard him anyway. "I can't run anymore."

It was, he thought dimly, a more interesting death than he would have imagined for himself. That didn't make it any less annoying.

The shriek of wet rubber reverberated through the garage, followed by an engine's growl. The creature's blind heads swung round as headlights carved away the shadows. For an instant they paused, backlit by the glare; then they melted like tar and dissolved.

A familiar glossy, storm-grey car screeched to a stop in front of Antja and Lailah slid out of the driver's side. Relief dizzied him— or maybe that was only hypoxia.

"Are you all right?" she called. A pale face watched them through the tinted glass of the passenger window. "Then let's get out of here before they come back."

"Liz—" Alex wheezed, even as Antja let out a strangled breath and whispered, "Oh God, Rainer." She pressed her blistered hand to her mouth and left a smear of blood and fluid behind.

"You'll be safer with us," Lailah said. Alex wasn't sure when they'd become an 'us', but he was in no condition to argue.

"She's right," Alex said, surprising himself. "You're hurt." Each word was more effort than the last. The world felt disconnected and far away.

Her eyes were black holes in the pallor of her face. "I can't." She brushed her fingers over his; his nails were shadowed lilac grey with cyanosis. "Take Liz and go."

The last thing he saw before he fainted was her back fading into the gloom.

"I DON'T KNOW what else to do," Rainer said. Whether he spoke to himself or to the empty shell in the hospital bed, he wasn't sure.

He paced in front of the window, his shoes squeaking faintly on the tiles. Watery shadows rippled across the floor, and rainlight rinsed the room dull and grey. Only the bed lamp burned against the gloom. Its yellow glow lent warmth and color to Blake's face, but it was an illusion—the truth was wan and cold and brittle.

Rainer hadn't been here since he'd arranged for the private room. He'd told himself he didn't want to draw attention to Blake, that his time was better spent finding a solution. In truth the sick knot in his chest whenever he looked at Blake was too much to endure. Even now his eyes strayed to the window more often than not.

Cowardice. He had to live with his actions. He forced himself to turn, to take the three strides to the bedside. He didn't take Blake's hand or touch his hollow cheek, though his fingers itched to do so. An uninvited caress might be more than Blake could forgive him, after everything else.

Machines dripped nourishment into him, but it wasn't enough; the arches of Blake's temples pressed sharp through papery skin, and Rainer could count the rings of his larynx. There were enchantments of stasis he could learn, ways to preserve the flesh beyond these tubes and wires—like Sleeping Beauty, or Brynhild in the fire—but without consciousness to reunite with the body, all they could do was prolong this cold unlife.

"I don't know what to do," he said again. Maybe Liz could accomplish what he couldn't, if he hadn't frightened her away last night. She wasn't bound by his oaths. Or protected by them.

He trained his eyes on Blake again, curling his fingers around the bed rail until his knuckles blanched. He teased Antja about her Catholic childhood, but he knew a cilice when he used one on himself.

"I am trying," he said softly. "Please believe that. And I'm sorry."

With that he turned away, his quarter hour of courage spent, and fled the hospital and its weight of grief and misery.

When he pulled into the narrow parking lot behind the gallery and turned off the car, it was all he could do not to lean his head on the steering wheel and weep. He couldn't go on like this, but his oaths weren't the sort to be forsworn. He had to find a way to serve that let him sleep at night. Would the King let him join a hermitage?

Rain snaked cold through his hair as he stepped out of the car. Only an hour past noon, but the alley was dark as dusk. His skin tightened as he hit the alarm button, fingers tingling. He paused, cupping the keys as he listened, but all he heard was the drum and rush of water. He shook his head, sending moisture trickling past his collar. Now wasn't the time to start jumping at shadows. His shoes splashed across flooded blacktop, the cuffs of his trousers slapping against leather.

The streetlamp that lit the parking lot buzzed and sputtered, sending shadows writhing along the walls. Some writhed more than others.

Rainer spun, following a black flicker at the edge of his vision. The sour taste of nerves coated his tongue as he murmured a warding spell. There—a ripple in the dark, gone as soon as he saw it. Clawed feet splashed and scraped on wet cement, but when he turned toward the sound it vanished.

The creature struck as the last syllable of the spell left his lips. The charm slowed its claws but couldn't stop them; instead of ripping his heart out with one strike it merely shredded his left shoulder. He fell, too stunned to cry out as he sprawled hard on the ground. Cold soaked his back. Heat soaked his chest. Rain stung his face as he struggled to breathe.

Two of them, identical. The darkness between stars made flesh. Whip-sharp tails lashed as they approached. Rainer scrambled backwards on three limbs, heels slipping in puddles, right palm scoring against asphalt. Warmth trickled down his left sleeve, cooling quickly. His arm was dead weight.

He had to focus, but the black shapes were mesmerizing as they closed on him, slow and playful as cats. Rainer stumbled toward the back stairs and fell on the lowest step. His blood swirled away in the rain, taking his strength with it. His own magic slipped fickle through his fingers. Drawing a painful breath, he reached deeper, for the power of the King.

It burned. Burned and froze the life from him. Blood thickened and slowed, sluggish as tar. He felt the darkness seeping across his eyes and fought the urge to retch.

The shadow-beasts paused, blind heads dipping as if they could sense the changes. As they tensed to strike, Rainer called the fire.

Smokeless yellow flame engulfed them, washing the alley black and gold. Alien flesh sizzled and popped. Fire was one of the few things that could hurt them, they'd discovered at the cabin. Too late to save anyone that night, but now he had the chance to repay his friends' deaths. The monsters staggered, leaking sparks and blood black as oil. Rain evaporated with a steaming hiss, but they made no sound at all as they burned.

Burned, but didn't stop their relentless approach. Black spots swam in front of Rainer's eyes. He'd lost too much blood.

And by the time they reached Vancouver, he'd actually thought he wouldn't end up dead in an alley. He tried to laugh and sobbed instead.

The back door flew open with a shriek and clang as his vision darkened. Antja called his name. Everything sounded dull and far away.

Silver light flared around him. A ward, hardly more to these creatures than a spider web, but it bought him a few more seconds. Time for Antja to grab his coat and haul him up the stairs. He screamed at the jolt, and the sound of his own pain was the last thing he heard.

16

PRICKS & SPINDLES

ALEX WOKE CRAMPED and stiff, his neck crooked at a painful angle. And cold—he couldn't remember the last time he hadn't been cold. His mouth was sour with sleep, dry and bitter with the lingering grit of albuterol. The air smelled of smoke.

He sat up straight in an uncomfortable chair, his shoes scuffing against wood. His memory was a distorted muddle of images: Antja's fire; Lailah leaning over him, pressing his inhaler into his mouth; a car the color of smoke; a familiar drive through twisting roads; Liz limp in Lailah's arms. He couldn't fit the pieces into a coherent whole.

He stood and stretched aching limbs. His neck popped loudly as he rolled his head. A blanket fell away from his legs, pooling on the floor. Movement triggered coughing, which set his head to throbbing in turn. He leaned against the chair until the spasm passed, closing his eyes against the pain in head and chest. His eyes ached and he groped for his glasses, only to remember that they were gone. Lost in the alley, and he hadn't thought to pack his extra pair.

The curtains were drawn, leaving the room around him a dim blur of warm-toned wallpaper and wooden furniture, the ceiling half-timbered in a way that might intend to be rustic. He hoped the bed was more comfortable than the chair—Liz lay there, lily-pale in the gloom. Her skin was cool when he took her hand, her pulse a slow and patient rhythm. He pinched the back of her wrist and watched blood return to whitened flesh, but between her pallor and the poor light, he couldn't tell if it took longer than it should.

Alex turned toward the window, stumbling over the edge of a carpet in the dark, and pulled aside the drapes. Light streamed in, weak and pale as skimmed milk between the shadows of snow-dusted evergreens, but still enough to make him wince. Slanting afternoon light—they'd been here at least a day. At least a day, and Liz still slept like some spindle-pricked princess.

"I hope you're not planning to sleep a hundred years," he murmured, bending down to brush her dry lips with his. Not prince enough.

Their luggage lay piled beside the door, and that was some comfort at least. Whatever new vicissitudes the day had in store, he could face them with clean teeth and clothes.

The door opened into a corridor, and he realized why so many things seemed familiar. The floor plan was nearly identical to Rainer's cabin. And that was where they must be, if he hadn't hallucinated what he could remember of the drive yesterday—back at Carroll Cove. The realization did very little to comfort him.

Smells drifted through the chilly air: smoke, coffee, toast. His stomach rumbled. He couldn't remember when he'd last eaten; the space between his ribs and spine felt hollowed out. But the foul taste in his mouth was worse than hunger, and he followed his memory of Rainer's cabin down the hall to the bathroom.

The hot water gave out too soon, but the steam lasted long enough to loosen ropes of slime in his lungs. He brushed his teeth, coughed up ribbons of dark phlegm, and brushed them again. His chest felt as if he'd been kicked and sat on and kicked some more. His face was stripped to skin and bone, eyes sunken and cheeks mottled with fever. His hands shook as he turned off the taps.

Maybe it was for the best that Liz was unconscious; he could never convince her that he wasn't as sick as he looked.

When he emerged, cleaner and warmer and layered in scarves and sweaters, music drifted from the front of the house. Something bright and poppy, incongruous against the grey chill and yesterday's half-remembered horrors. He followed the sound and smell of food down the hall.

A fire burned in the front room, and the blinds were open to a view of the cove. Lailah stood in the little kitchen, cracking eggs into a skillet. She'd abandoned the trench coat, and wore a black tank top and faded cargo pants, her hair twisted up in a sloppy clip. An ancient portable CD player sat on the counter, and she hummed along with the song. For a moment she seemed like a different person than the woman Alex had met in the cemetery; then she turned and he saw the outline of the holster at the small of her back. Her humming stopped when she saw him, and she reached out to turn down the music.

"Do you want breakfast?" she asked, scrambling the sizzling eggs.

Alex squinted at his watch. "At two in the afternoon?"

"It's the first meal of the day, isn't it? There's coffee." She gestured with one sharp elbow to a metal carafe on the counter while sliding chopped vegetables into the eggs.

"Thank you." The domesticity of it all was nearly as unnerving as guns and monsters.

He poured a mug and sat down at the table, letting the heat of the cup soak through his hands. A moment later Lailah slid a plate of toast and omelette in front of him.

"How's your friend?"

Alex frowned as he reached for the butter. "The same. What happened to the—" He broke off. There were no words that didn't sound ridiculous in the light of day.

"To the monsters?"

He started as a shadow stirred on the couch, sat up and resolved itself into a young woman. Blurry as a Degas sketch across the room, long black hair and sallow olive skin that would brown in the sun, dark clothes that didn't fit her. He remembered her vaguely from the funeral, and from their flight from the hotel. He thought her name was Rae.

"They're still out there," she continued, gesturing vaguely toward the windows. "Waiting." She sat down, but didn't touch the food Lailah passed her.

"Waiting for what?" Alex scraped butter over bread. The smell of peppers and mushrooms made his mouth water, until he looked an instant too long at a glistening thread of white veining the eggs. He reached for his coffee and tried not to cough. "What are they?"

"Hunters." Lailah sat next to Rae. "They're after maniacs. And now, apparently, you."

Alex ignored her expectantly cocked eyebrow. "Why haven't they come in?" He blinked against the memory of the black shapes bursting into the hotel, reached for the salt to cover his flinch.

"They can't. Not without an invitation. Hotels are too public— the rules don't apply there. And I know a few wards." Her eyes narrowed and flickered toward Rae. "You should eat. Both of you."

"I'm not hungry," Rae said, while Alex took a bite of toast. Her fingers fretted ceaselessly at the weave of her sweater.

"Food keeps your body working. The better your body works, the closer it keeps your soul."

They exchanged a conversation in a shadowed glance. Finally Rae snatched a piece of toast off Lailah's plate and took a deliberate bite.

Alex picked at his food, but the texture of anything but dry toast threatened nausea. He knew the fatigue and dizziness that weighed on him, knew them all too well. He needed sensible things like rest and fluids and warmth if he didn't want a hospital visit of his own. But he had left sense far behind.

The CD ended and silence settled over them once more. Lailah stacked her empty dishes in the sink. Alex caught her glancing more than once at the windows, and the still expanse of trees and water beyond.

"What are we doing out here?" he asked.

"It's remote," she said, drying her hands on a towel. "Not as many innocent bystanders if there's trouble. I sure as hell wasn't crowding all of you into my apartment." She flashed a lopsided smile. "Don't worry—we made sure the owners are out of town. Let's check on your friend."

Alex followed her down the hall, Rae padding behind them on silent bare feet. Liz hadn't moved. The rise and fall of her chest was invisible beneath the blankets; only the faint, infrequent twitch of her eyelids showed she lived. He bit back a protest as Rae sat on the edge of the bed and touched her face.

"What's wrong with her?" he asked instead.

"She's gone," Rae said softly. "She opened the door and now she's on the other side." Quiet envy filled her voice, and he thought of the maenad and shuddered.

"Can you do anything?"

"I tried to do what she's done, but it didn't work." Rae glanced at Lailah; the other woman shook her head sharply. "Without that... I don't know."

"I'm so bloody sick of hearing that lately." Alex raked his hands through his still-damp hair, wincing at the tender pain in his skull. "She can't last like this. She needs fluids, IVs..."

Lailah nodded, her thin mouth hooking down. "You'll do what you have to. But a hospital won't be any safer than that hotel room—invitation doesn't apply there, either."

She turned away before Alex could think of a reply. Rae trailed behind her, quiet as a shadow.

ALEX SAT BESIDE Liz for the rest of the afternoon. He wet her lips and triple-checked the warmth of the blankets and applied fresh ointment and bandages to her swollen hand, in between flipping through his thumb-worn copy of *Foucault's Pendulum* without reading a word.

The light died and the chill deepened. He knew he ought to turn on the lamp, find a blanket, find a place to sleep that wouldn't murder his neck, but the longer he sat the stronger his lassitude grew. If he kept perfectly still he could breathe—any movement might wake the terrible, tearing cough. The book slipped from numb fingers and he let it lie. Just a short rest, and then he would move...

He woke to voices and icy hands. Or maybe it was only that he was burning. He startled, and the spasm he'd feared threatened to rip his chest apart.

"Wake up," Lailah said, for what might have been the second

or third time. She brushed the hair back from his face and pried one eyelid back. In his feverish confusion, Alex thought her eyes gleamed in the shadows, pupils glowing like an animal's.

"He's sick," Rae said, leaning close behind her. "I can see it inside him."

"Wonderful."

Lailah looped an arm around Alex's waist and hauled him out of the chair. His head lolled against her shoulder, but he had no strength to spend on dignity. She half dragged, half carried him into the living room and laid him out on the couch, then shoved them both closer to the fire. The dying flames washed the room red and hellish, cast capering shadows across the ceiling. He closed his eyes against the sight, and opened them again to find Rae piling him with blankets while Lailah forced his head up and pressed a cup to his lips. The warmth of tea was welcome, but the first sip made him cough again. This time the salt-slime taste of phlegm was tinged with sour metal.

"Do you still think we don't need a hospital?" he asked, and regretted the effort.

Lailah snorted. "I didn't think you'd go so far to prove me wrong." She slid a pillow under his head and set the cup on the floor in easy reach. Not that he had the strength to lift it. "Just remember—if I take you to a doctor, it will mean leaving Liz alone."

It was a guilt trip worthy of his mother. He would have laughed, but all that came up was more mucus. "Well played," he whispered, and let his head fall.

If she replied, he wasn't awake to hear it.

Rae found Lailah in the bedroom late that night, sitting crosslegged on the bed and frowning at her phone. The light from the tiny screen washed her face cold and grey. She didn't look up as Rae eased the door shut behind her.

"What's wrong?"

"Besides the terrible service out here?" Lailah raised her head, her face twisted into an inhuman grimace in the shadows and pixel-light. "Rabia is reading me the riot act. There's trouble in the city, the kind I'm supposed to clean up."

"But you're stuck here with the strays." She sank onto the edge of the bed.

Another grimace. This one might have been a smile in a former life. "Someone has to look after you. Them." She encompassed the rest of the house in a gesture. "And it won't hurt Rabia to do her own damned wetwork for a change."

"Why do you do it?"

Lailah sighed, her broad shoulders slumping. "I joined a war because I thought it was the right thing to do. I nearly died." Her fingers brushed her scarred cheek and fell again. "When I didn't, I ended up drafted into another war."

"Is this one the right thing?"

"I wish I knew. But I'll keep fighting. It's all I'm good for anymore."

"Then why did you save me? Why rescue them?" Rae waved toward the far rooms, toward Alex and Liz.

"I was bleeding to death when Noor found me. She could have let me die. It might have been better if she had, but I wanted to live. So did you. How are your stitches?" she asked after a moment's silence.

"They're fine. I've been careful. Were they right? Rabia and Noor? That I'd bring you no joy?"

Lailah pressed a button and the phone went black. Darkness filled the room. "I'm not sorry I didn't shoot you, if that's what you mean. Not yet. How do you feel?"

"Weird," Rae admitted. "Restless. I feel... echoes." Laughter, dancing, firelight. The constant bacchanal chorus, waiting for her to join them. She leaned closer into Lailah's warmth.

"Do you understand it?" the other woman asked. Her breath drifted across Rae's cheek.

"It's mostly noise," she lied, grateful for the darkness that hid her expression. *The way is opening.* Rescuing Alex and Antja had distracted Lailah from her search for the door. Rae wasn't sure she wanted to remind her of it.

"Mostly?"

The mattress shifted with Lailah's weight. Rae caught a suggestion of movement as her eyes adjusted to the dark. "What's the matter? Do you think I'm dangerous?" Her smile felt like a stranger's. "You can always use the handcuffs again, if it will make you feel better."

Lailah's breath caught, held, left on a harsh sigh. "Rae—"

"Lailah." She crawled forward, pressing Lailah back, pinning her knees against the bed. The woman could have broken free in an instant, but for that moment Rae felt strong. Dangerous. "I'm cold."

This wasn't her. She didn't know who this was. But—as she dragged the borrowed sweater over her head and tossed it aside, as she moved forward to straddle Lailah's thighs, as she caught the other woman's hands and pressed them to her waist—she thought she wouldn't mind being this person for a while.

LATER, WHILE LAILAH slept, Rae slipped out of bed and eased the curtains aside. Her side throbbed; they hadn't been careful. Nail marks burned her back, and fresh bruises ached down the inside of her thighs.

The stars were louder than ever.

Beyond the window the wind rushed wild and cold. She could almost feel it tugging at her hair, sliding over her bare skin. Her reflection in the glass rippled like water. Rae raised a hand, but the ghost girl didn't. Instead she turned, lips moving soundlessly as she glanced over her shoulder.

Not her reflection at all. A taller woman, hooded and blindfolded. Her white dress fluttered in the breeze. Behind her a man sat cross-legged on a stone floor, shirtless in the cold. Gaunt and dark-haired, his arms and chest covered in swirling scars, the graceful looping script Rae still couldn't read.

The woman looked back at Rae, looked through her with bound eyes. Dark stains soaked the blindfold. From the cheekbones down she shared the maenad's face, but her smile was less cruel.

My sister's way is not the only way. Her lips moved, and the words shivered deep inside Rae's head. *There are other roads besides that of flesh and blood.*

"The road of needles," Rae whispered, "or the road of pins."
Her breath fogged the glass.

Exactly. Which one do you choose?

Rae reached out in wonder, but her hand touched the icy
windowpane and the vision shattered. She stood there, staring into
the darkness, until her teeth began to chatter. Finally she crawled
back into bed, huddling into Lailah's warmth until the starsong
faded enough to let her sleep.

WAKE UP.

The voice called Blake out of the dark, vanishing again as soon
as he reached for it, leaving him alone once more. The memory of
terror filled him, of cold and straps and mocking voices—

The cold, at least, was gone. He floated in softness, blood-
warm and sticky. Everything smelled of honey, raw and sweet and
cloying; the taste filled his mouth and made him want to gag. Only
his fingers responded when he tried to move, curling through thick
fluid. His eyes were sealed shut—when he forced them open the
world was a golden blur, like an insect staring out of amber.

Panic returned, hot and sharp, and he thrashed. He tried to
scream, but his mouth and nose and eyes were full of honey.
Shadows moved outside his amber prison, and he heard a voice as
if through deep water.

"It's too soon."

The light dimmed to the faintest orange glimmer, then died.
Blake dimmed with it.

"WAKE UP."

Hands again, more hands, shaking his sharply. His throat ached
as if he'd been screaming. "Blake, wake up. You're dreaming."

Black gave way to red and then to gold. Blake flinched away
from light and touch. The motion jerked him back into waking—
he could move again.

He raised his hands to his face. No honey this time, no hooks
and shattered bones. The stickiness on his skin was only sweat and

tears. He was whole. He convulsed in relief and buried his face in the sheets.

Sheets, pillows, bed—no water, no examining table, no warm waxen prison. Only cool, clean cloth. His stomach cramped and he swallowed bile; the sour taste eased the sweetness that filmed his tongue.

"It's all right. It was only a dream." He shuddered at the familiar rasp of Alain's voice. A dream. A black and drowning dream. That was all it had been—a nightmare. Horrors nested like matryoshka dolls, but now he was safe.

That certainty faltered as he opened his sticky eyes. A strange leafy ceiling spread above him, dripping with vines. Globes of light hung like fruit amongst the leaves. The walls were the color of amber, and as translucent. Shadows moved beyond them.

Alain stood beside the bed. His hair was black today, shading to viridian where the light touched it. The color matched the embroidered tendrils on his coat. He sat when Blake opened his eyes, a frown of concern giving way to a wry smile.

"Hey, Sleeping Beauty. About time you woke up."

Blake's shoulders shook, and a sound more mewl than sob scraped between his clenched teeth. He threw an arm around Alain's waist, pressing his sticky face against the other boy's thigh. "I dreamed—" The words wouldn't come. What had he dreamed? All he remembered was terror and pain and blackness.

"Shh," Alain whispered. "It's all right." He stroked Blake's back in slow circles. "I'm here. It's okay."

Blake's tears slowed and dried, leaving him raw-eyed and aching. Sheets the color of ripe plums snared his legs when he tried to sit up. Leaf shadows dappled the room, swaying gently though the air was still. The colors were too rich, over-saturated, and he wondered if he was feverish or if it was only a trick of his burning eyes. His sinuses ached, reminding him of those forgotten nightmares.

"Where are we?"

Alain's brow-ring flashed with his frown. "The palace. Don't you remember?"

A memory sparked but didn't catch. "I remember... a door. A storm and a door."

"That's right. You made the door. You opened it and brought us here."

"There were monsters—" He shuddered at the scattered images. Darkness given form and purpose.

"Don't worry." Alain wrapped an arm around his shoulders. "They can't find us now. We're safe here."

Blake curled into his warmth. Alain's scent was strange: musk and tangy sap, with a bitter hint of clove. His touch was familiar, though. Safe.

"Something's wrong," Blake murmured, the words muffled against Alain's shoulder. "Why can't I remember?"

"What you did wasn't easy. It will come back." Callused fingers stroked the back of Blake's neck, raising goosebumps. "Tomorrow we see the King, and he'll make everything right."

The King. It meant something. A promise he hadn't yet made. Memories slipped through his fingers, elusive and poisonous as mercury. "I can't—"

"It's all right." Alain kissed him, catching his lower lip between sharp teeth. His tongue tasted of honey. "It will all come back. Don't worry." The scattered lights swam like stars in the darkness of his eyes.

Shadows moved outside the amber room. Human shapes and inhuman, winged and gaunt, horned and crook-legged. "They're watching us," Blake said.

Alain's chuckle vibrated along Blake's collarbones, his tongue flickering hot against the sharp pulse in Blake's neck. "There's nothing they haven't seen before." He pushed Blake down, stripping back the clinging sheets.

"Don't—" His breath hitched as Alain trailed kisses down his stomach.

"Shh." Warm breath tickled the soft skin below his navel and his hands clenched in the sheets. "It's all right now."

It wasn't all right. It wasn't remotely all right. But his breath came too sharp and fast to speak.

They moved together on the vine-shadowed bed, and shadows watched them through the walls.

17

KINGDOM COME

D ARKNESS EBBED, WASHING Liz ashore like so much driftwood. Her limbs were heavy, her head soft and dull and dream-sticky. Cold stone gouged her shoulder blades and leeched the warmth from her flesh; her hands and feet were numb. Her skin was tender and sunburn-raw. The rush of her pulse deafened her.

No, not her own blood. A much vaster tide.

She pried her eyes open and moaned in wonder at the sky. Green as glass, green as poison, strewn with unfamiliar stars. Low and heavy and crushingly close. Clouds raced overhead, dark and purple as bruises, moving fast enough to dizzy her. She shut her eyes tight, tearing her nails on the stones as she fought for balance. The world was moving too fast, would shrug her off into the void.

No, she told herself, rolling onto her side in a fetal ball. She had to get up.

One by one her limbs uncurled. Every muscle ached, like the aftermath of a bad flu. Fighting nausea, she swallowed spit and waited for earth and sky to right themselves. Her mouth tasted of sour sleep and copper; a crust of dried blood itched against her cheek and upper lip. She scrubbed it away with the neck of her T-shirt as she sat up.

She sat on a stone quay. Black waves churned against the seawall, each breaker misting the air with a harsh chemical smell that stung her nose and throat as she breathed it in. Rust red fog rose from the water, thickening to bloody clouds on the horizon. Liz thought she saw the outline of a city in the distant haze, but staring too long only made her head ache. She turned to face the city behind her instead.

It sprawled like any city, the seawall lined with smaller buildings that might have been warehouses or shipyards—though she saw no boats in the water—or houses. Further in, the skyline swept up into the sky-piercing towers she'd seen before. No shining glass or steel here, no sharp modern angles. Grey and yellow stone, green and ivory-white, all sinuous curves and twists. Buildings sleek as bare bones, rooftops ridged like vertebrae, mosaics and roof tiles slick and pebbled as a lizard's skin. Organic. Skeletal. Visceral.

Carcosa. She had done it. She was here. Pride was lost to her stomach's seasick roll.

Twilight shadows filled the empty streets, and the poison sky rinsed everything with verdigris. Liz was glad not to face the angry red star, but without its heat the air was damp and algid. Not Vancouver's sharp-toothed winter chill, but enough to make her bones ache. She wore the T-shirt and underwear she'd fallen asleep in. Tourists never knew how to dress for the local weather.

"I won't be here long," she whispered, and winced as her voice carried through the still, damp air.

The street was paved with ochre stone, unwinding into the fog-shrouded heart of the city. To the palace. Towers loomed overhead, leaning together to whisper secrets, watching her with dark windows. Ivy and other vines clung thick to the walls, their leaves rasping a soft susurrus though no breeze stirred them. Streetlamps grew from the pavement, hissing with purple flames.

Liz walked carefully, but the stone still chewed her feet. She glanced at Blake's ring, but it was disinclined to be a compass or a key right now. Or a pair of shoes.

The fog thickened the farther she walked, and tiny flames flickered in the mist. Shadows passed in front of the lights, and running footsteps and distant voices echoed between the buildings. Liz never saw the runners and thought better of trying to follow them. Her neck and shoulders twisted stiff as rebar and her legs ached to run, but panic would only leave her lost and bleeding worse than she already was.

Were these the revelers she'd seen before, the ones who'd met Blake at the shore? They hadn't seemed shy then. Did Carcosa have inhabitants besides shadows and disembodied voices? Did she want to meet them if it did? Her right hand clenched until the ring carved an angry line in her flesh.

At the next crossroad she heard water—the splash of a fountain instead of the ocean's pulse. The violet light burned brighter in that direction. A trick? A mirage? Maybe, but she had to find something but empty streets and whispers or she'd lose her mind.

She rounded a curve and the street opened into a circular plaza lit by tall lamps. A fountain played in the center of the courtyard, a statue of a nude woman rising from the water. Her face was lovely and serene and spotted with lichen. Tubes and shunts jutted from her limbs and torso, trickling dark water from breasts and womb. Liz grimaced but moved closer, fascinated all the same. The lip of the fountain was thick with ivy; beneath the vines, a graceful looping script traced the stone, no alphabet she recognized.

As she leaned in to study the letters, movement flickered in the corner of her eye. She spun and nearly fell. Her heart lodged in her throat, and panic scalded her already-raw nerves.

A figure stood in the shadow on the other side of the fountain. He took a step closer, into the light, and her heartbeat roared in her ears. Deafened, she could only read the shape of her name on his lips.

"Blake?" She choked on his name.

He moved toward her, vines curling around his boots. The light washed his face a deathly grey, bruised his lips blue as anemones. "Liz? Is it really you?

It's a trick— But he reached for her and his hands were clammy and callused, solid and real. A sob bubbled up in her throat and he wrapped his arms around her and held her close.

"Blake." His name was a prayer on her lips. The softness of his hair, the fit of her cheek against his shoulder, the dry autumn scent of his skin. He brushed his lips against her hair and she sobbed harder.

"I heard you calling," he whispered. "I thought I was hallucinating."

"I dreamed of you. I saw you drowning. I saw the thing at the bottom—"

He hugged her tighter. "It's okay. It's over now."

She drew back, smearing tears across her cheeks. "We have to get out of here."

The corners of his mouth turned down. "I don't think I can."

"Of course you can. We're dreaming. We have to find a way to wake up."

He touched her face. "Liz, I don't think I can wake up. I don't think there's anything for me to wake up to."

"You're still alive!" She swallowed a lump of doubt. How much time had passed here? What might have happened in the waking world? Her head throbbed; her hands throbbed. "You're still alive," she whispered. "And we can't stay here. That thing wants to eat you."

"Liz. It did eat me."

He laid cool fingers against her lips before she could protest. "I drowned, and He was waiting at the bottom. He ate me, and spat me back onto the shore. This is my home now. I can't leave."

He raised a hand, and she saw the vines clinging to his wrist. Growing from him. Tendrils sank into his skin, binding him to the fountain.

Fresh tears blinded her and she shook her head. "I won't leave you here."

"No." He pulled her close again, pressing his lips against her forehead. "I know you won't."

Vines stirred around her feet, prickling against her calves like insect feet, twining slowly up her legs. She wanted to scream, but the sudden pain in her hands stole her voice. The left throbbed with her pulse, and the right burned so hot she thought her flesh must have already blackened.

"It's all right," Blake whispered, still holding her. All she could smell now was sap, and the bitter moisture from the fountain. "You can stay here with me. Isn't that what you really want?"

The vines reached her knees now, feelers pricking at her skin, searching for a way in.

"Just us," he continued. "No more fear, no more pain."

"You can't live without pain." But oh, how she wished she could. Just for a little while.

"Not out there, maybe. It's different here." His hands rested on her shoulders, the leaves on his wrists shivering against her neck.

Rest, they whispered. *Peace.*

"No." She drew back, knocking his hands away.

His smile faltered and grew sad. "Do you think you have a choice?"

She recoiled, but ivy trapped her feet and she fell. The jolt jarred both her hands and she screamed. The ring glowed. Silver melted, spilling across her hand to encase her in a gleaming glove, burning where it touched. With a shriek of pain and fear, she tore at the vines with that shining gauntlet. Leaves browned at its touch, tendrils shriveling.

"Liz!"

Blake—or whatever wore his face—reached for her, and she slapped his hand away. His skin blackened at the blow, withering like the vegetation.

"No," she said again, stronger this time, and ripped away another handful of vines. Beads of blood welled on her legs.

"No." With the third denial she was free, scrambling back across the stones. The vines retreated with an angry hiss, and the shape that had been Blake curled and crumbled into dust.

The ring was a ring once more, and the pain in her hand cooled and faded. With a sob, she pounded her fist against the ground to bring it back.

"You needn't go out of your way to injure yourself. This place is dangerous enough already."

She didn't startle at Seker's voice. Her nerves were worn through.

His sandals slapped softly against the stones. Liz straightened, wiping salt and snot from her face. She stared up at him for a moment, then took his offered hand and let him draw her to her feet.

"Did you see?"

He nodded, his face grave. "That was just a little treachery. The kind that grows throughout the city. Did you think it would be easy?"

"No," she said with a sigh. "I really didn't."

*   *   *

"WHY ARE YOU here?" she asked as they left the fountain behind. The words came out harsher than she intended. "You said you wouldn't stop me again."

"And I won't. I'm here to help you." Her eyes narrowed and he lifted his hands in a shrug. "I warned you, and you wouldn't be deterred. Now your presence here widens the breach between Carcosa and your dreamlands, your waking world. The damage is already done, and if you fail here, if you fall, the King will have two more souls for his retinue. So it would be best for everyone if you succeeded. And the sooner the better; your friend has been here too long already."

She lifted her chin and lengthened her stride, despite her bruised and bleeding feet. Seker smiled at her bravado.

She meant to stay stern and silent, but the hush grew too deep around them. "Is it always so deserted here?" she asked.

A breeze stirred, fluttering Seker's robes. "I don't think so. I imagine your friend's arrival is keeping the locals busy."

The wind picked up, thinning the smothering fog but worsening the cold. Liz clenched her jaw to stop her teeth from chattering. She stumbled on feet grown numb and Seker caught her elbow.

"You're not well," he said with a frown.

"I'm fine." She tried not to lean on him, not to fall in a heap at his feet. "Just c-cold."

He glanced at her bare, bloody legs. "I shouldn't wonder." He unclasped his linen mantle and wrapped it around her shoulders. The heat of his skin enveloped her, along with the scent of myrrh and oranges. The gold and lapis scarab glittered as he pinned the cloth in place.

"Thank you," Liz whispered.

Black eyes blinked. "Thank me when this is over, if you still feel the need."

They walked on. Her feet bled, her side stitched, and still they walked. Liz felt like Sisyphus without the stone. Maybe this was Tartarus after all.

"Who is the King?" she asked, anything to distract herself from the cold.

"Something very old, and he serves a power older still. The

Yellow King was human once—his master never was. Carcosa is dead and hollow, filled with shades and echoes. He wants something new, something fresh."

"The dreamlands? Earth?"

"Either. Both. He's never been particular."

"Why Blake?"

"The King fancies himself a patron of the arts. But he'll take anyone he can, anyone talented and foolish enough to find this place. He offers them visions; if they survive that, he gives them power. In exchange for service."

She couldn't imagine Blake offering to serve anything. But vision... Yes. That might tempt him.

"You know him. The King, I mean."

"I do, him and his master. I served once, too. No longer." Liz glanced up. Seker's face was a mask, cold and grim. He didn't meet her eyes.

She tried to think of other questions, but she was so cold, so tired. Her shoulders slumped, and then her head, until she watched her feet shuffle one in front of the other. That too faded into grey. Seker's hand on her arm roused her from her fugue. She stumbled, stubbing a toe on the pavement, and nearly fell.

"I—" She sagged in his grip. "I ca—" She bit back the word *can't*. She could, or all this had been for nothing.

"It's all right," Seker said, drawing her up. "We're here." He lifted her head with gentle fingers, turning her to face what lay ahead.

The castle rose before them, a phantasmagoria of pale stone. Bone-white and cream, yellow as old ivory, towers branching like fingers from a cupped palm. Some dripped with intricate reliefs, so many shapes that they blurred together like softening wax; others were honeycombed with windows—dark shapes crawled between the openings, tiny as ants with distance. Clouds shredded on spindle peaks.

Liz's breath rushed out as the sight drove back her fatigue. She stepped forward, but a wide chasm lay between them and the palace. Black water seethed at the bottom and the drifting fumes seared her nose. She retreated, rubbing her eyes.

"Do we fly across?"

"Flying might be easier, but no. That is our path."

She followed Seker's pointing hand and saw a bridge sagging between the chasm walls. An ominous looking thing, and it became no more reassuring the closer they came. A piecemeal creation—bones and grey boards, scraps of cloth and shards of glass, all bound in wire and rope and leather cords. It clattered like a windchime in the breeze.

A shape moved as they drew near, what she'd taken for a statue rising from its crouch to become a gaunt old man. Yves, she thought for a wild instant, but no. This man was taller, thinner, eyes sunken on either side of a beaky nose. He grinned, and his teeth were crooked and very sharp.

"What's this? Pilgrims?" His voice was the scrape of broken glass, the crunch of gravel being ground to dust. "Supplicants to the King?" He peered at Liz, and his eyes gleamed under heavy brows, the irises wide and yellow as a goat's, with the same sideways pupils. "You, at least. You I know of old," he said to Seker. "Wanderer, trickster, conjure man. Come begging at the tables of your betters."

Seker's face hardened. "We don't have time for games, old man. Let us pass."

The bridgekeeper cackled. "It's my bridge. We have as much time as I say we have. And as many games as I wish."

"Please," Liz said, stepping around Seker as he tried to hold her back. "I need to reach the castle. How do I cross?"

"You pay the toll, of course. The real question is, what do you have that I want?" The old man tapped his staff on the ground and sucked his teeth pensively. His coat was patchwork, like the bridge, rags of velvet and brocade, burlap and leather. The colors must have been vibrant once, but now they had faded to dirty yellows and greys.

"What *do* you want? I don't have much—" Liz spread her hands. She didn't have anything, not even pockets. Only Blake's ring and Seker's brooch, and those weren't hers to offer.

"Oh, you have plenty. Flesh and bone and blood. Hair. Eyes." He opened his coat with a flourish, like a fence unloading stolen watches. But instead of gold chains and fake Rolexes, the lining was pinned with bones and locks of hair. Phalanges, metacarpals, clavicles, all polished slick and gleaming. Red hair and golden and glossy black. A bit of pale leather, inked with part of a tattoo.

Liz swallowed. "I need those." Not her hair, she supposed, but it was mousy and tangled, nothing anyone else would want.

The man hrmphed and shrugged his coat shut. "Then what about all the bits and bobs swirling around in your head. You monkeys have more grey matter than you know what to do with. It only gets you into trouble. You know," he said to her blank stare, waggling one bony hand for emphasis. "Thoughts. Dreams. Jokes. Ideas."

"I don't know any jokes. What about—"

"No riddles," he said before she could finish. "Everyone thinks of riddles. My bridge is lousy with them. Riddled, even." He winked one inhuman eye and Liz winced.

"What, then?" she asked, biting back impatience.

The old man leaned in, wizened cheeks splitting in a smile. "I am fond of memories. No two are ever the same. Better than snowflakes."

"What kind of memories?"

"What sort do you have?" He waved her closer. "Come here, come here. I won't eat you. Have to show me the wares if you want to barter."

Her eyes narrowed. "Are you the King?"

He cackled again. "Clever girl. But no. I'm the bridgekeeper, the ferryman. The King is in his castle, and I'm here. He binds. I collect."

"Are the two of you the twins?"

"Curious little monkey, aren't you. No. The twins are in the castle with the King. Except when they aren't. They are the vine and the wine, the mania and the melancholy, the desire and the spasm."

"And between them falls the shadow?"

"Exactly! You'll learn, Curious George, you'll learn quickly here. Now step closer."

Seker's hand closed on her shoulder. "This is not a good idea, dreamer."

She shot him a glare. "Do you have a better one?"

The bridgekeeper's caprine eyes narrowed. "He thinks he can defeat me. Don't you, conjurer? And I'm sure you could, an old man like me. But this is my bridge. It does what I say. And it's the only way to reach the palace."

He snapped his fingers and the ground shuddered. Liz stumbled, her stomach flipping over. The black rock beneath the castle cracked and splintered, stretching as it shot upward, until it was no thicker than a wine stem and the top of the cliff was lost in the clouds. The bridge dangled from the heights, but now it was only gossamer threads thin as cats' footsteps and fish's breath, nothing that would bear weight.

"Do you see, monkey? This will be so much easier if you simply pay the toll."

Liz drew a breath and let it out slowly. Shrugging off Seker's hand, she stepped forward. "Fine. But just one memory."

"It will have to be a good one, then." He cupped her chin, long nails pinching her flesh. "Now show me your pretty pink brains."

He let his staff fall and wrapped his other hand over her skull. Liz twitched with a sudden vision of him cracking her head like an egg. Her lip trembled, and she shut her eyes against her reflection in his eyes, so tiny and scared.

She waited for pain, but what came instead was a dizzy floating sensation. A burst of color and meaningless noise. The sickening sensation of fingers picking through her brain, selecting images like beads from a bowl and holding them to the light.

How about this one?

"Excuse me."

Rubber soles squeak on warped linoleum, and Liz looks up at the boy standing beside her lab table. Tall and spindly, a worn leather biker jacket sagging over narrow shoulders, chin-length scarlet hair fading to rust and dirty blond at the roots. Fluorescent light washes his glasses white and blind. "Do you mind if I sit here?"

She shakes her head and he folds into the plastic chair like a string-cut puppet. "Thanks. I'm Alex." He smiles at her, this scarecrow boy, and his eyes are bright and blue behind his glasses.

No, she said. *No*. She might never see Alex again, but she wouldn't give him up. *Not like this. Not him.*

Fine. Again the nauseous swirling in her head. *Here's a pretty one—*

Red hair flattens beneath a brush, glinting copper and gold as curly strands pull straight. It bounces free at the end of the stroke, coiling over Lorna Drake's shoulders. Liz stands beside the old walnut vanity, turning a powder compact between her chubby fingers while her father watches them from the doorway.

Lorna winks as she reaches for her lipstick. "Remember your Chomsky, Elizabeth."

Not this, Liz thought, but her resolve weakened. Her parents were years dead, and so many of her memories of them had already dissolved. What was this moment compared to Blake?

Fine. Take it.

Good, good. But it's an older one, faded around the edges. Perhaps a little something extra....

One memory. That was the bargain.

Yes, yes. Only one memory. But something else, something small. A little spice. Lagniappe. A color, perhaps, or a scent or a flavor... Oh, no. A word. Yes, a word. Give me a word.

What kind of word?

Your favorite, of course.

Liz froze. She loved so many words: sesquipedalian, penultimate, numinous, liminal, spleen, cellar door—did that count as one word?—incandescent...

Pick one, the bridgekeeper said with a sigh, *or we'll be here all night. And nights in Carcosa are very long.*

It might have taken her that long to choose, but far in the distance she heard the waves of the black sea breaking against the shore, their rhythmic hiss and rush—

Susurrus, she said.

Done!

She expected a wrench, a tug, some feeling of dislocation, but there was only a grey haze enveloping her, passing through her, taking away—

Taking what?

Liz opened her eyes to see the bridgekeeper backing away, all his teeth bared in a grin. She sagged in Seker's arms, his strength the only thing holding her up.

"What happened?" she whispered.

"You made a very foolish bargain. But it's done now."

"Done indeed," the bridgekeeper said, retrieving his staff and gesturing with it toward the castle. It had returned to its original position, the swaying patchwork bridge in place once more. "You've paid the toll, Curious George, and now you may cross."

"Thank you. I think." Liz straightened, blinking until her vision focused. Her head was light and spinning. What had she lost, to dizzy her so?

The old man's staff came down with a crack as she and Seker started for the bridge. Liz turned to find the two men staring at one another.

"She paid the toll," the bridgekeeper said. "Not you."

Seker's lip curled. Nothing about him changed that Liz could recognize, but for an instant he seemed as inhuman as the old man. "You can't deny me. Not if you allow her. And you've already struck the bargain."

The air between them thickened with tension, electric and palpable, and Liz edged away. Finally the bridgekeeper shrugged his patchwork shoulders.

"I suppose not. You're a lamprey, and it's too much trouble to cut you out. Go with your pet. But don't think your tricks will work so easily against the King, conjure man." He stepped aside with a mocking bow.

The bridge creaked and swayed beneath her feet, planks shifting underfoot. The ropes of the railing unraveled in lazy coils. Strands of long red-gold hair threaded the cord, such a familiar color—

Liz closed her eyes against a wave of dizziness, then forced them open again as her toes curled on empty air. Acidic mist swirled up from the chasm, sighing between the boards and bones. Wind whined between the chasm walls like voices in pain.

"Don't stop," Seker said, close enough that she felt his warmth against her back. "It's not much further."

"Pet?" she asked, though she knew she might not like the answer.

Seker sighed. "I've thrown my lot in with humanity, for better or worse. Many of the older powers revile or ridicule me for it."

It wasn't much of an answer, but she didn't press. His company kept her moving. Maybe the old man was only trying to confuse her, to make her doubt an ally. If not...

If not, she would choose the devil she knew. Would choose any devil that gave her a chance to win Blake back.

She walked on.

Liz stumbled when the bridge ended, the sensation of solid ground unsettling after the pitch and sway. Her mouth was dry and sour, her skin raw and stinging.

"We're here," Seker said.

The palace soared above them, lost in the clouds. The walls looked even more like wax up close, every inch of stone covered by carvings. She looked closer, and her throat clenched. The carvings moved. Human and inhuman figures writhed in slow motion, twisting beneath a skin of black-veined marble. Faces contorted in agony and exultation; she wasn't sure which was worse. No gate or barbican stood to keep them out, only massive doors of yellow stone, covered with more undulating bodies.

Swallowing sour spit, Liz stepped forward. But before she reached the doors, the rustle of giant wings filled the air.

"The gatekeepers have arrived," Seker said.

Gargoyles, Liz thought as she watched two shapes plummet from the towers, aloft on wings the color of old mushrooms, but they weren't made of stone. The draft of their passage buffeted her as they landed; they reeked of honey and old death. Leathery sinew creaked as they furled their wings.

:What do you want here?: they asked in unison, a choral swell of voices that set Liz's teeth on edge. Their eyes flashed, full of darkness and scattered light.

"We desire entrance," Seker answered—Liz's voice was nowhere to be found. "And audience with your master."

:Our master is otherwise occupied:

"Nonetheless, we will enter." Liz couldn't see Seker's face, but she heard the mingled humor and impatience in his voice.

The creatures straightened on crooked legs. Taller than any

human, and the sweep of their wings only made them more imposing. Segmented tails lashed behind them. :We cannot allow that.:

Liz forced herself forward. "I paid the toll," she squeaked.

Two long heads swung toward her in unison. :Then you may stay here as long as you wish, until the doors open. But they do not open now:

Seker sighed. The air around him crackled, and Liz's ears ached with changing pressure. "Go inside, dreamer. I'll provide all the entertainment they need."

:Touch the door and we'll peel your skin to line our hives:

"You're welcome to try."

"I'm not leaving you alone," Liz said, shifting her weight. Seker stood between her and the guards. She was only a few yards from the doors.

He chuckled. "I can take care of myself. Go and find your friend. You don't have much time left."

She inched toward the door. The guards hissed, gaunt jaws clacking. Liz stared at their talons, the glistening barbs on their tails. "I can't—"

Seker turned, his eyes flashing. "Go now!"

She moved as if shoved, the force of his words hurling her toward the door. Carvings twisted as she touched the waxy surface, toothy mouths opening. Something shrieked behind her as she threw her weight against the door, but she didn't turn to look. The panel shifted and swung inward; teeth sank into her flesh. Liz screamed and tumbled inside.

The last thing she saw before the door swung shut was a flurry of grey wings and white linen. Then the entrance closed with an echoing boom and she was alone in the dark.

AN HOUR BEFORE dawn Rae stood beside Liz's bed, staring down at the sleeping girl. She wished she had her deck, familiar symbols to make sense of the confusion spinning around them. The voices and music were louder than ever, a constant chorus in the back of her head.

The auras were stronger, too, but only a faint nimbus of color hung around Liz. Except for her bandaged hand—that pulsed a dark and ugly red. Rae brushed her fingers over the girl's cold cheek and chapped lips. She might have been touching wax. The smell of mania clung to Liz's skin, mouth-watering sweetness. Rae swallowed hard against the craving.

"How did you do it?" She'd tried so hard to reach the stars and always failed, but this pale little mouse had opened the door and stepped through, easy as pie. "What do you see?"

Her only answer was a flicker of eyes beneath shadowed lids.

You can let her dream forever, a familiar voice crooned, nearly lost amid the starsong. *You can set her free.*

Rae's hand twitched toward her pocket and the knife there. Just a little pocketknife, Lailah's like everything else in the house, but the blade was sharp. She clenched her fists and took a clumsy step away from the bed. All the drapes and blinds were pulled to keep warmth in, and she stifled without the kiss of starlight.

No, she reminded herself, digging her nails into her palms. Glass and curtains kept the monsters out, kept them safe. No matter how badly her blood itched.

A shudder wracked her, strong enough to bring her to her knees, doubled over on the cold floorboards. Darkness spread through her veins, blue-black worms squirming under the skin of her wrists. Her teeth tingled and her mouth tasted of copper. Her jaw ached with the effort of holding back a wild bacchanal cry.

"What am I turning into?" she whispered, pressing her forehead to the floor. But she knew the answer, didn't she? She remembered the women in her visions, wild and fanged and bloody. She remembered Gemma's painting, the maenads tearing Orpheus to shreds.

He should have sung for them, the cruel voice whispered.

Her hand hurt, white-knuckled on the knife. Lamplight slid like golden water along the blade as she unfolded it. She pressed the tip against the inside of her arm, watch the soft flesh dimple. Skin dented, then popped. She prayed for red, but her blood, when it came, was black and sluggish.

Hissing, Rae tugged the blade, opening a line across her arm. Flesh parted, baring red tissue marbled with white. The sickly smell of mania wafted from the wound. A single dark drop of blood rolled down her wrist.

"All I wanted was to see," she murmured.

You will. You'll see and you'll touch and you'll taste.

A rustle of cloth drew her head up. On the bed, Liz convulsed once, chest hitching beneath the sheets. Rae stood, and her breath caught.

The girl's face was the color of sour milk, cheeks and temples shot through with black. She twitched again and the air smelled of blood and rot and honey.

End her suffering.

Mercy. The kind Lailah had refused to give her.

The woman in white's words echoed softly in her head. *There is another way. Another road, if you're willing to walk it.*

Shaking so badly she nearly sliced her fingers, Rae snapped the knife shut and tugged her sleeve over the gash in her arm. Yarn rasped against torn skin. Whatever road she walked, it wouldn't start like this. She yanked the bedroom door open and shouted for help.

Alex arrived first, a scarecrow shadow in the doorway. "What's happened?" His face was mottled with feverish color, eyes glassy, voice hoarse.

Would any of them make it out of this house alive?

"I don't know," Rae said, shaking off morbid speculation. "She's getting worse."

He sucked in a breath as he leaned over the bed. Liz's eyes twitched and her breath came short and sharp. Sweat plastered her hair to her black-veined cheeks, and her bandaged hand glistened with fresh moisture. Blood and pus dripped down her fingers as Alex peeled the wrapping back; he and Rae both turned their heads at the stench.

At least Liz still bled. Rae doubted Alex would take much comfort in that.

"I need bandages," he said. "A first-aid kit. Now!"

She stumbled back, colliding with Lailah. Rae ducked out of the way before anyone could notice how bad she looked. She huddled in the warm darkness of the living room, listening to Alex and Lailah argue, and trying not to think about the stars.

18

EURYDIKE

LIZ KNELT IN the darkness inside the palace, trembling on the cold stone floor. Her left arm throbbed to the shoulder: the door had bitten her, reopening the maenad's bite. Blood soaked the torn bandage, pooling in her palm and dripping off her fingers.

She wasn't sure how long she crouched there, watching that warm crimson trickle. Was time passing her by in the waking world? Would she wake to find Alex grown old and grey, find that he'd forgotten her? Would the world have changed? Would she wake at all?

Eventually Seker's warning roused her: she didn't have time to waste on fear. Neither did she have time to wait for him. And if the doors opened again and he wasn't the one who came through—She forced herself to stand and face the shadows ahead.

The entryway soared above her, arches and emptiness. The air was still and heavy, sweet without the alkaline breath of the sea. Lights glimmered high above her like green and violet fireflies, enough to give her some idea of the vast space, but not to illuminate it. The walls were orange where the light kissed them, veined and flecked with black, with the cool plasticky slickness of resin. Carven vines covered the floor in swirls and spirals, their leaves pricking her tender feet. Her blood seeped into the grooves, black as it ran into the shadows.

She wiped her hand on her shirt, trying not to stain Seker's mantle. She might not have thread or breadcrumbs, but at least she could leave a trail.

The dancing firefly lights led her down the corridor. Her soft footsteps carried through the still air. The quiet played tricks on her, until her own feet and harsh breath sounded like some panting beast pursuing her. She fought the urge to run; who knew what waited for her in the darkness ahead? After every dozen steps she touched her bloody fingers to the wall. Her feet bled too, but the vines drank it, hiding her footprints.

Liz tried to stay alert, but the endless walking left her drained and aching. She had begun to think the corridor would stretch forever when the light finally changed. A glass globe hung from the ceiling—or floated in midair; she wasn't sure which—illuminating a fork in the path. The hall split left and right, both branches black and featureless and identical.

She leaned against the wall, but the strange texture made her pull away again. Her sigh echoed through the sepulchral silence.

Another sigh answered from behind her, a dozen times louder. Hot breath blew across her neck, filming her skin with damp. The smell of beast filled the air, rank and pungent. It was a living smell, though, the stink of a barn—she took some comfort in that as she stood taut and trembling.

"You won't get far standing there," the beast said. Its voice vibrated behind her sternum, deep and rumbling. The floor shivered with its footsteps, the heavy *tok* of hooves on stone. "Which way do you choose?" His breath—she guessed male from the musk and the voice—wafted over her head, stirring her hair.

"Which way would you suggest?"

"That depends on what you're looking for. Are you here to kill monsters? To stop the black ships?"

"I only want to find my friend."

"Ah." His breath clouded in the cool air. "You're here to play Orpheus, then, and rescue fair Eurydike."

"That's right. Only with better results, I hope." Her bravado sounded forced, but it was better than hysteria.

The beast's laugh made her ears ring. "Orpheus was a fool.

Perhaps you're wiser. Do you know who I am?"

Liz didn't need to see the breadth of his horns to know the answer, the flashing eyes or cloven hooves wide as dinner plates. "You're the Minotaur."

She felt his weight shift behind her, felt his head tilt. His heat and pungent stink enveloped her. "That is what I am, one of many things. But that isn't what I asked. Who am I?"

A name. Did the Minotaur have a name? Of course he did—she must know it. The Bull of Minos, son of Pasiphae and the Cretan bull, imprisoned in the labyrinth until Theseus killed him... Follow the thread, follow it back.

"Asterion!" The name took all her breath to speak, left her chest aching where the word had been. "You're Asterion."

"Clever child." A great, thick-nailed hand closed on hers. "But this place has eaten so many clever children. Is your friend worth your life? Worth a thousand lives without the mercy of death?"

The cords in her neck stood taut as she lifted her chin. "Yes."

"Then go. Follow the right hand path. Follow your clew." He lifted her right hand, and Blake's ring pulsed with light. "The labyrinth won't harm you, but nowhere else in the palace will be so kind."

"Thank you." It might be a trick, a lie, but the little spark of hope lent her new strength.

"Hurry," the Minotaur said. "Your friend is safe while the music plays. As safe as anything can be, in this place. Hurry, and don't look back."

Liz ran.

She heard the music as she ran, the distant strains of an orchestra. The sound grew louder every time she stopped for breath, and the ember of hope burned brighter in her chest.

The labyrinth wound and twisted, and in the dim and fitful light the walls changed. Black amber became rough grey stone, which gave way in turn to low ossuary arches lined with polished skulls. Gold-veined marble became a shivering hedge maze, and her bleeding feet left dark prints on snow.

When the walls turned to mirrors, her concentration faltered. Her reflections ran past her in the glass, some brutally clear, others distorted as a carnival funhouse. Some didn't run at all, only watched her, a dozen unfamiliar variations of her own face.

Keep going, she told herself, but her lungs and legs and breasts ached from running, and it was too easy to slow her pace, to catch her breath while she studied this gallery of Lizes.

She saw a chubby little girl in pigtails, clutching a ragdoll cat to her chest. A teenager in a school uniform, a veil of blonde hair trailing over her face. Those she knew, but others she had never seen before. A middle-aged woman, her face creased with smiling lines as well as sad ones; a wedding band gleamed on one ink-stained finger.

It's a trick, a distraction. The music played in the distance and she had to keep running, but some of the faces were too fantastic to ignore. She saw herself robed in white linen, her hair draping her shoulders in tiny beaded plaits. Liz raised her hand to Seker's scarab brooch, and her reflection touched an identical jewel.

Opposite the white figure was a dark one. Older, maybe—certainly colder. Her face was grim and steady, no trace of shyness or fear. Black leather armor enclosed her, hard and slick as chitin. All her softness hidden away.

Here at last Liz halted. This. This was who she needed to be. She met her reflection's cool, wary eyes, raised her hand to the glass and touched her twin's fingertips.

"How do I become you?" she whispered.

The reflection didn't answer, but the glass rippled. Black bled like ink from the mirror, enveloping her fingers and spilling down her arm.

Liz made a soft wondering sound as darkness washed over her, gaining substance as it flowed. Armor weighed her limbs, cinched her waist and flattened her breasts. Boots hugged her aching feet, fitting snug around her calves. Only the mantle remained the same, the scarab glittering on her shoulder. Her reflection was only a reflection again, but she remembered those unflinching eyes.

My eyes.

She turned away from the mirror and her breath caught. Silence.

The music had stopped.

She ran again.

THE LIGHT OF a thousand candles lit the ballroom, a thousand stars reflected in the green amber vault of the ceiling. Blake stared at the wide sea-green dome, searching for any hint of the sky beyond. All he found was the mirrored image of the room below, distorted as if through deep water, a chaos of color and music.

Dancers moved across the polished floor, dressed for an elaborate masquerade. Hooved figures and horned, winged and tailed. Shaggy pelts and sleek, glittering scales. They moved in threes and fours, following the rhythm of an odd, syncopated waltz. Many had asked Blake to join them, but even watching the steps dizzied him.

He leaned against the wall and closed his eyes, but that only made the dizziness worse. He felt drunk, though he hadn't touched anything he'd been offered. The air was heady with wine and beeswax and perfume. Colors blurred across his vision. Crystal chandeliers and jeweled costumes threw back shards of fire, and the faces of the dancers swam and slipped whenever he tried to study them.

On the far side of the room, beyond the dancers, stood the throne dais, enclosed in black velvet draperies. The curtains wouldn't be drawn until the King arrived.

He wasn't sure how long he'd stood here, watching the dancers. He couldn't judge the passage of time at all since he'd woken in the amber room. He and Alain had spent hours there, or days; the sheets stank of sex and sweat and honey by the time silent attendants had arrived to see them bathed and clothed. The ballroom had windows, the first he'd seen anywhere in the palace, but the thick stained glass panes offered no glimpse of the world outside.

Maybe there was no world beyond, only the abyss.

Dancers swung past him, their laughter carrying above the music. A slender creature with grey-green skin turned his way, its tentacled face framed by a tall upturned collar. One tentacle rose, swaying as if in greeting. Blake nodded in response and the dancer's partner—naked save for a crown of leaves—giggled.

He turned away from the spectacle, leaning his head against the cold glass of a window. He almost missed the endless black depths of his nightmares; he had trusted those.

An unexpected touch fell feather-light and teasing across the back of his neck. Blake spun, hands clenching as a surge of angry panic scalded him. Only Alain, slim and sleek in plum-dark brocade. His hair was dyed to match, woven through with ivy.

Was it, an ugly little voice whispered—*was it only Alain?* Everything was the same, down to the pattern of his calluses and the scar on his navel from an old piercing. But that cool little smile, the laughter in his dark eyes... If this wasn't Alain, who was the stranger wearing his lover's face?

Doubt couldn't stop the desire that tightened Blake's skin as Alain pressed him against the wall for a kiss. The heat left him breathless and reeling, and the questioning voice was lost beneath the sharp pulse of want.

"Soon," Alain whispered as Blake's hands tightened in his hair. "It's almost over." He trailed his fingers down Blake's chest, the sharpness of his nails a muffled promise. "Are you nervous?"

"Yes."

Alain's mouth twisted in sympathy, but it didn't reach his eyes. "Don't worry. Soon everything will be as it should be." Another kiss silenced Blake's questions, left him braced against the wall for support.

A woman all in white cut through the crowd, the dancers peeling away from her like skin from a blade. A cowl and blindfold hid the upper half of her face. Her chin and throat were nearly as pale as the cloth, rinsed with blue ultramarine tones. He felt her regard despite her blinded eyes, but when she spoke it was to Alain.

"It's time."

The music died as if at her cue, leaving the dancers faltering through their last steps. The candles dimmed, and golden flames cooled to violet. The rattle of chains carried through the wide room, and the curtains surrounding the dais parted. A murmur swept the crowd, nearly lost beneath the heavy rustle of velvet.

The King sat in a twisted throne, his face lost in the shadows of his gilt-edged cowl. His robes were the color of old ivory, heavy with golden thread. Blake could see nothing of the man beneath, save for one long, pale hand on the armrest of the black chair. Ghastly gargoyle creatures crouched before the throne, skeletal things wrought of leather and bone. Avian and insectile, neither and both. They knelt motionless, except for the rattle of their barbed tails. The crowd knelt as one with the sound of a wave. Blake would have fallen, too, but Alain held him up.

The pale hand rose, beckoning. The guards stepped aside, creaking as they moved. Blake's pulse closed his throat, deafened him with its roar. Alain led him forward, one hand on the small of his back.

The King's presence grew heavier as they crossed the room, pressing down on Blake's shoulders. By the time he reached the foot of the steps, he couldn't bear it. His legs buckled and he fell, bruising his knees on stone. Alain bowed deeply, and the woman in white curtsied amid a puddle of skirts.

That hand lifted again, and the woman rose and climbed the steps. She knelt beside the throne, facing the audience, and the King grasped her shoulder. She shuddered. In the cold purple light her lips looked blue and drowned.

"**Welcome, Chosen.**" That voice was never meant to come from her slender throat. It echoed through the room, through Blake's skull.

He stood, though his legs shook, fighting the urge to look for a face beneath the hood. The hand on the woman's shoulder was grey, desiccated.

"**You have come to complete the oath.**"

It wasn't a question, but he nodded all the same. His throat was dry, his tongue dead in his mouth.

You don't have to say anything. He'll know.

Who had said that to him? Someone far away, in a life he'd forgotten. His stomach cramped, and if he'd eaten anything today he would have vomited it all over the shining steps. Sweat slicked his palms, prickled his scalp. Alain squeezed his arm, reassurance or a warning.

I don't like the storm.

Who had said that?

"Come, then," the King said through the woman's mouth. "Receive the sign."

The King unwound himself from the thorny embrace of his chair and stood. He beckoned, and Blake went, shaking so hard he could scarcely walk. The smell of bone and roses washed over him, crawling into his mouth and nose. His heart raced as though it meant to escape the prison of his ribs.

The King raised his long gaunt hands and threw back his hood. From the darkness where his face should be, light unfolded.

The world slipped.

Blake wept, enfolded in an angel's flaming wings. His blood boiled, searing through every vein, burning away imperfections.

He understood now what Rainer had meant. Words meant nothing here, only intent. This oath was unspeakable, unspoken. He had only to give himself entirely to the King and be reborn.

Had Rainer done this, too? He remembered Rainer now, Vancouver, all the things the abyss had tried to wash away.

He swore a shadow of this oath. The voice rang through him. Painful, but he had already passed through pain into something else. **He was so loyal, so eager, but he didn't truly understand. You are the only mortal to take the oath in my presence in... spans and spans of time, as you mayfly creatures measure it. You have the chance to be so much more.**

The sign burned behind his eyes, the glowing sigil Rainer had shown him. It surged inside him like a choirsong, the cacophony of a thousand fractured voices. For an instant he understood it—a name, a song not meant to be heard by human ears, let alone spoken. For a fraction of a heartbeat he saw past the angel's devouring light to the darkness beyond. The King, the angel, the shining brilliance was a bright spark against a vast shadow, an anglerfish lure for the timeless presence brooding in the depths of the abyss.

Complete the oath.

He balanced on a knife edge between fear and wonder when the sound of his name shattered the vision. Blake staggered, sagging in the King's skeletal embrace. His hand closed on the King's sleeve and rotten cloth disintegrated at his touch, revealing withered grey flesh beneath.

"Blake!"

The crash of a door slamming shut echoed through the room, followed by a roar of sound.

"Stop her," Alain shouted.

Blake twisted to see the cause of the commotion, falling to his knees as the King released him. A woman strode across the room and the crowd drew back to let her pass, pressing close in her wake to gawk. Despite Alain's command, no one laid a hand on her as she approached the dais. She wore no mask, only black armor and a white mantle; her boots echoed on the tiles. She lifted her face toward the throne, and Blake's jaw slackened as he recognized her.

"Liz?"

He didn't know how he could be surprised after everything he'd seen and felt and dreamt in this place, but still he gaped.

Her eyes widened as she took in the scene on the dais, but her gaze fixed firm on him. "It's me. I've come to take you home."

"He is home," Alain said, stepping in front of her.

Liz turned, and her voice was cold and harsh. "Who are you?"

Blake tried to step down, but the King's robes clung to him like cobwebs. "You've met Alain—"

She made a sharp gesture with her right hand, leaving a tracer of silver light in its wake. "Alain is dead. I went to his funeral. This isn't him."

Blake opened his mouth to deny it, but his teeth snapped shut on the words.

Alain looked up at the King, and the frown twisting his face wasn't one Blake knew. "Will you permit this?"

The King's narrow shoulders hitched, but it was the blindfolded woman who voiced his rumbling chuckle. **"It amuses me. Deal with her as you see fit."**

Blake shook off the clinging robes and descended the steps. Liz met him at the bottom. Her hair was tangled, her pale face flushed. A blood-soaked bandage wrapped her left hand. Her hazel eyes were wide, lashes spiky as if she'd been crying. He started to reach for her, but jerked his hand back again.

"Is it really you?"

She sighed, and her eyes flickered as if they wanted to roll. "It's really me."

His fists clenched. "You say Alain isn't real. How can I trust you?"

"Because I've fought my way here through dangers untold and hardships unnumbered. Because I brought this." She held up her right hand and he saw his ring, the ring she'd given him, shining loose around her thumb. "And because I'm getting you out of here whether you trust me or not."

Her voice cracked on the last word, a hitch of breath full of worry and impatient determination. The sound caught in his chest like a hook and pulled him forward. He threw his arms around her and the unfamiliar bulk of armor, tucking her head under his chin. She smelled of blood and sweat and fear and the fading sweetness of vanilla shampoo.

"I missed you," he murmured against her hair.

She shook; he thought she was crying until he heard her laugh. "You could have asked me to visit. You didn't have to nearly get yourself killed."

"This is very sweet," Alain said. "But now isn't the time."

Blake turned, and once again doubt paralyzed him. "Who are you?"

Alain's face crumpled, a miserable expression that twisted in Blake's gut like a knife. Then he laughed, and the pain fell away like a mask.

"This game is boring me. Your friend is right. Alain is dead and buried. I'm all you have left of him. But I'll keep wearing his face if you ask me nicely. We can still have fun together."

Blake recoiled, his stomach churning. "Who are you?"

The false Alain stepped closer. "I'm your lover now, aren't I? And more. I've seen all the dark ugly things inside you, more than anyone else ever has." One sharp-nailed hand reached up to stroke Blake's cheek.

He moved without thinking. It wasn't until Alain sprawled on the floor in front of him and the dull warmth of pain spread through his knuckles that Blake realized what he'd done. The crack of flesh against flesh hung in the air. Alain—Alain's face—stared up at him, dark eyes wide with shock, blood trickling from a split lip. Blake's hand ached, and the taste of sour metal filled his mouth. His cheeks burned.

Was this what it felt like? This rush?

His knees gave way and he doubled over retching. His stomach was empty, but it heaved all the same, strings of spit and bile dripping onto the floor.

Laughter washed over him, cold and mocking. He knew that laugh, and it wasn't Alain's. He retched harder.

Hands closed on his coat, hauling him up. "You can be a predator, darling, or you can be prey. It's a pity you seem disposed to the latter. Perhaps the King can cure you of that. If not, well... better sport for the rest of us."

Liz grabbed Alain's arm and tried to pull him away. Instead he backhanded her with casual viciousness and sent her sprawling across the tiles.

"I'm glad you're here, after all," he said. "You can keep my friends company. This was a boring party anyway." He whistled sharply, and an answering howl rose from the dancers.

"Now," he said to Blake. "Let's finish what you started."

Blake struggled, but the false Alain was too strong, carrying him up the stairs as if he were a child. Something moved inside him, something more than his own helpless panic: a coil of darkness, some lingering taint of the abyss. Black and cold and alien, but it gave him strength.

He smashed his skull into Alain's face and kicked. Their legs tangled and both of them spilled down the stairs. Blake's head bounced off stone and the world exploded into white starbursts. He landed blind and dizzy. Alain fell across him, pinning him to the floor. All Blake could do was lie limp and pray he didn't fall to pieces.

Alain's voice whispered in his ear. "Aren't you tired of being a victim? Anyone's meat, to use or save or throw away. This place could make you so much more, if you'd only let it."

Blood roared in Blake's ears, leaked down his face. Darkness sang to him and he wanted so badly to listen.

The door crashed open again, and a new voice carried over the shrieking din. "Enough!"

Blake knew that voice. It burned through the pain-haze, drew him back from the edge of unconsciousness.

I'm not helpless, he told himself. *Not a child. Not prey.*

He drew a breath, choked and spat blood. He heaved Alain's weight aside and pushed himself up, fighting the urge to vomit again. Blood trickled into one eye, splashing bright as rubies against the floor. Through red-webbed lashes he watched a white-robed man cross the room.

"You've had your entertainment," the man said, looking up at the throne. His voice was the velvet warmth from Blake's dreams. "Now if you'll excuse us, it's time these children went home."

The gargoyles on the dais had held so still that Blake had almost forgotten them—now they stirred, unfurling wings the color of decay. **:You trespass:** They spoke in unison. The woman in white had vanished from the dais, leaving the King alone in his chair.

"I don't belong here, it's true, but neither do your guests. Give them to me and I'll trouble you no more."

Blake heard the thunder of wings, but Alain leaned over him, blocking his view. "Let them play. You didn't answer my question." His smile bared too many teeth. "Don't you want to be something more? Or do you like being fragile and broken?"

In response, Blake punched him again. Something crunched—his hand or Alain's face, he wasn't sure which. Pain traveled up his arm, warm and sweet. "How's that?"

The false Alain grinned. Blood black as tar leaked from his nose, seeped between his sharp, sharp teeth. "Much better! I knew you had it in you somewhere." He lunged, quick as a snake, too fast for Blake to dodge. But instead of a blow, he pulled Blake close and kissed him.

Sharp teeth shredded Blake's lips and Alain's tongue slid hot against his, bittersweet and sticky with blood. Hands slipped under his coat, tugging at his shirt buttons. Thread snapped; nails scraped his skin. And even now, after everything, he arched into the touch with a gasp, inhaling Alain's bloody breath. He clenched a hand in Alain's hair, dragging his face away.

"Yes," the impostor hissed, the cables in his neck standing taut. "That's it. Hit me. Hurt me. Isn't that what you want? Isn't that what you know best?"

Blake rolled, pinning the false Alain against the floor. His hands ached with the effort of not giving him what he asked for. "No."

"Then run." Alain lay back, hands held wide in a gesture of surrender. Purple-black hair drifted around his blood-streaked face. "Who knows, maybe you'll even win free. But every time you think of your poor dead boy, you'll really be thinking of me."

Blake's vision tunneled until all he could see was blood on ecru skin, the jump of Alain's pulse in his slender throat. This was what it looked like from the other side.

His fists clenched. But if he gave in, he wouldn't stop. And that was exactly what the impostor wanted. Instead he scrambled to his feet and ran to help Liz.

Alain's mocking laughter followed him.

LIZ FOUGHT, BUT the crowd kept coming. They wore suits and gowns, satin and velvet and jewels, but beneath the finery they were the same bacchanal procession she'd glimpsed in the streets of Carcosa. Hooved and horned and clawed, men with goat legs or goat heads, women with hyena teeth. They howled and laughed as they surrounded her.

The ring blazed on her hand, sword and shield all at once. Bone and cartilage crunched as she drove her boot into a muzzled face. Adrenaline sang in her blood, and for one terrible moment she felt strong. Her veins burned, a sensation that moved through panic and into something wild and electric.

But even armed and armored, there was only one of her and too many of them. Talons tangled in her hair; teeth scraped against leather, tore through it to reach the flesh beneath. Maenads and satyrs fell beneath her shining blade, but more came on, wave after wave. Liz screamed and kicked and bit, drove her elbow into something's ribs and broke a laughing woman's nose.

The laughter never stopped. It wasn't until her throat began to ache that she realized she was laughing too. Her skin felt wrong, too tight and tingling, blood surging hot. Was this desire? The lust that drove the world? Sex and death and madness—Carcosa would teach her all of them if it could.

The wall of leering faces opened and clutching hands gave way. For an instant Liz felt alone and bereft, cold without the press of flesh. Then she fell and cracked her head on the tiles. Colors burst behind her eyes and a roar of static drowned the cries of the bacchante.

With doubled vision she watched Blake break through the crowd. Two Blakes tossed bodies aside. Two Blakes throttled two unlucky satyrs. Blood splashed his hands and face, clotted in his hair; she couldn't tell how much of it was his. She tried to shout, but his name was a wet sound in her throat. She spat pink-streaked phlegm and called again.

"Blake!"

He turned and it took all her resolve not to flinch. Black oozed across his eyes like tar, swallowing grey and white alike. Dark veins stood out in his sunken cheeks. "Let him go," she said, climbing painfully to her feet. "It's not worth it."

He looked down at the body sagging in his grip and flung it away with a shudder. "You're hurt." Even his voice was darker, thicker.

"I'll be fine." Probably a lie, but she didn't have time to inventory her wounds. Blood trickled down her face and throat, dripped from her hands, but her throbbing left hand eclipsed any lesser pain. The white mantle was a lost cause, but the scarab pin still gleamed on her shoulder.

She expected the bacchante to attack again, but they were breaking up into a dozen writhing brawls and tangles, or shrieking and swinging one another around in a dance. Across the room, Seker stood before the throne, beset by the King's winged guards.

Her vision, already swimming, blurred again. Where Seker had been she saw a swirling darkness, a thousand eyes gleaming red and gold and green amid a vast tenebrous shape. Then the moment passed and he was a man again.

"Who is that?" Blake asked, spitting blood.

"Seker. He's a friend. I hope. He's with me, either way." She reached out to wipe at his bloody face, but only smeared more gore between them. Silver gleamed beneath crimson, and she twisted the ring off her swelling thumb.

"This is yours."

He took it from her and slipped it onto his finger. "How did you—"

"I'll explain later. You didn't eat any pomegranates, did you?"

His smile looked like a grimace, but he laughed. "No."

"Then let's get out of here."

Hand in hand they ran. It wasn't until they reached the doors that Liz realized her mistake: running meant prey, and the hunters had given chase once more. The door swung shut on the sound of pursuit, and they fled into the halls of the labyrinth.

The maze had changed. The mirrors had vanished, as had the bloody handprints she'd left on the way in. No thread to lead them back. The corridor branched and they stumbled up a narrow flight of stairs.

"How do we get out of here?" Blake gasped.

"Do you have the silver shoes?"

"Damn. I thought you did."

They laughed because they had to, though it wasted precious breath. They climbed, and ran, and climbed again, while howls and laughter grew closer at their heels. Her legs burned; her lungs burned; Blake's footsteps began to falter.

She stumbled when the stair ended. They stood on a broad balcony overlooking the sea. Only a narrow ledge of stone stood between them and the long drop to the black water below. There was nowhere to go but back, or down.

Liz let out a sobbing breath. Beside her, Blake moaned. They stood side by side, staring out at the drop.

"We tried," he whispered.

"We're not finished yet." But she could barely stand. Dream or no dream, she hurt all over, and blood loss left her cold and queasy. Could she fight again when the hunters reached them?

"This is my fault," Blake said. "You never should have come after me."

Liz straightened. The cold chemical wind whipped her hair into her eyes. "Don't be an idiot. I'm not giving up."

Snarls and howls drifted up the stairs, the echoes of feet and hooves. Liz inched closer to the railing and looked down. The sea below was lost in haze and distance. Beyond the black water, a crimson line burned across the horizon. Aldebaran was rising. She swallowed. "This is a dream."

Blake's eyes narrowed, a familiar gesture around alien black irises. "Liz—"

"How do you wake up from a dream?"

"You're not serious."

"Do you have a better idea?" She set one foot on the low railing, bracing herself against the wind. The snarling din of the bacchante was almost on them. She held out her hand.

Blake took it. Blood pasted their skin together. He stepped onto the ledge.

"One, two, and through."

They stepped into nothing.

ALEX TRIED TO keep a vigil beside Liz that night, but eventually exhaustion stole over him and he drowsed in the uncomfortable chair by the bed.

He woke with a start hours later, a ceramic crash echoing in his ears. He'd dropped a mug of tea; shards and cold dregs splattered the floor at his feet. But that wasn't the only thing that had woken him—something had changed.

Liz's breath. The harsh rasp that had lulled him to sleep had stilled.

His pulse spiked. He'd waited too long—

"Alex?"

He froze, nerves stretched and charged with shock and fear. For a moment he wasn't sure the sound was a human voice, let alone his name. Then he leaned forward, reaching for the lamp, dreading what the light would reveal.

"Liz?" He flinched from the sudden brightness, flinched again when he saw the pallor of her face. But a natural pallor, no black veins or sallow tones. Her eyes were open, glittering bright as glass.

"Liz—" He fell to his knees beside the bed, heedless of the broken cup. He caught her hand, pressing careful fingers against the vein in her wrist. Her pulse was quick, but stronger than it had been. Her hair and skin were damp with sweat, but her brow had lost its fevered heat. The room still stank of illness, but the bandages on her left hand were clean, smelling sharply of antibiotic oinment. "Are you all right?"

Of all the stupid things to ask, but her chapped lips cracked with a smile and her fingers tightened around his. She whispered his name. Then she was asleep again, still gripping his hand.

19
OPEN TO THE DARK

"It's no use. He's still flatline."

"It's been five minutes."

Blake woke to darkness and voices. The darkness filled him—it would burst through his eyes if he opened them, tear open his throat if he tried to scream. His skin was too tight, his skull too small to hold all the pain. The voices moved around him, shouting things he couldn't understand. Hands touched him, always hands, an endlessly repeating hell of hands.

"Clear!"

Electricity hit him, a kick to the chest, searing every nerve. The world washed white as he convulsed. A scream clawed its way up from the pit of his stomach, ripping out of his mouth with such force he thought his jaw would break. Fire raced under his skin, through his veins, burning him to ash. Other voices joined the scream, all underscored by a shrill mechanical shriek.

Then it stopped, a silence so abrupt he felt deaf. Blake opened his eyes, but the world was a kaleidoscope of spinning lights and shadow. The hands were gone, but tentacles still held him, worming under his skin. A slick plastic tube ripped out of his nose as he flailed, and he gagged as it snaked up his throat. Another stung his arm as he ripped it away, and the smell of blood blossomed bright and hot. Beneath that he smelled harsh chemical disinfectant.

A hospital. How had he ended up here?

He yanked at another tube on his thigh, realizing his mistake too late. Warning pressure gave way to pain, like fishhooks through his groin, and the smell of urine cut through the layered stink. He opened his mouth to scream but vomited instead, doubling over the cold metal bed-rail. Watery bile dripped down his chin.

His legs folded beneath him when he tried to stand and he sprawled on the floor, curling helplessly around the agony in his crotch. The fluorescent lights stuttered fitfully. People shouted in the distance and running footsteps shivered through the cold linoleum. Cramps knotted his calves.

He groped for the edge of the bed, a chair, anything to pull himself up. Instead his hand fell on flesh, and he jerked away with a startled yelp. A woman in hospital scrubs curled on the floor an arm's reach away, her wide eyes fixed somewhere beyond him. Her mouth moved, shaping words, but no sound came out. Blood trickled sluggishly from her nose, dripping into her mouth and down her chin. Blake reached for her, moved his hand in front of her eyes, but she didn't react. When he sat up, he saw two other bodies fallen beside the bed, another woman and a man: they didn't move at all.

Blake bit his lip against a whimper, turning away from the woman's blind stare. Tears filmed his eyes, turning everything into a flickering blur. Blood oozed from his wrist; pink-streaked piss leaked down his thigh; a dull ache throbbed behind his sternum. Finally he hooked one hand on the bed frame and pulled himself to his knees. He was too weak to stand, let alone run, but if he didn't get away from the pain and the lights and the noise he would start sobbing and never stop.

Something stirred inside him, cold and dark. An anesthetic tingle spread through his limbs, soothing his cramping legs, steadying him as he hauled himself to his feet. He didn't trust this strange chilly strength, but it whispered at him to run, and he couldn't argue with that.

He flung open doors and cabinets until he found his clothes, leaning against the wall as he struggled into jeans and sweater. His fingers trembled too badly to lace his boots.

The corridor was a confusion of shouting and alarms and running nurses. No one bothered him as he staggered down the hall, except to push past. What had happened? He didn't stop to ask. All that mattered was escape. Through the maze of hallways and clamor of the lobby, into the clean, scathing night.

Lions Gate, he realized as he reached the sidewalk. North Van. City lights blazed white and gold, blue and green, mirrored in the black water of Burrard Inlet. A chiaroscuro blur through his watering eyes.

His strength didn't last long. A block from the hospital he slipped on icy pavement and sprawled into a gutter full of frozen slush. He crawled across the sidewalk, too weak to stand again, and huddled against a dark shop front. Sirens screamed nearby.

The sky over Lions Gate seethed with shadows, winged shapes spiraling through the clouds like giant bats.

The monsters from the cabin.

Headlights cut the night open. Blake flinched, expecting an ambulance, police, but the car that pulled up to the curb was sleek and black, its windows midnight mirrors. The back door swung open.

"Get in," a man called.

Blake moved closer in spite of himself, drawn by rich, familiar tones. The door opened wider and the streetlight slanted across the curve of a shaven head, gleamed in one pearl-black eye.

"Please," the man Liz had called Seker said. "Get in. Unless you came all this way to freeze to death."

Blake laughed. Or maybe it was a sob. He climbed into the warmth of the car.

Liz floated on the edge of sleep, drifting in a warm red sea. She didn't hurt; she wasn't afraid. That was important, but she couldn't remember what had ever scared or pained her. Surf beat in her ears. There was a word for that soft whispering sound, a word she used to know, but it was a hole in her memory now, like the empty socket of a tooth. The sensation filled her with a sadness she couldn't explain.

You did it, didn't you? Alice's wet voice coiled around her. *You solved the puzzle, faced the dragon, saved the princess. Now what? Closure? Resolution? Happily ever after?* The words were mocking, but veined with something soft and wistful.

Liz woke with a dizzy start, all her peace undone. Tears leaked down her cheeks. "It doesn't work that way," she whispered. She wasn't sure if she was talking to Alice or herself.

The room was dark and silent. Blankets weighed on her, stifling, but the air drifting across her face was cold. Her skin itched with dried sweat; her scalp crawled.

What had happened? The last thing she remembered was Blake's hand in hers, the rush of falling and the whiplash crack of tumbling out of the dreamlands. Her joints ached and her muscles felt weak and stiff, as if she hadn't moved them in days. Her head was stuffed with something—old socks, by the taste in her mouth—and her tongue was a slab of dry meat. Sore back, numb toes, aching bladder: her body's list of complaints grew longer with every passing minute.

Where was she? Not the hotel, not a hospital. Not Carcosa, and that was what really mattered. As her eyes adjusted to the gloom, she recognized Alex's familiar outline slumped in a chair at the foot of the bed, his head propped on one hand.

Her good hand twitched, nails snagging on the weave of the blanket. She held something in her palm, a small, unfamiliar shape. Her knuckles crackled as she opened her fingers. A gold and lapis scarab bounced against her chest, gleaming in the dim light. Blake's ring was gone.

She made a soft, wondering noise and Alex stirred. Liz closed her hand around the brooch again and tucked it out of sight.

"Liz—" Something inside her untwisted as he said her name.

"I did it," she said. Dry lips cracked and stung. She'd never been so thirsty.

"What did you do, besides scare me half to fucking death?" His voice was tired and thin.

"I found Blake." She tried to sit up, but slumped against the pillows again, weak as a newborn kitten. Movement woke the pain in her left hand, sharp and hot and sickening. She twitched her fingers and gasped as torn skin stretched. Rosettes of blood spotted the bandage.

Alex switched on a lamp and she winced at the sight of his face. His eyes were shadowed and sunken, naked without his glasses. His hair hung lank against pale, splotchy cheeks. She could see the effort each breath cost him.

"You're sick."

He waved it aside with an angry gesture. "That doesn't matter. Why didn't you tell me? Why didn't you talk to me before..."

Liz propped herself up again, with better success this time. "Because you would have tried to stop me, and I couldn't explain it to you."

"You could have tried."

Her lips thinned. "Would you have tried to believe me?"

He frowned and rubbed his temples. "Tried, yes. Succeeded... I don't know. I'm sorry, sorry for the things I said before."

She reached out, slow and careful with her wounded hand, and brushed her fingertips against his. "I'm sorry too. But... Can you help me out of bed? I really need to use the bathroom."

THE BLACK CAR carried Blake away from the sirens and chaos, purring through the wet streets. Blake slumped against the soft leather seat and watched the city lights bleed through the haze. Seker studied him silently; the driver—a pale man in tinted glasses—didn't speak either. He wasn't sure where he expected the car to take them. Eventually he realized it wasn't going anywhere, only circling through the city. Waiting for him? He knew he should be alert, ready to run, but his head sagged against the cushions. Turning to look at his rescuer took all the strength he had.

Streetlights swept rhythmically across tinted windows, revealing his face in flashes. Strong cheekbones, deep-set eyes, a wide, amused mouth. A face Blake would have itched to paint a month ago; now the thought left him cold and unsettled. The white robes he'd glimpsed in the palace were gone, replaced by a tailored dark suit.

"Is your name really Seker?" It wasn't what he'd meant to say. The words scraped out of his aching throat, slurred as if he was drunk. The thought of drinking reminded him how painfully thirsty he was.

"It sounds silly here in the real world, doesn't it?" His voice was as deep and rich as Blake remembered. He said *real* as though it were a private joke. One hand slipped into his inside pocket, slowly enough that Blake didn't flinch. He took the offered card and tilted it toward the light. Shadows lined the embossed letters. *Sebastian Sands*, it read, beside a stylized scarab. On the back, in smaller type, was a phone number.

Sands reached down into the darkness and Blake tensed, but when the man straightened he held a bottle of water, its plastic seal still intact. Anything else he could have refused, but his tongue curled at the sight. Condensation slicked his hand as he accepted it; he didn't notice the chill. He shuddered as the first swallow soothed his throat and lined his hollow stomach with cold.

"Thank you." Plastic dented under his fingers as he lowered the half empty bottle. "For helping us."

Seker—Sands—dipped his head in acknowledgement. "Your friend did most of the work. My assistance was minimal."

"Liz. Is she—"

"She'll be fine. She has people to take care of her. You, however, look terrible."

Even in the dark car that much was obvious. His hands were pale and gaunt around the water bottle. Shadows pooled between bone and tendon. A crust of blood stained his left wrist where he'd ripped the IV out, and a fresh bruise purpled beneath it; his groin still ached as if he'd been racked. His palms and knees were dark with grime, jeans clinging damp to his legs. The water couldn't entirely rinse away the lingering taste of bile. Over the aroma of leather and citrus cologne that filled the car, he could smell himself—greasy hair and skin, piss and sickness. Humiliating, but he was too tired and raw to feel the sting.

"Would you like something to eat?" Sands asked.

Blake swallowed. A drink of water. A cup of coffee. A hot meal. Then the snare of debt would close around him.

"Why?" he asked before Sands could go on. "Why did you help us? Why are you helping me now? What do you want?"

"I wanted you out of Carcosa. Now I want to keep you alive. Which would be easier to manage if you'd eat something, but we'll skip that for now."

Every mention of food reminded him how hollow he felt. How long had machines pumped paste and fluids into him to keep him alive? Plastic creaked as his hands tightened.

"That's all? Simple altruism? Just like Rainer?"

Sands sighed. "Morgenstern is a fool, little better than a dilettante. Though in fairness, he never meant to hurt you. He merely courted you with gifts he didn't understand." He tilted his head, one eye flashing as light slid across his face. "As for my altruism, I wouldn't call it simple. More a long-term investment. Some day I'll ask for your help. But for now I want you safe, and away from Carcosa and its king. Can you accept that?"

"Do I have a choice?"

Sands' mouth quirked, a hint of a smile in the shadows. "You always have a choice. You can refuse to help me, when I ask. Though I hope that you'll at least consider it. Tonight, however, all I want is to be sure you don't end up dead in a gutter."

Blake turned back to the window, leaning his forehead against the glass. The chill soothed the band of pain that circled his skull. He squeezed his eyes shut as they turned onto Lions Gate Bridge; water was the last thing he wanted to see.

Blake dragged a hand across his eyes, pretending it was fatigue instead of tears he fought. "What happened to us at the cabin?" he croaked, swallowing the taste of salt. "Where did the monsters come from?"

"From the dark places between dreams," Sands said after a moment. "They're hunters."

"Hunting who?"

"They came to stop Morgenstern's invocation. But now—" He reached out and took Blake's hand, turning it over to expose the veins in his wrist. Blue now, but Blake felt the shadow inside him, waiting. "You're marked now. You escaped Carcosa, but you carry a piece of it within you. The King will be drawn to it. His enemies will be drawn to exterminate it."

"To exterminate me."

"Only if they find you." Sands smiled. He let go of Blake's wrist, but the warmth of his touch lingered. "I can keep you safe. We can leave the city. Tonight, if you like. Anywhere you want to go."

Blake fought a shudder. It would be so nice to say yes. To let someone else take care of him. To trust. But he should have learned that lesson eighteen years ago; he wasn't about to forget it again now.

"I appreciate everything you've done, but I can't do that. Not now. There are things I need to do, people I need to talk to. Alone," he added, before Sands could offer.

He waited for anger, refusal, violence. But after a frowning silence, the man nodded. "If that's what you wish. You have my card. If you ever need my assistance—"

Blake nodded. "I'll call. You can let me out here. Please."

The car slowed, sliding neatly up to the curb.

"You'll need these," Sands said. He reached inside his coat again, this time retrieving a lumpy envelope. Metal clinked as Blake took it, spilled cold into his palm. Leather slid after. His keys and passport and wallet—warped now and water stained.

"And while we're at it, you might as well take this too." Sands shrugged out of his coat and held it out.

Blake hesitated, his hand on the door handle. He could feel the cold waiting for him. "I'll be fine."

Sands raised an eyebrow. "You've survived terrible things. That doesn't mean you can't get hypothermia. It's a coat, not an obligation."

"I—" His fingers closed on heavy wool. The smell of incense and oranges clung to the fabric. "Thank you."

"Be careful."

The door closed on his warning and the car pulled away, leaving Blake shivering on the sidewalk.

LIZ'S SENSE OF accomplishment lasted almost an hour, long enough to wash her hair awkwardly with one hand and for the bath water to cool. Alex sat with her, explaining as best he could what had happened since she took the mania. He wouldn't admit it, but she suspected he was also making sure she didn't pass out in the bathtub.

But when they came out of the bathroom, tension floated through the front of the house like strands of a spiderweb. Lailah sat at the tiny kitchen table, her gun stripped to metal bones. Rae—who Liz had met briefly only a few days ago, though it felt much longer now—perched on the arm of the couch, her arms wrapped tight around her.

Rae looked up as they walked in. Her hair trailed like a black veil across her face and beneath it her eyes were dark and sunken. A chill settled in the empty pit of Liz's stomach as she met the other girl's gaze.

"It isn't over," she whispered.

Rae shook her head, sending her hair flying. "You thought it would be? If you and Blake woke up, it would be a miracle cure? Nothing's changed. No," she corrected herself with another shake of her head. "It's still changed. It's still changing. The monsters are still out there, waiting."

Before anyone could speak, Lailah's phone buzzed. Liz flinched at the sharp rattle, and Lailah's frown stretched into a snarl. She turned away to hold a short conversation punctuated by curses.

"Lions Gate lost power an hour ago," she said when she ended the call. "Even the backup generators. No one knows what happened, but people are dead. That was just about the time you woke up."

The towel slipped off Liz's hair, snaking down her shoulder to pool on the floor. "Blake?"

"Missing." Lailah turned back to her gun, reassembling the pieces into their killing shape. "I don't give a damn about your friend, but whatever's happening in the city, happening to Rae, he's in the middle of it. We have to find him." She punctuated the last word by slapping the clip into her pistol, and all the dread Liz thought she'd left behind in Carcosa surged fresh.

Rae stared down at her hands as if she didn't recognize them. "The door is opening."

"Oh." Liz's face drained cold with realization. "The door. The door to Carcosa. Blake painted it. It's on display in the gallery."

Lailah holstered the gun at the small of her back. Her smile was harsh and sharp. "Get dressed."

RAINER DRIFTED BELOW the pain, as he had drifted for days. It waited for him, red and ugly, and it was simpler to hold his breath and sink.

When he did surface, Antja was with him, changing his bandages, feeding him tea and broth, humming charms to speed mending flesh. Sometimes she wept. He reached for her then, though movement twisted a hot knife in his shoulder, but she always pulled away.

He never should have involved her in this—the Brotherhood, the gallery, the intrigues of the world beneath the world—should never have wooed her with tricks and magic lessons. Once, burning with fever, he tried to tell her all of that. Delirium rode him, and he wasn't sure if the words made any sense, or even what language he spoke. She only kissed him, and her lips tasted of magic. The spell settled over him, warm and soft, and he drifted into the dark once more.

THE FEVER EASED; flesh and muscle knit back into their proper shapes, itching and burning as tissues healed. Rainer still drifted, but the darkness changed. He had felt the presence of the King since he first swore his oath at sixteen, a faint spark in the back of his mind, so familiar that it went unnoticed unless he sought it out. Now that spark burned brighter, stronger than he'd ever known. It whispered to him like a siren.

He woke drenched in cold sweat, alert for the first time in days. His vision was too sharp, colors brittle and razor-edged, and his pulse sang in his ears. Flowers of dried blood and other fluids spotted his bandages, but he could move his left arm again.

Antja was in the kitchen. She started when he called to her, and something clattered into the sink. Her eyes were shadowed, her hair lank and tangled over her shoulders. She knelt beside the bed, pressing him down when he tried to sit and laying a cool hand against his forehead.

"*Gott sei dank*," she whispered, and her voice was low and rough.

"It's all right," he told her, folding his hands over hers. She winced; her palm was raw and pink, puffy with healing blisters. "The worst is over."

She laughed, short and harsh, but kissed his hands before she pulled away. "The worst is never over. You should know that by now."

Something was out of place in the room, but it took him a moment to recognize it: her bags were packed. Not just Antja's luggage but his, piled in the middle of the floor.

"You're leaving?" Not that he could blame her, but the words took the wind out of him all the same.

"We're leaving. As soon as you're well enough to travel. Vancouver isn't safe anymore."

"How long have I been unconscious?"

"Three days. It's been quiet, but something is wrong. Something is coming."

"I can't leave. I promised Blake—" He winced and she looked away. When she turned back her face was the cool mask he'd come to dread.

"I saw Liz three days ago. Just before I came here. She took a whole vial of mania. She's a vegetable now, just like Blake. So what else do you think you'll be able to do?"

Rainer closed his eyes, as if that could stop the news. His last hope. Blake's last. "I'm sorry," he whispered, and he wasn't sure who he meant the words for.

"Rest," Antja said. "You're still weak, and I need to clean up. We can talk about this later."

The bathroom door shut and water gurgled through the pipes. Rainer lay back, trying to take her advice. But as his eyes sagged close, a flash of red by the door caught his attention and jerked him awake again. The alarm panel. Someone was in the gallery.

Sometimes he envied Antja her prayers.

20

DISINTEGRATION

BLAKE WALKED SOUTH across Granville Bridge, hands clenched in the pockets of his borrowed coat. The street glittered with Christmas lights, but signs in the shop windows advertised Boxing Day sales. The newspapers said it was the twenty-seventh. He had lost three weeks.

Snow drifted in lazy spirals from the dusty rose sky. Well after midnight, he guessed, from the depth of the stillness. The streets were deserted. Coffee cups piled in drifts by overflowing trashcans, and stray receipts and bits of wrapping fluttered soggy on the sidewalks. Only the lull of the holidays, but it felt as though he'd woken to find the world emptied in his absence.

Behind the clouds, the stars brooded. The cold, inky thing inside him sensed their gaze too, and stirred.

Was this what Rainer had meant when he'd spoken of his gift? It wasn't what Blake had imagined. But he never could have imagined any of this.

The gallery was dark and locked tight, but he saw a sliver of light in the upstairs window. The faceless angel above the door stared down at him. His hand closed on his keys, metal gouging his palm. What would he say to Rainer? He wanted the strength of anger, but all he felt was tired and lost.

As he stood on the sidewalk searching for words, a car door

shut across the street, then a second and a third. Footsteps started toward him, and he turned at the incredulous sound of his name.

"Blake?"

Stephen York's eyes widened as he approached. "Son of a bitch. You're alive." Jason followed behind him, huddled against the cold, and another man Blake didn't recognize.

"I admit, we didn't think you'd make it. Especially after Lions Gate blew up. Lucky you got out."

"Lucky," Blake repeated, trying not to think of the nurse's staring face. A warning sensation prickled down his back, a sensation he'd long since learned to listen to. Stephen had always set his alarms shivering, and now he was outnumbered. "What are you doing here?"

"Just stopping in to talk to Rainer. Have you seen him yet?" When Blake shook his head, Stephen grinned. "Good. It will be a happy surprise."

All Blake's instincts screamed at him to run. But he was too slow; Stephen's hand slipped out of his coat pocket and the streetlamp gleamed yellow against the barrel of a gun. "Let's go up together."

Stephen's hand closed on Blake's arm, steering him toward the narrow alley that led behind the gallery. Blake didn't look at the gun, but he felt its pressure against his side. After Carcosa and the King, a gun felt like a toy, not anything that should frighten him. Which wasn't enough to make him risk a hole in the gut, though.

"I thought Canadians were politer than this," he said, rolling his eyes.

"We all have our breaking points. I would have thought you'd be on my side, after what Rainer did to you. Not to mention Gemma and Robert and Alain."

Blake almost asked about Robert and Gemma, but decided not to give Stephen the satisfaction. Besides, he remembered the smell of blood, the screams, before Alain had dragged him to the water. He could use his imagination. Since Stephen hadn't mentioned Antja, she must be alive.

"If you thought I'd be on your side," he said instead, "why is there a gun pointed at me?"

"No point in taking chances."

Stephen's voice was smooth as ever, but Blake heard the darker undercurrents; he was dead as soon as Rainer was. If not first. The shadow moved inside him, flaring like a cobra's hood.

Hinges squealed as Blake opened the back door. The blinking red light of the alarm panel broke the darkness inside; it chirped and quieted when he punched in his code.

"Wait for me," Stephen told his companions. *Me* instead of *us* settled Blake's suspicions. The two men just nodded. Jason shivered, sallow in the sodium light; he didn't meet Blake's eyes. The other man looked through him as if he were already dead.

Blake went first up the stairs. He could think of a dozen action movie scenarios for getting the gun away from Stephen, but he doubted any of them would survive contact with reality. A tingling itch started in his hands—like a nicotine itch, but he hadn't had a cigarette in years and rarely missed them. It spread up his arms and throat, across his cheeks. He looked at his hand on the railing and saw a network of black veins beneath his skin. His stomach lurched, but in the next heartbeat the vision was gone, a trick of shadows and uncertain light.

"What do you want?" he asked. Let Stephen think the fear in his voice was for the gun; he wished it were.

"I have a lot invested in Vancouver. I thought Rainer could help me, but I was wrong. He'll get himself killed with his crazy cultist bullshit, and a lot of other people too. It's bad for business."

A thin stripe of light glowed under the door of the loft. Stephen's eyes narrowed and the smell of ozone drifted through the air; the hair on Blake's arms stood on end.

"Open it," Stephen told him.

Static sparked under his hand as he turned the knob. Blake jerked, teeth closing on the inside of his cheek.

He started again when he saw Rainer. The man's sleek self-possession was gone. His cheeks were pale and hollow, eyes sunken, hair matted. He leaned on the bar as though he couldn't stand without it. Bandages wrapped his left shoulder, and ugly mottled bruises crept past the edge of the gauze. His jaw slackened when he saw Blake.

"Blake." Rainer's voice broke on his name, and Blake's chest tightened. He drew a breath, but Stephen spoke first.

"Good evening." The gun barrel pressed against Blake's shoulder, pushing him gently into the room. "I've brought you a present."

Rainer's eyes narrowed to electric slivers. "What have you done to him?"

"Nothing yet, but that reminds me—"

Stephen's empty hand moved. Blake tensed for a blow, but instead the man grabbed his jaw and twisted his head around until their eyes met. "Don't move."

The words echoed through his skull. He tried to flinch, but his muscles were locked and rigid. A shivery taste like biting aluminum foil spread through his mouth.

"What are you doing here?" Rainer asked. He straightened, but one hand gripped the edge of the bar, white-knuckled.

"I thought I should check up on you. And it looks like I was right." Stephen flicked a finger toward Rainer's shoulder. The gun didn't waver. "Your friends from the cabin? I still haven't figured out how they got in. Our philosophical differences aside, I know you can build a ward. And I'm sure you think it was me, but it wasn't. So which of your friends sold you out, do you think?"

Stephen paused, glancing around the room. Blake followed the sweep of his gaze—his eyes, at least, he still controlled—to the pile of bags on the floor. "Leaving town? Pity, if you'd thought of that a week ago I would have let you go. But now I'd rather not take that chance."

The smell of ozone returned and the room blurred like a heat shimmer. The air between Rainer and Stephen crackled; the hair on Blake's nape stood on end. He looked past the suitcases, and noticed other details Stephen ignored: a woman's coat draped across the couch, and light glowing beneath the closed bathroom door. He fought against Stephen's compulsion, but the more he tried the more his muscles cramped and burned. The cold thing inside him could still move—he felt it coiling and uncoiling through him, testing the limits of its prison.

Stephen's head swung as if under a blow and he took a step back. Blake, still struggling, fell to his knees, biting his cheek bloody as charley horses knotted both his legs. Under the roar of his pulse he heard a distant crack, then another—like a car backfiring, but he doubted it was that innocent. Stephen steadied himself and gave a shaky laugh.

"Is that it? I didn't even need a hostage."

On his hands and knees, Blake felt a warm draft, smelled steam and shampoo. Light moved across the floor, then vanished abruptly.

Stephen flinched again and a dark trickle oozed from one nostril. His mouth pressed to a white line. Rainer took a step forward and Stephen fell back. Blake's breath caught.

Then Rainer's legs buckled and he slumped against the bar. A bottle tottered and fell, spraying glass and the sharp scent of whiskey through the room.

"Nice try," Stephen said, his voice strained, "but give this up before you embarrass everyone. Anyway, bullets trump magic." He raised the gun.

The cold shadow spread through him, lending him strength, and in that instant Blake could move again. He lunged at Stephen, catching him hard at the knees. They both sprawled across the floor.

Thunder cracked, but the pressure that caught Blake in the face was an elbow, not a bullet. His head snapped back and blood filled his mouth, thick and sickly sweet. Dark spots swam across his eyes. He scrambled backward and fell, waiting for the next shot.

But Stephen was empty handed.

"Looking for this?" Antja asked.

Stephen raised a hand, shock stripping away his slick veneer. "Antja—"

Thunder roared again and his head burst in a warm red spray. Blood and thicker things splattered Blake's face.

Antja stood over them, hair dripping down the shoulders of her bathrobe, hands white-knuckled on the gun. The barrel never wavered.

Blake stared at the wet red ruin that had been a man's face. The smell of copper and raw meat filled his nose, followed by the pungent stink of urine; the taste slid down his throat as he swallowed.

"I don't think he's getting up," he finally said.

Antja blinked and lowered the gun to her side. "No." She looked down at Blake and her mouth twitched. "Hello."

He laughed once and his whole body trembled. He scrubbed a hand across his face, wincing as gore smeared. His nose throbbed, and blood trickled sluggishly from both nostrils.

"Hi." Muscles screamed as he stood, his calves still twitching with cramp. Goosebumps rippled down his skin. At first he thought it was shock, until he felt the icy draft. Stephen's bullet had gone through a window.

Blake and Antja turned to Rainer, who had regained his feet. His face was paler than ever, and a crimson stain like a Rorschach blot seeped across his bandage. Antja dropped the gun on the table and ran to him before he fell again.

"Are you hurt?"

"Not badly. No worse than before, anyway. You?"

"I'm fine." She helped Rainer into a chair and stepped back, straightening her damp robe.

Blake started forward, stopped short. "What the hell happened to me?"

"I'm sorry," Rainer whispered. "I never meant for you to be hurt. For anyone—"

"Alain is dead." He fought a shudder; he hadn't put the words together since Liz spoke them in Carcosa. "So are a lot of other people."

No one spared a glance for Stephen's cooling body.

"What happened to me?" Blake asked again. "That thing—your King, your angel—he put something in me. It's still there." He moved closer and Antja fell back, her face tight and pale.

Rainer stood, leaning hard on the chair. Blake smelled blood and sweat and the crackling ozone scent that he realized must be magic. He met Rainer's snow-shadow eyes and the shadow in him stirred once more, this time in recognition. Rainer's eyes darkened, and Blake knew he felt it too.

He reached out and cupped Rainer's cheek. His fingers tingled at the touch, and gooseflesh rippled across Rainer's chest. Beneath the other man's skin, Blake felt the same darkness moving. But so much less. A noonday shadow compared to the bottom of a lightless well.

Blake's stomach tightened and he nearly leaned into the touch. Instead he pulled away, his pulse beating sharp in his throat. Rainer's eyes were wide and nearly black.

Before either of them could speak, the floor beneath them shuddered and a howl tore the air.

No one spoke as Lailah's smoke-colored car cut through the slick streets toward downtown. Liz sat in the backseat next to Rae, clutching her seatbelt at every too-sharp turn. Alex had given up complaining after the third stomach-lurching swerve. Now he hunched in the passenger seat, his hand white-knuckled on the overhead handle.

It wasn't until they reached the bridge that Rae reached across the seat and caught Liz's hand. The girl's eyes were wide and dark—too dark, as if her pupils had swallowed her irises and were spreading across her sclera. Liz tried not to shudder.

"What was it like?" Rae asked. Her voice was all but lost beneath the engine and hiss of the tires.

"Awful. In every sense of the word." During her bath she had found thin welts criss-crossing her arms and stomach. Echoes of the wounds she'd taken in Carcosa. "Terrible. But"—the admission caught in her throat—"it was beautiful too."

Rae made a choked little noise and turned away. She tugged the sleeves of her sweater over her hands, but not before Liz saw the darkness creeping under her skin. Lailah's eyes flickered in the rearview mirror; her hands tightened on the wheel.

The downtown streets were quiet, even for two days after Christmas. Did other people feel the unnatural tension in the air? Did they have the sense to avoid it?

Light glowed in the gallery's upstairs windows. Slush sprayed from the tires as Lailah swung through the alley and into the narrow parking lot. Liz had her hand on the door before the car finished braking. The night air sliced through her coat and sweater, but the chill she felt went deeper than that.

Two men stood by the back door, no one Liz recognized. One huddled unhappily against stair rail, arms folded across his chest.

The other moved forward. His hands were open at his sides, but there was nothing friendly in the set of his shoulders.

"Who are you?" Lailah asked.

His lips moved but he didn't answer. The light shifted around him, the yellow sodium glare gathering in his hands. He raised a hand, a glow like a dying star cradled in his palm.

Lailah was faster. The gun spoke like thunder and the man fell. Blood trickled black across the snowy asphalt and his light flickered and died.

"Fucking magicians," she muttered.

The second man shouted, his voice high and young. Hardly more than a teenager. Liz's stomach tightened, but she was too slow. Lailah fired again and he fell to his knees.

Rae shrieked, short and sharp, and bolted forward. "Jason?"

The young man looked up from the wet ruin of his chest and his eyes widened. "Rae?" A dark bubble burst on his lips, leaking down his chin. "What—" He sank back against the door, while tendrils of blood snaked across the stairs. Rae knelt beside him, brushing a shaking hand against his face. Her fingers came away red and wet.

Lailah's face was a cold mask in the jaundiced light. "We need to go."

Rae's eyes were lost in shadow. Her throat convulsed. "I'm sorry," she whispered to the dead boy.

Liz caught Alex's hand. He trembled with cold or rage or both, but let her pull him toward the door. She heard him swallow as they stepped around the spreading puddles of blood. The cold numbed Liz's nose, but not enough to mask the smell.

As they stepped over the boy's body slumped on the threshold, a shot echoed upstairs. Liz started, slipping in a smear of melted snow and thicker fluids. Alex caught her before she could fall. A few heartbeats later the sound repeated.

Lailah held her back again when Liz wanted to run. The other woman took the stairs cautiously, scanning the shadows all around them. They reached the second floor landing without any more shots.

But as they stood before the door into the gallery, Liz heard something else. Something worse. A high, ululating wail that stood her hair on end. The cry of the bacchante.

"The door," she whispered. "Blake's door. It's in there."

A crash reverberated through the stairwell and they all jumped, but it was only the upstairs door flying open. Lailah spun and aimed; Liz grabbed for her arm, but her fingers closed on air.

Blake froze at the top of the stairs, his face pale beneath smeared blood. Liz's breath rushed out at the sight of him.

"Christ," Alex breathed. Then, louder, "Put the fucking gun down."

Lailah's eyes narrowed, but she lowered the pistol. Rainer and Antja followed Blake onto the landing. Rainer was shirtless, bloody and bandaged, and Antja wore a coat pulled over a bathrobe and a bag slung over one shoulder. She slipped one hand into her pocket, and Liz caught the now-familiar shape of a gun.

Blake took the steps two at a time and pulled up short in front of Liz. Beneath the blood his face was even thinner than when she'd last seen him in the hospital. But his eyes were open. His grin crinkled the gore drying on his face. Her sinuses prickled as Liz stepped into his arms and hugged him until he grunted. The pressure set her left hand burning again, but she ignored it.

Lailah shoved past them to glare at Rainer. "Open that door."

"I'm surprised you haven't shot it open already," Antja said dryly.

"I didn't bring a shotgun. Do it and hurry. Something bad is happening in there."

Antja's hand closed on Rainer's arm. "We need to get out of here."

"Not until you clean up your fucking mess," Lailah snapped.

Rainer's shoulders sagged. "She's right." He shrugged off Antja's hand, leaning hard on the railing. The door opened at his touch.

A draft exhaled from the gallery, warmer than the night and damp, smelling of blood and wine and sap. And beneath that, a bitter chemical reek that was all too familiar; the wind off the black sea. Light rippled across the walls, and the cries of the bacchante carried through the twisting corridors of the exhibit.

Liz's good hand clenched on the cold stair rail, her palm slippery with sweat. Panic seared the veins in her throat. But she had faced Carcosa once already, alone. She could do it again.

Lailah shoved Rainer through the door first and followed close behind. Antja hesitated, one hand trembling on the strap of her bag.

Alex's hand closed on Liz's sleeve, but he looked at Antja when he spoke. "This isn't your problem anymore."

"No," Blake answered. "It's mine. I made the door. I have to close it."

He stepped through the door. Liz followed, leaving Alex and Antja cursing softly behind her.

The outline of the gallery remained, but it was already changing around them. Vines snaked across the walls, dripped quivering from the light fixtures. The walls pulsed, and the floor shivered. What should have been firm tile beneath Liz's boots was softer, yielding. Where paintings had hung the walls now opened into windows, each one looking into a different nightmare view. Liz kept her eyes straight ahead. Rainer and Lailah had already vanished into the maze.

"I am never letting you plan a vacation again," Alex muttered as he fell in beside her. She pretended her watering eyes were the fault of the draft.

The air grew warmer and wetter the deeper they went, stinging Liz's throat with every breath. Alex began to cough. They balked when they reached the arches. What had been plaster now glistened slick as wet bone. Red tendrils writhed across their surface, meshing to form a pulsing web of tissue. The walls expanded and contracted with the rhythm of the draft, and fluid seeped across the floor. Behind them, the ivy had devoured the lights, leaving only the sulfurous glow ahead to guide them.

From the other end of the tunnel, someone shouted. A woman's laughter answered. Beside her, Liz felt Blake shudder.

"Keep going." Antja shouldered ahead. "It will only get worse."

Moisture squelched beneath Liz's feet as she followed; mephitic fumes seared her lungs. Alex gagged, but kept moving.

Antja's breath caught as they turned the last corner, an instant's warning. Then Liz looked up and saw the door.

It was still a painting, barely, but the canvas had stretched to fill the room. The great stone door stood all the way open now, framing a view of towers and black water, and the gathered horde of the bacchante.

RAE FELT STRONGER with every breath of the damp, acrid air. The smell of Jason's blood lingered in her nose; it had sickened her at first, but now saliva pooled on her tongue. Soon, the voices promised. Soon she would have all the blood she wanted.

She was a danger to everyone. Lailah had to know it, too. Was a bullet waiting for her at the end of the hall? The part of her that cared was growing weaker and quieter with every step into the labyrinth.

Then they reached the heart of the maze, and the vista waiting there, and Rae nearly threw back her head and screamed with joy. She didn't need the stars anymore—Carcosa was coming here.

Rainer knelt before the threshold, and Lailah sprawled on the floor, struggling against the vines that ensnared her. But Rae could only stare at the woman standing over them.

Tall and voluptuous, cinched and corseted by plum-black leather. Ivy threaded her wild dark hair, a crown of leaves tangled in the coils. Move vines inked the chalk-white flesh of her arms and shoulders. Her eyes were wide and black and starlit. Rae shuddered as she recognized the maenad from her visions, the leader of the hunt.

"Look, Chosen," the woman said to Rainer. One white hand cupped his chin and tilted his head back. Vines slithered down her arm to brush his face. "Look at what you've helped accomplish. You've earned your place in the King's court."

Her eyes rose and met Rae's. "And you, little bird. I've been waiting for you." She held out a hand and Rae went. Lailah screamed her name. "My sister and I have been arguing over you, but I know what you want."

Her hand closed on the back of Rae's neck, pulling her into a bittersweet cyanide kiss. Rae's fists closed in the vines of the woman's hair; her lips tore on sharp teeth. The heat of it was stronger than anything she'd ever felt, stronger than mania. She pressed herself against the taller woman, aching for the scrape of teeth, the touch of taloned hands. If the maenad had torn her apart, she would have screamed encouragement.

Instead the woman let her go with a bloody, teasing smile. "Soon," she promised. "You'll join the revels, and all the flesh and blood you've ever wanted will be yours for the taking. Just as soon as I'm finished here. For now, entertain yourself."

Rae shuddered and licked her lips, tasting her blood and the maenad's, black and bitter. Her teeth shivered as they sharpened. She followed the casual sweep of the woman's hand, to where Lailah still writhed against her prison of vines. Blood from a split lip streaked her chin, shining in the flickering light.

"Rae—"

Rae dropped to her knees beside Lailah and took the woman's face in her hands. Shuddering, she licked the blood from Lailah's mouth. "It's all right," she whispered. "You knew it would come to this."

Lailah snarled, but the more she struggled, the tighter the vines wound around her. The black gun lay on the floor beside her, just out of reach. The sight of her helpless sent a queasy thrill of lust through Rae.

My sister's way is not the only way.

Rae leaned close, pressing her face into the crook of Lailah's neck. The woman's pulse jumped against her lips. The smell of salt and blood dizzied her. "This isn't what I wanted," she whispered. She ran her tongue down Lailah's throat, and heard the bacchante cheering her on. Her hand closed on the gun.

She rocked back on her heels and raised the gun. "There's another way."

The sight clacked against her teeth, gouged the roof of her mouth. The taste of bitter oil and metal filled her mouth. Lailah's eyes widened and her mouth opened on a cry.

Thunder set her free.

Rae flew.

* * *

As RAE CROUCHED beside Lailah, the ivy-crowned woman turned to Blake. Liz shuddered at her sharp-toothed smile.

"And here's the artist himself. I misjudged you, I admit. I thought you were another pretty pet, but you're worth more than that. Not that I wouldn't keep you on a leash all the same."

Blake stood stiff and trembling. Flesh sank against bone, and the veins in his cheeks darkened to ink. Liz recoiled before she could stop herself.

"You don't belong here," he said, his voice low and rough.

"Neither do you, anymore. You belong with us now." She held out her hand. "Come home. We have a lot of catching up to do."

"Go fuck yourself."

The woman laughed. "Come and help me. I'll wear his face again if you want me to." Her features rippled with vine shadows, and Alain stood framed in the light of the doorway. Blake flinched; behind them, Antja's breath hissed through clenched teeth. Rainer opened his mouth, but a tendril of ivy curled between his teeth to gag him.

"Come with me," the false Alain said. "If you do, I'll close the door behind us and your friends will be safe."

No, Liz tried to say, but all that came out was a silent breath. Her hand closed on Blake's sleeve, and she felt the tension shivering through him.

"Do you mean that?" he asked.

"Cross my heart and hope to die. This"—a wave of his—her—hand encompassed the door, the room, the gallery—"is a rare opportunity, but I'll give it up for you. Come home, come willing, and your friends and this city can keep their illusion of safety a while longer."

Out of the corner of her eye, Liz saw Rae lean back on her heels, Lailah's gun in her hand. Her breath caught as she realized what was happening; she tried to shout, but all that came out was a squeak.

The shot shook the room. Rae jerked once as her blood sprayed the painted door, then toppled slowly at Lailah's side. The false Alain's lips peeled back in a snarl.

"Pathetic," she hissed. For an instant her true face showed, but the mask was in place when she turned back to Blake. "But a perfect example of what will happen to your friends if you refuse me." Behind her, the hunters clawed at the fabric of the door. Canvas stretched. Changed. Behind them, Carcosa's painted sky had begun to brighten. "Decide. My friends won't wait forever."

Out of the corner of her eye, Liz saw Lailah move. One hand was free and reaching for her gun. Liz glanced away. In time to see Alex grab Antja's arm and drag her close. Liz couldn't hear the words he whispered in the woman's ear, but she read the shape of them on his grey-tinged lips.

Oils burn.

"I'll go," Blake said. His chest deflated with the words, as if the cost of them left him hollow.

The maenad's stolen face stretched in a smile and she held out her hand. Lailah's hand closed on her gun. Even expecting it, the sound was deafening. The false Alain's knee burst in a spray of black blood. As she staggered, Rainer caught her other leg and sent her sprawling. Fire crackled around Antja's fingertips, sputtered and popped as she pressed her burning hand against the canvas. For an instant nothing happened—then a wave of flame swept the room. Liz gasped, and regretted it as heat rushed into her lungs.

The woman shrieked, and in the light of the burning painting her face was her own again. Vines writhed and crisped and the smell of seared vegetation joined the chemical reek of oil paints. The surface of the canvas bubbled and seethed, and the bacchante drew back from the fire.

Lailah fired again but the shot went wild. Antja's aim was better; blood blossomed across the maenad's shoulder. Then Rainer was in the way, grappling with her on the threshold. They shouted, but Liz couldn't understand the words over the echo of the gun.

Vines burst from the woman's skin to ensnare the room. Liz spun in front of Blake, hooking her ankle through his and knocking him down. The tendril aimed for him coiled around her throat instead, sharp as a whip. Dark spots swam in front of her eyes as it tugged her backward. Then Alex was there, tearing the strand away, and Liz sagged breathlessly against his shoulder.

Facing the red darkness of the corridor, she saw the wave of shadows coming. They ran on all fours along the floor and the walls, a sleek boneless surge, wings furled to fit through the hall. Beautiful and terrible and unstoppable.

Liz drew another lungful of searing, smoky air and leapt forward, dragging Alex with her as she flung herself on top of Blake. The shadows rushed past them and the draft of their wings was cold and clean. She twisted around in time to see the monsters fall over the woman, black and silent. Rainer fell to his knees as dark blood sprayed the room, sizzling as it burned. Wings like slices of midnight eclipsed the burning door.

She never knew, afterward, if it was an accident or not. Rainer looked up from the threshold, looked from Antja to Blake and back again. Liz thought he smiled, but she was never sure of that either. He pushed himself up—into the path of a razored black tail as it whipped through the air.

The tip sank into his back and out his chest. A bubble of blood burst on his lips as he gasped. Blake jerked, and Liz felt rather than heard his choked sound of dismay. Antja screamed and emptied her pistol into the creature, but the bullets passed through inky flesh without so much as a ripple.

The last vines retreated, clutching at anything in reach as they were sucked through the disintegrating door. Liz dodged a flailing coil and Blake batted another aside. Sparks and flakes of burning canvas drifted through the air, crisping hair and searing skin as they landed. Whether the fire undid their tenebrous shapes, or if they simply retreated now that their purpose was fulfilled, the shadow-creatures melted into nothing. The flames licking the canvas frame blazed higher, mushrooming across the ceiling. The heat withered Liz's lungs, singed the fine hair on her face.

Antja stood silhouetted against the apocalyptic light as the flames rolled toward her. Then Lailah flung an arm around her, knocking her out of their reach.

"Run!" she shouted.

They ran.

Fire raced them down the hall, consuming partitions and paintings and sculptures, rolling in greedy waves across the ceiling. Alex collapsed, one hand clawing at his chest; Liz and Blake grabbed him and dragged him on. Something groaned and crashed behind them.

The shock of the night air drove Liz to her knees in dirty snow, shredding her hands on ice and blacktop. Tears dripped off her cheeks and she couldn't stop coughing. Yellow light and black smoke bled from the top of the gallery, staining the night. Sirens wailed in the distance. Antja wailed. Snow spun through the glow of the sodium lamps.

Blake offered her a hand, still supporting Alex with one arm. His face was a mask of blood and soot. Silver flashed on his outstretched hand, the ring nearly lost under ash and filth. His eyes were human again.

21

CODA

IF BLAKE HAD been less hollow and numb, he would never have gone back to Carroll Cove. But by the time he realized where they were going, he was slumped against Liz in the back seat with no strength left to argue. Dawn was a bruise in the east when they climbed the steps of a different cabin, an ache behind his eyes. He collapsed onto the couch like his strings had been cut. He had no strength to take off his coat—Sands' coat. Beneath the reek of smoke and blood caught in the wool, he smelled oranges and incense. The scent followed him into the dark.

He woke later to silence and morning light. At least he thought he was awake; his eyes were open, staring into a darkened corner, but his limbs wouldn't move. Sleep fog faded, replaced by the prickling certainty that he was being watched.

Hypnagogia. Alex had taught him the word. The transition between sleep and waking, prone to hallucinations and sleep paralysis. Night terrors, even in the daylight. That knowledge did nothing to quell the shivering dread that spread beneath his skin. Something was watching him, waiting in the dark, moving closer—

Pale sunlight slanted between the curtains. Beyond that watery line, shadows stirred. Blake waited for the winged monsters to emerge from the gloom and end this once and for all, as they had for Rainer. But the slender shape that stepped into the light was even worse.

The light fell through Alain as he drifted forward; he cast no shadow on the floor. His eyes were black and lightless beneath a fall of bleach-streaked hair.

You'll really be thinking of me, the maenad had taunted. But staring at the specter in front of him, Blake didn't think any nightmare could be worse than the simple knowledge of what he'd lost. His eyes stung and watered, and he couldn't wipe the tears away.

"I held on," Alain whispered. "I held on tight. But you let go." His voice was soft and dark and rougher than ever, but Blake wasn't sure if his lips were moving.

"It wasn't your fault," he went on. "But that doesn't make it any warmer here. I'm always drowning now. Drowning in you."

Then he was gone. Lazy dust motes danced through the cold light and Blake wept silently into the cushions.

A KNOCK AT the door woke Alex, soft and insistent, dragging him out of a dreamless sleep. Dawnlight edged the curtains, and Liz curled next to him, one arm limp and warm across his stomach. She didn't stir as he slid out of bed and fumbled for his clothes in the gloom. Last night's clothes—his nose wrinkled at the clinging stench of smoke.

He expected to find Lailah in the hall, or Blake. Instead it was Antja looking up at him. She had refused their invitation to come back to the cabin last night, instead taking Rainer's car and disappearing before the fire trucks arrived; he hadn't thought he would see her again. The wan light showed her bruised, burn-welted face, the singed ends of her hair. Alex doubted she'd slept.

"Lailah let me in," she said. Alex winced at the hoarse scrape of her voice. "She's outside." She nodded toward the water. In the shadows of the front room, Blake lay motionless on the sofa.

Alex opened his mouth and shut it again uselessly. Concern was too clumsy a thing, pity too cruel. The light brightened by inches and the silence stretched.

"You're leaving today," she said at last. He nodded. "So am I. But I wanted to give you something first."

She lifted a bag off her shoulder. The same one she'd rescued from the gallery, he thought. He took it, feeling the familiar weight and shape of books through the leather. "What are these?"

"Nothing I want. They were— I don't want them. You might not either, but I suspect you'll take better care of them."

"Thank you. I think." He forced down a cough. "Antja, I'm sorry—"

She shook her head, a quick, violent, gesture, and he broke off.

"I wish I could say it was nice to have met you," she said with a bitter smile. "Maybe some other time. But thank you all the same."

He reached to adjust his glasses, but caught himself mid-gesture. His hand curled at his side. "What will you do?"

"I don't know. Go somewhere warm. We'd talked about..." She shook her head again.

Alex swallowed. "Good luck."

"You too. I think you'll need it as much as I do." She lifted a hand as if she meant to touch him, but dropped it. Her weight shifted and she paused on the brink of turning away. "Rainer always thought that magic was inherited. A birthright. I don't believe that."

"What do you believe?" he asked after a long pause.

"That it's contagious. It slips past your defenses and changes you. And we're all infected now." She cast one last tired smile over her shoulder. "Good bye."

He didn't follow her out, but he stood in the hall until the sound of her car faded into the distance.

THE CEMETERY LAY under a white shroud, silent save for the creak and sway of trees. The afternoon sky was the color of milk, while dusk spread violet grey as pigeon wings in the east. Their flight left in three hours. This was the only stop Blake had asked to make.

Snow crunched under his boots as he crossed the lawn. His hair, still damp from a hasty shower, froze in tendrils against his scalp.

That was nothing, though, to the greater chill coiled inside him. Liz thought it was over, but he new better; the shadowy thing was still inside him, parasite or symbiont. His piece of Carcosa. Quiescent, at least, since the gallery burned.

He frowned at the smooth, rolling grounds as he navigated between graves. Cemeteries should have standing markers, statues and obelisks and brooding mausoleums. Something to remember— not these bland, homogenous stones. Flowers broke the drift of snow over Alain's grave, wilted and crusted with ice. Someone would come soon to take them away.

Gone. As simple as that. Nothing left now but memories and nightmares, and a haunting that may or may not have been real.

Blake swallowed, his throat tight. His eyes were dry, though. All the tears had leaked out of him this morning. He thought he should leave something, but what would be the use? It would be gone with the flowers. Besides, graves were for the living, and he already knew he wouldn't come back.

There was nowhere for him to go back to. Not in Vancouver, and not in Connecticut.

Slow footsteps crunched behind him, pulling him out of his fugue. Blake squared his shoulders, rehearsing what he would say to Liz. She would understand, at least. He could always trust her to understand. But when he turned he found not Liz but Alex. His mouth snapped shut, all his half-formed thoughts dying unvoiced.

They stood in silence, not quite meeting one another's eyes. Lazy snowflakes spiraled down, snagging in Alex's hair, on the shoulders of his coat. He looked half a corpse in the wan light, his eyes sunken and bruised, naked without his glasses, and one cheek spotted with welts.

"You're thinking of staying," he said at last. His breath whistled softly.

"Not staying," Blake said. "Not here."

Alex flicked a hand in dismissal. "But you don't plan on coming home."

Blake stiffened at his tone. "How can I? It's too dangerous."

One eyebrow quirked. "Is that what you're telling yourself?"

Heat rose in Blake's face. "Alain died because of me! What

happened at the gallery—Rae and Rainer—that was because of me. This thing is still inside me, and I don't know what it will do next. I don't know what I'll do. How can you expect me to go home knowing I'd put everyone around me in danger?"

"It's easier to be alone. Not to trust. To walk away and tell yourself it's for the best. I understand that." Alex raised a hand before Blake could reply. "I don't know if everything that happened was because of you. Maybe it was. What I do know is that Liz nearly died for you. If you leave now, you'll throw that in her face. You'll break her heart. And if you do that I'll—" He broke off, forcing his strained, angry voice low again. "I'll do something stupid that will embarrass us both." He tugged his coat straight self-consciously.

"It isn't that simple. What if the next person I hurt is Liz? Do you want that on your conscience? Because I sure as hell don't."

Alex's eyes narrowed. Then he smiled sardonically. "Push me away all you like. It's Liz I'm concerned about."

"You don't understand." Blake's jaw clenched. Christ, he sounded like a damned teenager.

"I don't know what you experienced, it's true. I can't know. But I know what Liz went through to find you. Hell. And she'll do it again. She's made her choice. I may not like it, but I have to respect it. And you should too."

Blake drew a breath and let it out again. It hung shimmering in the air before the wind unraveled it.

"Liz won't give up on you," Alex went on, his voice softening. "And I won't give up on Liz. We're bloody well stuck with each other. We might as well make the best of it. Lailah, on the other hand, will probably leave us to freeze if we stand out here much longer. And I've had enough of the cold."

He turned toward the car. After a moment, Blake followed. He might regret it, but he was tired of the cold too.

Liz raised her eyebrows in a silent question as he slid into the back seat: *are you all right?* Blake nodded. It felt less like a lie than he'd thought it would. She reached for his hand, and he returned the gentle pressure.

"Let's go home."

ACKNOWLEDGEMENTS

This novel has been a labor of love, despair, and grim determination, more than any other I've written to date. So many people have suffered with me through the drafts. I'm indebted to Steven Downum, Elizabeth Bear, Jaime Lee Moyer, Leah Bobet, Jodi Meadows, Kathryn Allen, Marissa Lingen, Ian Tregillis, Cathy Freeze, Siobhan Carroll, Cory Skerry, Jamie Rosen, Lisa Deguchi, Deva Fagan, and everyone in the Online Writing Workshop and the Bat City Novelocracy. And of course, my indefatigable agent Jennifer Jackson, Michael Curry, David Moore, Jonathan Oliver, and Jeffrey Alan Love.

I'm also grateful to Matt Andrews for his help with the Bete Noire recipe. I have consumed many of them.